WHAT HAPPENED TO THE BIG APPLE?

Where the ship had been standing there was now just an old pier. Ali had also disappeared just before his eyes. Jim had to find McManus—he would know what happened.

He ran across the West Side highway. There was no traffic. He ran up to 44th Street, past stoops where people sat frozen in position, barely watching him. There were no stores. No delis. Nothing open for business.

Then Jim heard the crowd. Hordes of people stood around a black truck, begging for food from gaurds dressed in stiff uniforms. An image came to his mind: Those living skeletons who blinked against the light and cameras of the GIs as the first Nazi concentration camps were liberated. Pathetic men and women, now androgynous, seeming beyond the pale of normal existence. These creatures were like that.

Someone grabbed Jim's shoulder. Briefly, he hoped that it was Ali. But when he spun around, he saw he couldn't have been more wrong. . . .

TIME WARRIOR NOVEL #3

Day of the Snake
Matthew J. Costello

A ROC BOOK

To Michael E. Costello—brother and friend.

ROC
Published by the Penguin Group
Penguin Books USA Inc., 375 Hudson Street,
New York, New York 10014, U.S.A.
Penguin Books Ltd, 27 Wrights Lane,
London W8 5TZ, England
Penguin Books Australia Ltd, Ringwood,
Victoria, Australia
Penguin Books Canada Ltd, 10 Alcorn Avenue,
Toronto, Ontario, Canada M4V 3B2
Penguin Books (N.Z.) Ltd, 182-190 Wairau Road,
Auckland 10, New Zealand

Penguin Books Ltd, Registered Offices:
Harmondsworth, Middlesex, England

First published by Roc, an imprint of New American Library, a division of
Penguin Books USA Inc.

First Printing, July, 1992
10 9 8 7 6 5 4 3 2 1

 Roc is a trademark of New American Library,
a division of Penguin Books USA Inc.

Printed in the United States of America

1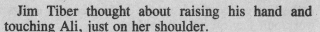

Jim Tiber thought about raising his hand and touching Ali, just on her shoulder.

Something reassuring, something that would close the gap suddenly created by the gusty wind blowing off the Hudson, that—and his words.

But, as if sensing what he was about to do, Ali stepped away, closer to the metal railing, the painting flaking even as she grabbed it.

His attempt to soothe her frustrated, Jim took a breath. The air was cold but still ripe with the unhealthy stew that was the lower Hudson. He saw people looking at them, a few tourists, and the Sabrett's hot dog man, already scarfed and bundled against the wonders of a New York winter. The street people watched the real life drama unfold.

Words, Jim thought . . . never my forte. But worth a shot.

"Ali, I don't see what you're getting all crazy about. It's just for a year and—"

He heard her exhale, a noisy sigh that spoke volumes about her icy temperament.

She didn't, of course, deign to look at him.

"C'mon," he tried, searching for a lighthearted tone.

Once again misjudging the expanse that now separated them.

"It's a stupid waste. Stupid—" she paused, and looked over at him tellingly, delivering the fatal blow right to his eyes. "And cowardly."

Jim nodded. By this time, her points were all too clear in his mind. Now that he had his Master's, now that he finally had his thesis on the early Beatles accepted—with a little behind-the-scenes push from Professor Lindstrom, it was time for him to—

Yes, boys and girls, *time to write*.

Grab the old keyboard and fulfill my destiny.

That's what I'm supposed to do, Jim knew.

So what do I do instead? I take a teaching position in the University of Wisconsin. Just to see how things work out. Pay off my school loan.

Taking me away from writing.

And from Ali.

And angering her more?

Jim didn't have a clue.

"It's just a year," Jim said. "Look, Ali, I need some time, and some income, to see what I really want to do." He thought about trying to touch her shoulder again. But it seemed a formidable precipice. His hand froze in space, then finally twisted into a half-hearted gesture.

He referred to that other reason she was opposed to his leaving, a reason she wouldn't ever admit . . .

"I'll come see you. And you can come out and see me."

She turned sharply, delivering another cutting glance. "I'm sorry. I have no interest in an academic toiling in the cornfields . . ."

"They don't grow corn in Madison."

Ali turned away from the water, looking right at him. Am I crazy, Jim thought, or is there the tiniest beginnings of a smile blooming on her face?

A giant gust sent her rich, brown hair flying forward, covering her eyes. She's absolutely beautiful, Jim thought. Absolutely. And it's hard to imagine that after everything we've done together—all a blur now, too dreamlike to be real—that they could end up like this, just another pair of New York lovers breaking up over some stupid career decision.

And—for a moment—he looked past her, at the giant gray ship behind her.

At the U.S.S. *Intrepid,* the floating sea, air and space museum that they had just visited. But, following their ever-icier dialogue, he couldn't remember a thing he saw.

Some World War II fighters jutted off the edge of the carrier. From his vantage point, they formed a crown for Ali's head. A small boy leaned against the railing waving down.

The wind whipped Ali's hair the other way.

Her sparkling blue eyes were powerful, undeniable in their hold on him.

"I thought," she said at last, "that you wanted *more*. I thought that you had enough of classrooms, curriculums." She paused, and Jim braced himself for a telling salvo. "I thought that you wanted something *real* from your life."

Jim stepped closer.

And he thought:

We've made love in my apartment at Columbia. At her apartment.

But also in Nazi Germany, in the very bowels of Hitler's Reich Chancellery—both of us in different bodies. And I've held her close to me as she nearly bled to death as the Tet Offensive was about to change the Vietnam War forever.

Maybe it's all been too much.

He smiled. There's just so much strain that a relationship can stand. It's not time travel that's so bad.

No. But coming back—reentry—has been hard.

Jim knew that Ali was all set to continue her work

with McManus, working on other vagaries of the time stream. And she wants me to stay here.

So why do I want to go?

Just for a job?

Or do I need some breathing space? he wondered.

The wind blew a tiny fleck into his left eye. It stung, and a tear quickly appeared.

He rubbed at it, blurring Ali who kept him fixed, as if she could see the thoughts in his mind. Another gust—and damn, his other eye stung. He wiped at it, the Hudson River, the *Intrepid,* Ali, all going blurry.

(And he seemed to feel something then. Something more that just a damp, chilling wind. Something that went deeper, in through his skin, slicing into him. He felt queasy, as if he was on the great ship, rolling ever so slightly in the swells as the Altantic knocked heads with the great river.)

He kept rubbing.

"Damn," he said. "I can't see. The wind—"

Another rub.

And Ali wasn't there.

He said the word aloud, moving his lips, slowly. *Ali. Ali* . . . As if he'd lose the word, the image itself, if he didn't repeat it.

Ali was gone.

And gone too, he noticed, was the giant aircraft carrier . . .

Jim Tiber stood frozen for a moment, looking down at the railing, now needing more that just a paint job. Now it was rusted, crumbling, tilting down towards the water.

"No," Jim said, his mind rifling through a file of possibilities, coming up with absolutely nothing.

There was a ship right here, he thought. A damn big ship, an aircraft carrier and—

Now there was just an old pier. It was still a chilling, gun-metal grey morning. At least the weather hadn't changed. But inside the rotted timbers of the pier, rustling about in the shadows made by the decrepit roof, Jim saw figures shambling around. He watched them, and then—he thought that they saw him.

And they were coming towards him.

Jim spun around. Great. he thought, I know what this is. All that jumping around in time. It's made me lose my mind, just as McManus feared it would. There is no Ali. I'm just a crazy person now, another New York nut. Where's my cardboard box, my shopping cart filled with rags?

He took a breath, tasting salt and something oily and foul on his lips.

There was no Ali.

She's dead. Somewhere in Time.

Somewhere back in Berlin, or Saigon.

That must be it.

No, he thought.

He reached into his back pocket and felt something.

(Please, he prayed. Let it be there. I know it shouldn't be there. But, God, let it be there.)

He pulled out the brochure.

"Visit the U.S.S. *Intrepid*," it said. There was a picture of the carrier. He flipped it open. There were pictures of the planes, the helicopters, all the things that he had just seen, just minutes before.

He heard a board creak behind him.

Jim didn't realize that he was leaning against the rusted railing. He pushed away from it and some of the metal—thin and sere as ancient cloth—snapped. He heard a plop as a chunk was gobbled by the churning river.

Jim looked over his shoulder.

Those people, he thought, those zombie-like figures on the pier, were coming towards him.

Gotta get out of here, he thought. Got to get a move on, do something. Find Ali—

What the hell happened to her?

And find McManus. Jim took a breath. He'll know what happened.

Jim tried to think, tried to figure out what could be going on. But this, he thought, wasn't like getting a flat. No, it wasn't like hearing a popping sound, and then feeling the steering go all wobbly and then—clever you!—deducing that a tire has just been punctured.

No. At this point, no hypotheses were forthcoming.

Absolutely none.

I'll get uptown, he thought. Get to the Time Lab. The beginnings of a plan . . .

And with a creaking board only feet away, Jim ran across the West Side Highway, barely noticing that there was something odd about it. He ran full-out, his hand clutching the brochure, anchoring his sanity.

As long as I have this, I have proof, he thought.

He ran fast, dogging traffic.

Even though there was no traffic.

Not a single car.

He ran up to 44th Street, passing boarded-up buildings, past stoops where people sat frozen into position, barely watching him.

He saw no stores. No delis. No coffee shops.

Nothing open for business.

There were parked cars here. But they looked old and useless. Most were without tires, sitting on rusted rims, the seat benches long ago ripped out, the glass broken.

Something's very wrong here, he thought.

Very wrong.

He got to Tenth Avenue, looking for a bus, a cab, something to take him uptown.

But this street was also deserted. Scraps of paper danced around the deserted and cracked avenue. He squeezed the *Intrepid* brochure.

For the first time he asked himself the question.

If the *Intrepid* is gone—God, if Ali is gone—if something has changed everything.

Then how come I still have this . . . this piece of paper in my hand? It shouldn't exist. Not if time has been changed . . .

He kept running, even harder now, across the avenue, then down a dark block littered with more corpses of automobiles. He heard grunting sounds from the alcoves of buildings. Hungry sounds. And snickering as if he was putting a show on for everybody.

And he had this thought:

If everything has been changed . . . how come *I* haven't been changed?

A grayish-black lump lay on the sidewalk in front of him and he glanced at it for only a second as he jumped over it. He couldn't risk stopping . . . getting caught by something stumbling out of one of those buildings, leaping up from one of those shadowy alcoves.

But he saw the grayish-black fur, and the matted blood, and—

The dead rat looked as if someone had turned it inside out.

Getting all the meat out, all the good, nutritious parts.

Waste not, want not, he thought.

And then, as he reached Ninth Avenue and a gas station that seemed as ancient and abandoned as the Temple of Giza, he saw a faded billboard across the street. A man with a broad smile, a shining face. Thin white hair, combed back. His hands were out, as if gesturing at the city's streets themselves.

And the billboard read, WASTE NOT, WANT NOT.
The thought that I just had, he thought.

His foot hit a crack in the sidewalk, and he stum-
bled forward, almost falling, his left foot quickly
kicking out to stop the fall.

Don't want to fall here. No way. They'd get me
for sure. They would—

Who'd get me? he wondered.

I must know something about this. After all, I'm
here. I have to know something about—

Then he heard it.

Noise. A tremendous roar coming from just—

Jim stepped out into the street.

Yes, just from one block ahead.

There were people.

And maybe answers.

He jogged across Ninth Avenue, starting to feel
his wind give out. I've got to get to those people.

Because there are no cabs, he knew now. No
busses.

And he was sure that when he finally got to a subway entrance that it certainly wouldn't be any place
that he'd enter.

He *knew* that.

The noise of the crowd grew with his steps. He
heard the crowd's voices, cheering as if they were at
a sporting event. And then an amplified voice speaking to the crowd. Jim tried to make some of it out.

It was all a wildly echoing blur until he got near
the corner and could see the people.

Hundreds of them, thousands of them, gathered
around—

He stopped.

Froze.

It was a large black truck.

And there were guards in all-black outfits, and
each had a white circle with a white "R" embla-

zoned on the front.

The crowd was screaming, yelling, and—

No. Jim licked his lips. They are begging.

Jim heard a crack. One of the guards perched atop the back of the truck fired at the crowd.

What? Jim thought. What the hell is this?

A warning shot, he thought. But no. Not a warning shot.

And he knew that now—

(Oh, I've lost it, he thought. I've lost my mind. Or this is hell and I've been a very bad boy.)

No, he knew that it wasn't a warning shot because the crowd squealed as if the home team just got a goal. And they moved, huddled around the person the guard had just shot. More screams, squeals, and—

Jim stepped back.

I swear I hear eating sounds, Jim thought. I swear I hear it, above all this noise, and the speakers monotonously ordering the crowd to "Line Up!" And "Wait Your Turn!" and "Waste Not, Want Not."

Above all of the noise, Jim heard tearing sounds, and slurping, and—

Losing it, no doubt about it.

Jim laughed. Not a funny laugh. Something, yes, from the hysterical family of laughs.

What's happened to the Big Apple?

"There will be no food, no food!" the amplified voice screamed. "Not until there is order and a line."

This must be what it's like at the zoo, Jim thought. When it's feeding time and the lions get kinda edgy, walking back and forth, licking their chops, jumping on each other, as the keepers take forever to throw out the great chunks of fatty beef.

When all the lions want to do is jump on the keepers and bite into something really fresh.

"No food—not until there's a line, not until—"

Jim stared at the back of the big truck. He noticed that the truck was black and it also had the same symbol, a white circle with a bright white "R" in the center.

"R" for revolting. Or ridiculous, and—

One of the guards seemed to look up. Seemed to, because the helmet had a black plastic faceguard that covered the guard's eyes, his entire face.

But Jim felt his stare.

And that guard tapped a guard next to him.

Jim smiled.

Just not hungry, gang, he wanted to say.

Why, I just passed up a juicy rat not more than a half a block back.

Jim stepped back.

The guards were still, talking to each other. I'd hate to give in to my paranoia, Jim thought. But I'm pretty sure that they're talking about me.

But then some movement from inside the truck broke up their tête-è-tête. Some workers, dressed in black but without weapons or the little symbol that made the guards look like trademark logos, hauled something red and heavy to the edge of the truck.

Jim barely noticed the crowd, but now he looked at them—the clothing hanging off their skeletal bodies, their bony hands reaching up to the back of the truck as if "amen-ing" some charismatic preacher . . .

He got a good look at them.

Only one image came to mind.

Those living skeletons who blinked against the light and cameras of the GIs as the first Nazi concentration camps were liberated. Pathetic birdlike men and women, now androgynous, and seemingly beyond the pale of normal existence.

These creatures were like that.

Jim felt frozen.

And someone touched him.

Touched his back, his shoulder. *Grabbed* his shoulder.

For one brief second, he hoped, prayed that this was Ali.

Somehow they had been separated, but now she was here. Now everything was okay. Together, they'd get this all figured out.

But—when he spun around—he saw that he couldn't have been more wrong . . .

2 ═══════

Dr. Elliot McManus heard a buzzing sound.

His hand reached out and flailed at the end table in search of the insistent alarm clock.

He hit a glass and sent it tumbling to his bedroom floor. And then his pen and notebook—always by his side—also tumbled down.

The buzzing kept up, and McManus realized that he'd have to open his eyes.

As the filmy blur cleared, he looked around for his clock. He found it hiding on a corner of the bedside table. Twelve o'clock . . . somewhere near midnight. Or maybe noon.

And it wasn't buzzing at all.

Something else was.

"I'll need my glasses for that," he said. Years of solitary thought and work had conditioned him to welcome the sound of his own voice . . . even when his voice sounded different. He treated it as if it was actually another person.

He could get into a nice loud argument with himself quite easily.

The buzzing—off, then on, an alarm of some kind—was beginning to get to him.

"Now where are my glasses?" he asked.

He looked around, his near-sightedness rendering the room a shadowy blur.

But a thin shaft of light cut through the edge of his curtains, telling him that it was probably midday and—at the same time—illuminating his glasses, sitting on his desk.

He got up—the air was cold and the thin rug chilled his feet. He picked up his glasses and almost sighed as he finally could see.

The buzzing, he didn't have to remind himself. Got to do something about this infernal buzzing.

He looked down at his desk.

There was his computer, linked up to the new Fujitsu Mainframe at Columbia and, next to it—

Another device. A small gray box. It looked rather like a modem but he couldn't—for the life of him—remember what it was.

"Isn't that funny?" he said aloud.

Not laughing at all.

The gray box kept buzzing. And there was a tiny, red light that flashed on and off.

The scientist pulled up a chair and sat in front of his computer.

Why don't I know what this is? he wondered. He looked up staring blankly into the cloistered darkness of the room, thinking. What in the world is this thing?

He turned on a light over his desk.

And he saw his room.

The walls were yellow with age, decades late for painting. The rug was dirt brown, worn to bare spots, and tattered and frayed at the edges.

Something about this room wasn't right.

That, and this stupid buzzing . . . he thought.

He looked at the gray device.

Well, he thought, it's obviously attached to the computer. Yes, perhaps it has something to do with the computer.

He turned on his machine.

The screen flickered to life.

And he was right. The device did have something to do with his computer.

As the letters appeared on the screen, he was—for a moment—shocked by what he saw.

But only for a moment . . .

Jim spun around.

"Ali," he said, hoping she'd be there. Or hoping that he'd find himself twisted in his bedsheets, about to escape a very nasty dream.

It wasn't Ali, though. It was a man. Or something. The mouth was black with crooked teeth. The stench of the man made Jim gag. The ripped and filthy clothes dripped off the man. But his grip was strong.

Jim half-expected the creature to ask him for a quarter. Need to get some coffee, bub.

But that wasn't quite what he was after.

The man's hand held Jim's shoulder hard. And then the second skeletal hand reached up and grabbed Jim's other shoulder and held him there, locked, with an incredible, almost unbelievable force.

And the man opened his mouth, a gummy pit with all sorts of foul-looking stuff dangling from the stalagmites and stalactites formed by the man's fangs.

Belatedly, a remarkable thought occurred to Jim.

He's going to bite me.

As the man lunged, the thought became even clearer.

He wants to eat me.

Perhaps he nailed that rat back aways—and it didn't sate his appetite.

Jim staggered backwards, thinking for a second that he was stupidly moving towards a whole crowd of hungry men. There's no way that black meat truck could hold enough people to keep that crowd happy.

No way.

The man's grip didn't loosen. With practiced strength, the skeleton man dug his talonlike fingers into Jim's shoulder. The pain made pink bubbles explode in Jim's brain.

The fetid mouth, its aroma almost deadly enough by itself, leaned close to Jim, inches away from Jim's exposed neck.

And though the painful fireworks show was still running in Jim's head, finally he moved quickly.

I've got to get this animal off me, he thought.

Jim brought his arms up sharply, trying to knock the man's hands loose. His first shot did nothing, but Jim grunted—the man's slobbering face dripping a browning goo—right next to his!

Jim brought his arms up again, and this time the man's fingers popped free—surely taking some of my skin with them, Jim thought.

Jim stepped back—the loud speakers yelling at the crowd, their frenzied cheers and moans and exited yells sounding like visiting day at the madhouse.

Mr. Mad Mouth looked down at his empty hands, disappointed.

Like a kingfisher emerging from a murky pond *sans* the silvery bass it thought it had speared.

Then the creature snarled. He made an animal sound, and Jim felt even more scared than before.

He is an animal, Jim thought. A hungry animal, and he'll do anything to get fed. Anything . . .

Wish I knew Kung-Fu, Jim thought. Or Tai Chi, or Lao Tsu, something oriental and devastating.

The man leapt forward, surprisingly agile considering the fact that he looked dead. And Jim performed the one special attack that he learned in the back alleys of his old neighborhood.

He kicked the man where the two Vs of his legs met. With remarkably good aim, Jim watched his foot crash into the ghoul's family jewels.

With little effect.

The man's leap was stopped. But his treasure horde

of jewels had long given way to a dead zone down there.

And Jim knew: one on one, this guy is going to eat me alive.

Literally.

The man's eyes widened, as if he too recognized that fact.

But with the few feet of distance that Jim had gained, he wondered about something.

How fast can this ugly fuck run?

Not too damn fast, Jim guessed.

And with that hopeful thought, Jim turned and did an outside run, flying past the man, pumping with his arms.

But he didn't look back, afraid that he'd see the man just as he was about to bring Jim down like a dumb-ass gazelle.

If he's going to get me, Jim thought, I don't want to see.

He kept running, past other cadaverous creatures huddled together on the steps of decrepit brownstones, past alcoves left by abandoned Chinese restaurants.

Jim reached Ninth Avenue.

Still, he didn't look around.

He just kept running, to 45th Street, 46th Street, the wonderful west side of New York, looking now like Berlin after the Russians got through mauling it, or Nagasaki after the world changed forever.

And as Jim ran, his lungs burning, his knees starting to feel weird and wobbly, he kept telling himself, quietly, I've got to get to the Time Lab.

I've got to get to the Time Lab.

Because—*everything's* screwed up now.

McManus—of course, he thought. That's who I am. I remember now.

And he took one last look at the screen.

How easily we forget, he smiled to himself. He shut off the computer. This aspect of time-stream manipulation would have to be carefully studied, he told himself. Later, when it's all put back the way it should be.

If it can be put back.

And then he sat for a second debating his next action.

"Oh, well," he said, and he picked up the gray device, his link with the shielded Time Lab. He ripped the wires out of the back, and threw it against the wall. The plastic case shattered open, and he watched the memory board pop out. He got up, grabbed the board and slipped it into his pocket.

"Wouldn't do to have this getting away," he said to himself.

Then he opened a drawer of his desk and pulled out a map.

"Good," he said, glad to see that it was still there. Can't depend on anything now, he knew.

Not after these changes.

He opened the map and his finger travelled through some unfamiliar terrain. Where there used to be Central Park was now something called RevCom 1, "authorized personnel only," if you please. Up north, up in the Bronx, he saw another open expanse, labeled RevCom 2.

"They used to be parks," he said. His voice sounded tired and angry. Not for the first time, he wondered whether he was going to be able to do this. It gets ever so much more complicated . . .

He thought of Jim, Ali . . . where were they? How ever would he find them?

"I should have made better plans," he scolded himself. "I should have prepared for all contingencies. This . . . this is inexcusable."

He checked the map. There were blocks that were

circled with thick black lines. Forbidden Zones, they were labeled.

Perhaps the best place to go, McManus thought.

He saw that the George Washington Bridge was still on the map. He read the label, "Not Open for Citizen Use."

And then his finger travelled further.

To the castle.

It was still on the map.

"Good," McManus purred. There were no guarantees that everything was okay, he knew. But, thank heavens, *it's* still here.

"Okay," he said. He pulled on some pants draped on the back of his chair. They were rough and scratchy, and way too baggy even by McManus's own generous standards. And then a shirt, an even coarser brown material. He saw black shoes that looked as if they were made of cardboard.

I'll have to watch them, he guessed. They could give out anytime.

I need a weapon, he thought, something to protect myself.

He walked out into the tiny kitchen area and opened a drawer. There were two knives in a sickly yellow utensil tray, one a dull butter knife, the other a thin, ineffective-looking knife with a serrated edge.

McManus picked up the knife. It wasn't much. But it was all he had.

He held the knife up in the air.

"Banzai!" he said. He shook his head in disgust, and stuck the knife in his back pocket.

Let the battle begin, he said. And he opened the door and left his tiny apartment.

This is Lincoln Center, Jim thought, standing there.

Culture Land. Home to the Metropolitan Opera, the Philharmonic, the American Ballet.

But not in this world.

The main building, the Met—once flanked by two wondrous Chagall paintings—was a bombed-out shell. It looks, Jim thought, like the Alamo. The other buildings looked even worse, black from tremendous fires that must have turned the theater's insides into a charnel house.

He had to wonder if anyone had been inside when they caught fire.

Jim had stopped only a few seconds, but then he spotted a guard dressed in regulation black strolling around the corner.

"Citizen, halt!" the guard yelled.

Jim guessed that following his order wouldn't be such a good idea. He turned and ran.

Jim could feel the gun aimed at his back.

He counted.

Thinking: I've seen combat, Jake. I've been in the desert with Rommel. I've hacked my way through the Vietnamese jungle.

And I'm not about to die in the busted-up plaza of Lincoln Center.

He counted.

One. Two.

A breath . . .

Jim imagined the guard pulling back on the trigger. Wondering, what kind of kick-ass weapon did the guy have?

Three.

Jim hit the ground, rolling, twisting around, rolling down the steps to Broadway.

The Ginger Man used to be across the street, he thought. Nice bistro for a Bass Ale and some chunky fries, about all his budget allowed.

He heard the bullet fly over his head.

Not an ordinary bullet from the sound of its high pitch scream. Some kind of rocket bullet . . .

Citizen. What was all this "citizen" bullshit?

And as Jim bumped down the steps to what was once the street but was now just a sea of broken asphalt, he thought:

I know what this is like.

It's just like *Things to Come* . . . the marvelous film with William Cameron Menzies' grim view of H.G. Wells' world gone to the dogs. Post-World War whatever, when civilization was no more.

That's what this is like. Except there was this difference:

Somebody had some civilization.

Somebody had it together enough to have jet-powered rifles, and snappy neo-Nazi uniforms with cute Trademark symbols, and brooding black trucks loaded with meat . . .

Of some kind.

There was civilization.

Not here certainly, but *somewhere*.

Jim still had a good thirty blocks to go. He looked east, to where the park was, and he thought: that might be the way to go.

Central Park.

It's got to be safer than these streets.

He crawled behind an upturned piece of asphalt, and checked that his pursuer was not following him.

And then Jim got up and started walking to the park.

On his way north, McManus had only one nasty encounter.

Two women, one white, the other black—sisters at heart—cornered him as he neared Riverside Drive. One tottered in front of him while the other circled to the back.

McManus tried talking to them.

"Now don't go getting any ideas," he said to them. "Don't try anything."

But his calm, rational words only made them grin more crazily than before.

He brandished his knife.

They giggled.

And McManus guessed that they had dealt with far worse.

Well, he thought, I haven't come this far to be stopped by two hags staging a new age Macbeth.

McManus grinned back.

"Alright, ladies." He smiled even more broadly. "C'mon, let's play games."

The words sounded all too false, McManus observed. I'm not cut out for this adventurer's image.

The woman in front made a lunge.

A false attack, it turned out, as the one in back quickly tried to leap on him.

McManus managed to move his own rather gaunt body out of the way before the attacking woman landed with what he feared might be fatal accuracy.

McManus tripped, and the knife, unfortunately, tumbled from his hand.

The woman in the front spied the loose blade. She applied all her brain power to figuring out whether to go for McManus or the blade.

A delay that McManus decided to take advantage of.

He jumped up and waited for the crone to fall upon the knife. Then, fighting back his more chivalrous urges, he planted a kick on her side that resounded with a satisfying ommph.

As that hag rolled over, McManus snatched up the knife and swung around just as hag #2 lunged at him . . .

Into the knife.

Her face registered confusion and surprise.

Incongruously, she grinned.

McManus smiled back.

A flutter of fear took flight in his stomach. By god,

he thought, the knife missed her vital organs. A horrible miracle!

But then she melted away, sliding off him, pulling the implanted knife down as she slid to the ground.

McManus hesitated a second and thought about withdrawing the blade. Might need it later, he thought.

But that was far too messy a prospect.

Besides—he could see the George Washington Bridge just ahead. With no traffic.

That's *one* improvement he thought.

He looked back at the knife.

I'm close. Very close . . .

And he decided to do without the knife.

A decision that he hoped he didn't regret.

Jim crouched in a basement entrance and looked at the park. Or what was once the park.

There was a chain-link fence, painted black, of course, such a fashionable color. The fence was twenty feet high and crowned with what Jim assumed was electrified barb wire. He saw the ubiquitous guards walking around, their faces hidden behind opaque glass. And there were some dogs too, lean and mean Dobermans.

And Jim quickly figured out that the park was not the way to make it up to Columbia.

He started crawling backwards, from one basement entrance to another, kicking away rats. A withered hand clutched him, too feebly to be a real threat.

And Jim had to wonder.

What the hell is it going to be like on the good old campus of my alma mater, Columbia University?

He didn't know that, much as he might have wished it otherwise, it would exceed his wildest expectations . . .

3━━━━━

Jim ran . . .

Past whole blocks, bombed and burned down to
the ground, past elevated subway tracks jutting out
into the air, useless, a relic from better times, past
stands of young trees growing through the cracked
sidewalks, the hopeless fields of rubble . . .

It grew dark.

Without the warming glow of the city's million
lights flickering to life.

And Jim came to Columbia University.

Or what should have been Columbia University.

At first, he thought he had the wrong street. Street
signs had all but disappeared, and—at around 100th
Street, just before the outcrop of rock that is the
Morningside area—he started counting the streets.

At one point, he thought it was raining.

He felt a drop of water hit his cheek. He rubbed
at it. And then there was another. One trickled down
to his lip, salty, tangy, shocking him with the real-
ization that he was wrong.

He had to laugh at that.

It wasn't rain . . .

I'm crying. Stressed out.

Didn't know I cared that much about the place.
Just a school. Half a dozen years out of my life.
What's the big deal? What the hell is the—

He stopped.

If I use my imagination, he thought, if I squint my eyes and really look at the open stretch ahead, I can almost see the buildings the way they were . . . the Low Library, West Hall, even the Tower, the newest monument to technology and heavy corporate funding.

All gone.

A cold, foul wind blew across the open plane.

He heard a sound. A soft moan. A pitiful sound. And then he realized that he was making that sound.

Jim tried to caution himself. Hold on. Hang in there. This just isn't real, this is just the way things are now, that's all. It's not real.

But as soon as he told himself that, he knew he was wrong, completely full of it.

Once time is changed, it's changed, pal. Unless someone can change it back. And, from experience, Jim knew that wasn't too damn easy.

The wind snapped at him, laced with a salty, stinging tang from the East River.

What the hell has happened to New York, he wondered? Bombed into submission? A new post-war Berlin, only now no Marshall Plan to rebuild it. Because whoever won just didn't give a f—

He saw something.

Behind the shell of the library.

Another building.

At first he assumed that it must be just another ruins . . . until he realized what building it must be—

Had to be.

It's the Time Lab, Jim thought exultantly. The Time Lab. And then he let himself fantasize, to hope that—God—the Time Lab has been untouched. Of course, it's protected from the time stream, shielded. Whatever happened to all the rest, couldn't happen to the Time Lab.

He started walking fast, and then running, leaping over the giant cracks in the cement walkway that used to be filled with students complaining about bad courses and boring teachers.

And as he ran, circling around the hull of the library—with only one pillar still standing in front, the steps a jumble of broken concrete—he heard something.

A deep, low and throaty rumble.

Coming from the east, coming from where the FDR Drive used to be.

He looked over, a faint alarm beginning to sound inside his head.

He was almost past the library. He could see the Time Lab.

And it was perfect. The squat red building, looking almost black in the gloom of twilight. And the fence, the mesh looking pristine as it circled the building, protecting it.

The low rumble grew louder.

And he turned and saw the trucks.

Three of them . . . black trucks, rumbling along what was once 125th Street, what once rocked to the ethnic jumble of a dozen different countries.

The black trucks! Sounding almost scared, desperate as they rumbled right towards the Time Lab.

No, Jim thought.

He slowed, just a bit.

Because the trucks seemed so much faster.

"No," he said. And in that instant he figured out what had happened. The Time Lab had been protected. So while nouveau New York was being created, it had no effect on the lab.

He slowed to a walk.

There was no way he could get there ahead of the trucks. None at all.

He watched the trucks separate, one going behind the building, while the other two flanked the sides.

Jim stood there, oblivious to the fact that they might see him, might look over and catch him watching them.

What were they going to do?

Well, that was obvious. Now wasn't it? Jim thought.

The Time Lab had been protected. But now, like anything else, it was in *this* world. And someone, whoever controlled the trademark army, the guys with the big "R"'s on their chests, knew that the lab had to be taken out.

The trucks stopped. The back doors opened, the metal rattling noisily, the sound carrying cleanly over the windy and open expanse.

Voices, orders being given, and then dozens of the black suits jumping to the ground, deploying themselves around the edge of the Time Lab.

The Time Transference Device is in there, Jim thought. The only way to set things right, the only way to end this nightmare. And more—McManus is in there, and Lindstrom, and—

No, he told himself. Ali couldn't be in there.

Please, God. If there is a God. Don't let Ali be in there.

They had long cannons, two men to a cannon. Sleek bazookas.

A single voice rang across the open field, giving orders.

Jim rubbed at his hair. Helpless. Watching.

The voice again. The words indistinguishable.

And again—

And the cannon rang out, giant burps, followed by the crash as the shells smashed into the Time Lab. A huge cloud of smoke erupted from the top of the building. In an instant it was on fire.

"No," Jim moaned.

And then the voice, terrible in its steely calm, giving the order to fire again.

The cannons blasted the building, sending one of the side walls collapsing inward. Smoke and dust surrounded the building, and now the cannons were firing at will. And Jim saw a perfectly formed flame begin to bloom on the top of the building, licking at the night air.

He fell to his knees.

It seemed like the only thing he could do.

He brought his hands up to his ears, to block the cannonading, the firecrackerlike explosions.

The flames grew larger. And the building, the smoky pyre, grew smaller. Like the witch in *The Wizard of Oz,* melting away to nothingness.

It's all over, Jim thought. There's nothing we can do now.

This is the world now.

He opened his mouth, as if he was going to scream, or call out, begging for something to free him from this vision.

When a hand quickly covered his mouth . . .

It was a small hand, with thin fingers that barely covered his mouth, barely muffled his cry. Jim turned around. The person was silhouetted by the brilliant purple glow of early evening.

He saw Ali.

She smiled. And then pulled her hand away.

"I thought that you were going to cry out," she said. "I thought that you might scream."

"I—I can't believe that you're here." Jim turned, looked back at the lab. "I thought that you were in *there.*"

"I was going to the Time Lab when I saw the trucks."

"You know about them?"

"Yes."

Jim had a chance to see Ali a bit, his eyes adjusting to the faint backlight. There was something different about her, something—

"Ali, did something happen? Did something happen to you?"

She turned away. "No. Nothing. Nothing . . . I'm fine." She grabbed his hand, and he felt a desperation in her tug. "Come over here, behind the library wall," she said.

Jim let himself be led by her, knowing that she wasn't telling him something.

She wasn't telling him what had happened to her after the change.

Ali led him around the building until they could just barely hear the shouts of the guards, the cracking of the wood and plaster as it burned, sizzling away on the devastated campus.

"You remember?" Jim asked. "What we did, the other times. In Germany . . . in Vietnam?"

He could see her eyes, and filled with red lines, puffy and wet. He thought of the cadaverous creatures who prowled the city—

And Ali.

"Yes," she said. "I mean, it wasn't all there, not at first. I didn't remember everything. But—"

Jim gave her hand a squeeze. "Where did you go? What happened to you?"

She shrugged. It was cold, and Jim wanted to put his arm around her and hold her close.

"Whatever this new history is—my new history— I ended up inside this building. There were men there—" she paused. "I worked for them, I think, I *did* things for them . . ."

She shivered. Jim knew better than to touch her. Not now.

"I had to escape. I remembered bits and pieces of what we did. But there were holes." She looked right at him. "But we shouldn't know anything, should we? Why aren't we absorbed—" she gestured at the city, ever more shrouded by the dark—"in this new history?"

Jim shrugged. "I don't know. That's what should have happened. I even—" he dug into his back pocket—"still have this!" He pulled out the *Intrepid* brochure.

Which, he saw, was now blank.

Jim looked down at it, totally dumbfounded.

"What is it?" said Ali, as Jim tilted it up and down trying to catch whatever little light there was. But it was just a piece of white glossy paper.

"Hey . . . it was the *Intrepid* brochure." He touched her shoulder. "I still had it and—you do remember going on the ship, don't you?"

Ali nodded.

"I—I didn't understand how I could still have it, now that the *Intrepid* is gone, now that it maybe never existed at all. How could I have the brochure?. . ."

"And now, apparently, you don't," Ali said.

Jim looked down at the now-blank brochure.

He shook his head. "I thought McManus might have explained all this." Jim looked back to where the Time Lab was degenerating into rubble. "And now that's impossible."

They both said nothing for a moment.

Finally, Ali reached out for him, her hands closing around his, grabbing him hard. "Jim, what if we're alone? What if there's nothing we can do?"

Jim tried to think of something to say, something hopeful, something to give them a plan.

His mouth opened but nothing came out.

He shook his head and, with Ali still holding onto him, he went to kiss her. But she turned away.

It's then that he saw the bloody streaks on her hands. The bloody swatches were cracked, like the mud of a dried river bed.

I'm not going to ask about that, he thought. Not now. Not until she's ready to tell me.

"We'll do something, Ali," he said. "Something . . . there's got to be something we can do . . ."

Then—much too late—he heard steps from behind him. The push of heavy feet scraping at rocks on the ground, treading carefully over the clutter of broken concrete.

"Of course there is," a voice whispered. "In fact, there's more to do than you might bargain for . . ."

Jim's fingers leaped from Ali and then searched the ground for a rock. So damn primitive, he thought. Living like cave people, ready to kill or be killed.

His fist closed on a jagged stone and he raised his hand.

When, belatedly, he recognized the quiet, thoughtful timbre of that voice.

It was—

"Lindstrom," Ali whispered.

Dr. Flynn Lindstrom, the Time Lab's reluctant historian, the man who told them how to weave back to normal the unraveled skein of time. A brilliant man who worked wonders—as long as he was kept well clear from any spirits.

Jim stood up.

"What are you doing here?" Jim asked. "We thought that you were inside the Time Lab, with McManus?"

Lindstrom laughed. "No. Now that would have been a fine end to things, eh, Alessandra? All our work down the tubes, so to speak, just because we were found in the lab, unprotected." Lindstrom laughed.

Ali grabbed his arm.

"So you mean Dr. McManus isn't inside the Time Lab?"

"No. Nor is Dr. Beck."

Jim heard voices. He moved to the edge of the shattered library wall and looked back at the lab.

The soldiers were lining up and boarding their terror trucks.

"They're done," Jim said.

"Yes," Lindstrom said, his voice deep and concerned. "And it's not too safe to stay here. If the Corps doesn't spot us, then the Packs might chance upon us. I wouldn't give much for our chances at night."

"The Corps?" Jim asked. "What's the 'Corps'?"

Ali huddled close to him. "The Packs . . . are those—?"

Lindstrom chuckled, but without his normal reassuring heartiness. Just trying to keep our spirits up, Jim guessed. And keep us sane.

"I'll explain everything—" another small chuckle—"or nearly everything. But please, can we get a move on?"

Jim nodded, then, with his first step, he asked, "Where? Where are we going?"

"To the Cloisters . . ." Lindstrom said. Lindstrom marched out across the field of rubble. "The Cloisters . . . worth a visit . . . even in these rather horrible times . . ."

"It's a castle," Lindstrom said, squinting into the darkness.

They were by the river, crouching behind a fat maple tree in what Jim guessed must be Riverside Park. He held Ali tight as he looked around, waiting for a hungry band of Fun City residents to pounce upon them.

"Worried about the Packs, are you?" Lindstrom asked. "They won't come here, not by the bridge." The George Washington Bridge was ahead, barely visible. There were no lights on. There was just the slightly darker outline of the bridge.

Lindstrom's smile caught some faint light bouncing off the river. "They know that they'd be shot, no questions. It's just too heavily patrolled here."

"So what are we doing here?" Ali asked.

"Not getting caught, I should hope. You see, we have a link to their communications network, our own form of Ultra, if you will. We know the schedule the Corps follows. If we stay here another few minutes, we should be fine . . ."

Jim sighed. Fine, Lindstrom says. That seemed doubtful . . .

We're huddled here like cartoon characters hiding from the Big Bad Wolf. The park seemed deserted, but every now and then Jim thought he heard a moan or a scream coming from somewhere deeper into the overgrown park.

Lindstrom raised a finger.

"There. Listen . . . it's one of their trucks passing by. Another minute or two, and we should be able to press on. No talking, mind you, but—"

"You were talking about the Cloisters?"

Lindstrom turned to Ali. "Yes. Marvelous place, actually a collection of medieval cloisters, a wonderful Romanesque chapel, a chapter house—simply beautiful. Why, the Unicorn tapestries alone—"

Jim interrupted. "Professor Lindstrom, I'm not sure that this is a good time for an artistic appreciation of the Cloisters."

"Hmmph," Lindstrom grunted. "Just as well," he said flatly. "there's nothing left. The tapestries, Campin's altarpiece, all gone, looted, vanished . . ."

Jim knew that this was all leading to something, namely the reason they were going to the Cloisters. But he resigned himself to the fact that Lindstrom would have to take his own meandering time to get to the point.

"You see," Lindstrom said, his voice devoid of

artistic rapture, "McManus knew that—inevitably—the scoundrels who were playing with time would change their tactics."

"I thought we had beaten them," Jim said.

Lindstrom laughed. "Hardly, my boy. But I'll let McManus tell you that sad story. Anyway, he knew that they would move again. Only this time they would move against the Time Lab, immediately and decisively with the first changes in time."

"These are only the first changes?" Ali said. "You mean there's *more* to come?"

Lindstrom's great head, his bushy beard, nodded in the gloom. "Apparently. Anyway—"

Lindstrom cocked his head to the side, and then put a schoolmarmish finger up to his lips.

Trucks. Two, maybe three of them, Jim guessed from the sounds.

Jim waited, huddled against the tree, aware of the smells of the dirt, the river, his own chilling sweat.

The sounds faded.

Lindstrom stood up.

"Come on," he said. "We have to hurry now. We've got to get past the bridge, then onto the road—unfortunately—all the way up to the Cloisters." Lindstrom got up and started off.

"But what's there?" Jim hissed, hurrying to catch up with him.

"Oh," Lindstrom said, turning back just slightly, "I thought that you had figured that one out, my boy. The Time Lab, of course. We moved the whole operation there, secretly, of course, well before this happened."

"And McManus is there?" Ali asked.

Lindstrom shook his head.

"I don't know. I hope to heavens he is, Alessandra. Because—"

An ominous pause, Jim noted.

''Well, let's not dwell on that little scenario, shall we?''

And then Lindstrom kept walking towards the dark bridge.

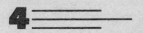
4

"It's beautiful," Ali whispered.

She clutched Jim's hand and squeezed it tight. It was hard to believe that she hadn't visited the museum before. Now, silhouetted by the deep purple of the night, the Cloisters looked gorgeous, a gothic monument on the Hudson.

Lindstrom cleared his throat.

"I think everything looks okay," he said. "You know," he said, "I once did a short monograph on the Unicorn tapestries, how the hunt for the mythical unicorn reflected the changing medieval society fate . . ." Lindstrom paused and cocked his head proudly. "Rather good work, if I do say so myself."

He sighed.

"Well, let's go."

Lindstrom stood up and briskly strolled off into the dark like some determined Berliner out to buy a dinner sausage and a newspaper.

"He's going to get us killed," Ali said.

"C'mon," Jim said, tugging at her. Lindstrom was their only ticket out of this mess. While Jim didn't trust Lindstrom's reconnoitering skills, he knew that they had no choice.

He pulled Ali along, into the gloom, towards the castle.

Which now looked more like a ruins. The basic

structure of the Cloisters was still there—the towers, the open courtyard, the great wall. But the parapet was pitted as if it had been shelled by the Saracens, and there were gaping pits in the outer walls. Dark holes where the windows had been shattered.

He had a hard time thinking that the Time Lab was in there.

That it was still operational.

A disturbing thought occurred to him.

Maybe Lindstrom's crazy. Maybe the old history professor lost it in the last time shift. And he's dragged us here, to the site of his academic success. And he'll lead us inside, talking to the dank walls, chattering with the rats (big fat ones, enjoying the run of the manse), totally mad, a victim of lost time.

Ali's hand had slipped away. Jim suddenly found himself rushing forward and grabbing it again, holding her tight.

"Stay with me, Ali. Stay with me . . . I'm not too sure about this . . ."

Lindstrom walked up to the main entrance to the Cloisters, to the huge metal doors that stretched to the first parapet.

Hope you have the right key, Jim thought.

He heard Lindstrom muttering to himself.

Good, he thought. Now the old man is talking to himself. That's a good sign, real good.

Jim looked around nervously. The air was frigid, and he could feel his nervous sweat turning cold and clammy under his clothes.

And as he turned, he saw something glistening on the walls of this castle on the Hudson.

He saw it, just barely, just catching the tiny amount of ambient light.

Words, painted across the bricks. The paint could have been red, or green, or black, it was impossible to tell in this gloom.

But—for some reason—Jim immediately assumed they were red.

Big, bold words written in red.

Death to the R!

"Look," Jim said, squeezing Ali's hand.

(And was it his imagination, or was Ali pulling against him, trying to tug her hand away, as if the physical contact itself felt bad? And Jim wondered where she had been before they met at the old Time Lab . . . what had really happened to her?)

Jim went over to Lindstrom who was furiously working his fingers on the edge of the door.

"Lindstrom," Jim hissed.

The professor said nothing.

"Lindstrom!" Jim said louder. The history professor turned slightly towards Jim. "What do those words mean?"

Lindstrom shook his head. Jim wasn't sure whether the professor was shaking his head at the door . . . or what. "I can't—" Lindstrom said, breathing hard. "I can't get this door open. It was always open just a crack. But now—"

And Jim revived his earlier hypothesis. Namely, that Lindstrom is crazy. And, quite obviously, he's brought us up here to get killed.

"The words, Lindstrom. What do they mean. What the hell does 'Death to R' mean?"

Lindstrom removed his fingers from the giant metal door, like a kid unable to crack a cookie jar.

"I can't get the door open," Lindstrom announced, his eyes filmy and wet in the blackness.

We've got to get out of here, Jim thought. It's a damn wild goose chase, and we're the geese.

He turned to Ali, to tell her.

But she wasn't there.

She was at the wall of the Cloisters, looking up at the painted words.

Jim watched her turn and look at him.

She had the look of a startled deer. Frozen by terror, unable to move. What made her do that, he wondered. What scared Ali . . . ?

But then he heard the sound. A foot stepping on some leaves, coming from the side of the building.

And Jim opened his mouth, ready to scream for them all to run, to get out of here before it was too late.

(He remembered how well the guard's rifles worked, with nifty high-speed bullets that cut the hungry crowd down with an ear-piercing whistle.)

His mouth opened.

Too late. Because somebody was already there, at the corner, then next to Ali, standing next to her.

Holding her tight . . .

Jim moved. In seconds he ran from Lindstrom and the door, to where Ali was standing, next to a spectral figure, skeleton thin, holding her.

Stupid man, Jim cursed Lindstrom. He's gone crazy and we get to pay for it.

He readied himself to leap on the figure.

I'll grab his throat, Jim thought. Wrap my hands around his windpipe and squeeze until—

The figure spoke.

In a voice that—for a moment—Jim didn't recognize. Until, just as Jim was about to land, it sunk in. The sound of the voice, the odd formality of it, the memory of the cheerful way it sounded when delivering the most incredibly strange facts.

It was McManus.

Jim stopped.

Rather like Wily Coyote just before reaching the cliff's edge.

"McManus," Jim said, too loudly.

The physicist shushed him. "Please, Jim. Not so loud. The park gets very, er, active, as the night wears on."

Lindstrom came over to them.

"McManus! there's something wrong with the door. I can't—"

McManus brought a finger up to his lips. "No, there isn't. There was too much activity out here. I thought we'd better find a *better* way to get inside." McManus turned to Ali. "It's very good to see you, Alessandra." McManus gave out a tiny laugh. "Not to say essential . . ."

Jim shifted his weight.

"Oh, and good to see you, Tiber. Very good. Now, let's get out of the cold, shall we?"

Jim reached out and grabbed McManus's arm as he turned.

"What's this graffiti mean?" Jim said. "Death to—"

"To 'R.' Yes. But please, Jim—I'll explain everything, but it will all make a lot more sense if you allow me to start from the beginning. And then you'll understand it all." Another small laugh. "Or nearly all . . ."

Lindstrom came beside Jim and patted his shoulder in a fatherly way meant, Jim assumed, to reassure him.

Which it didn't.

Because with every turn in this little game they were playing, from the deserts of North Africa to the jungles of Vietnam, things seemed to be turning worse.

Not better.

"C'mon, Jim," Lindstrom whispered. "Maybe I can find the castle's wine cellar."

Jim shrugged, and let himself be led along.

McManus's entrance was no entrance at all. He led them around to the side wall, and then back, to a small courtyard that seemed to end in a dead-end of flat stone.

But McManus picked up a heavy plank that lay on the ground and Jim saw something that looked like a manhole.

"I had Toland wire it," McManus said. "It's not exactly a foolproof alarm system, but we'll know if anyone should try breaking in. If we move fast, we should have enough time . . ."

Ali shivered beside Jim.

"There's that word again," she said.

Yes, *time* . . . Jim thought. There was always plenty of it, or too little. And maybe one of these *times* there will be none at all.

McManus used a pole to work the metal cover off. He grunted and Jim moved to help him. The lid slid off, and then to the side.

"The alarm is sounding now . . ." McManus said. "But Toland will know it's us."

When the lid was off, McManus gestured at the opening. Ever the chevalier, he graciously helped Ali into the black opening.

More craziness, Jim wondered. Maybe both McManus and Lindstrom have gone crackers.

But then Lindstrom hurried in, and McManus put his hand on Jim's back. "Come on, Jim. Let us show you what we've done."

Jim nodded, trying to hear the sounds of craziness in McManus's voice.

For a moment, he imagined being led into some dungeonlike cell, with its candles, rats, and a case of Amontillado to help weather the end of the world.

Jim slid into the hole, and the smells rewarded his apprehension. He heard the metal lid being slid back into place and then a bolt of some kind being thrown. It was black, and only McManus's voice urging the party to hurry got them moving.

Moving, stepping into slimy puddles until he heard Ali call out.

"I see something," she said.

And then Jim saw it. The tiniest crack of light. As they got closer, Jim saw the barest outline of stairs and then, at the top, a door.

Where, Jim hoped, it would be drier.

He heard Ali, and then Lindstrom clomping up the stairs.

Jim banged his shin against the first step.

"Ouch," he said.

"Okay?" McManus asked, the round tones of his voice making him sound like a professionally considerate funeral director.

"I'm fine," Jim said.

Jim clomped up the stairs. Suddenly the door at the top opened, and blinding light filled the stairwell and Jim saw how nasty-looking it was down here. As bad as it smelled, it looked even worse.

(And for that second—the smells, the blackness, the feeling of being trapped seemed to hit him with something like a memory. But no, he immediately recognized, not a memory. It was something else, something from the—

"I was getting worried," a voice boomed from the open door.

"No fear," McManus said from behind Jim. "Just took them a while to get here."

Jim saw Toland's large frame, and the rifle slung to his side. He didn't know which he was happier to see, the burly security guard from the Time Lab or his gun. But Toland was out of uniform, and Jim was getting impatient to hear what had happened.

Toland clasped Jim's hand as he walked by. "Good to have you back with us," Toland said, as if Jim had just returned from a bit of R&R.

And Jim entered the brilliant glare that—except for the cramped space, stone walls, low ceiling, and tangy odors—looked very much like the Time Lab . . .

* * *

"Yes, we've brought everything here, everything that we needed." McManus stood in the center of the room, looking taller than normal due to the low ceilings. Dr. Marianne Beck, her face showing clearly how much she worried about McManus, stood just behind him. Dr. Julian Jacob, master of the tachyon generator, smiled at them as if they had all taken a nice evening's walk, and then hurried to the safety of his precious controls.

"The Cloisters was already wired with sufficient power since everything from major art acquisitions to maintenance was computer driven."

"And the tachyon generator?" Ali asked.

Good question, thought Jim. Just how did they get the generator here?

"That *was* difficult, eh, Dr. Lindstrom?"

Lindstrom grunted from behind his terminal. Jim heard him tapping at his keys, scrolling through pages on his monitor.

McManus continued . . . "I worked through the office of the curator of the Metropolitan Museum of Art, Monsieur Andre Dassain. Once Dassain understood the enormity of what we were facing—and who better to put the whole thing in historical perspective?—he gave us every assistance. The Cloisters was a perfect spot. We coordinated the transfer with a major landscaping project on the southwest slope, facing the Hudson River. The tachyon generator was buried in the ground, rather quickly. A smaller lab, with lines running to the particle generator was set up here, completely shielded of course . . ."

McManus smiled.

"We are immune to changes in the outside world."

"But why?" Ali asked. "What made you move it?"

McManus looked over at Lindstrom. Lindstrom kept at his pecking, and then, aware of the eyes on him, he looked up. "Oh . . . yes," he said gruffly. "Well, do you remember that moment right after you were reunited, back at the lab—"

"After the Iron Men's attempt to capture the American Embassy during the Tet Offensive," McManus added.

Jim nodded.

Lindstrom cleared his throat. "Well, you'll remember that everything was back to normal. Everything, that is, except for one small piece of data."

"Which was?" Jim said.

He noticed Toland move away from them, over to a wall filled with monitors and oscilloscopes, as if there was a terminal heart patient in the room.

Toland seemed uneasy.

Lindstrom stood up. "A small glitch that somehow connected Watergate and the Middle Ages . . . the early Middle Ages," Lindstrom said meaningfully.

"I don't get it," Ali said. "Everything was put right. You said so."

Lindstrom nodded, and stroked his bushy beard. "Yes. That's true. It was all put right. But still there was this connection that popped up in the screen. Something appeared wrong with Watergate, with the testimony—"

Jim saw McManus raise his hand. He pursed his lips as if Lindstrom was about to say too much.

There's something funny going on here, Jim thought.

Something very funny . . .

Lindstrom stopped talking.

McManus picked up the ball. "It took us awhile to figure out what was wrong—"

"And the scale of it!" Lindstrom added, not without a reproving glance from McManus.

"We found out enough to know that the Time Lab

itself was in danger, imminent danger," McManus said. "It had to be moved."

"Why didn't you tell us?"

Now McManus looked over to Lindstrom, looking for some help explaining what must be a difficult problem.

"You see, Alessandra," Lindstrom said, "if we told you of our plans we'd be affecting the present without knowing what was happening. We restricted the information—our concerns—to just ourselves, and Dr. Beck, of course . . . and Toland."

Jim waited, feeling their embarrassment.

Embarrassment, because that plan of action hadn't turned out too well.

"So the Iron Men struck again? They dabbled with the past, and that's how all that craziness outside came about?" Jim asked.

"Yes," McManus said. "And no."

"What Elliot is trying to say is that, this time, something *different* is happening—" Lindstrom caught himself. "Well, maybe not *so* different."

Jim saw McManus shake his head at Lindstrom's inability to keep what must be a secret.

Then he watched Toland at the monitors. The guard slipped on a pair of headphones. Jim imagined him listening to the rustling sounds outside the castle walls, the sounds of squirrels darting nervously around, crows calling to the black night, and other sounds . . .

Toland seemed *concerned* . . .

"It's not the Iron Men?" Ali asked, referring to KGB maniacs who were playing with the past.

"Oh," McManus said. "It is the Iron Men." He laughed hollowly. Nobody else got the joke. "But it's—" he looked at Lindstrom, and Jim knew that here were lots of things being held back . . .

"It's trouble from the future," McManus said flatly. And he smiled now. "I'm afraid that the Iron

Men are getting help from the future . . . and it's going to make your work that much harder . . .''

It took but a second for the words to completely register with Jim.

Your work. Funny, he thought, but I never considered this a *job.*

Jim started to ask a question.

But Toland came over to them, pushing his cordless headphones off his head.

''I've got something, Dr. McManus.''

And for the moment, all other concerns were forgotten.

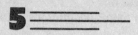

5

"At the main entrance," Toland said. *"There.* You can see them on camera one."

At the sound of Toland's voice—lowered to a chilling whisper—everyone crowded to the bank of monitors. The screens were all red and black.

Toland tapped one of the screens, and Jim saw a black shape, and then another, dark blurs gliding across one screen, and then onto another.

"I don't see anything," Lindstrom said, leaning forward. "Just a lot of—"

"The infrared's hard to see," McManus said to Toland, quietly. "Is there anything you can—?"

Toland nodded. He reached down to a small control panel in front of him. "Sure. I can digitally enhance the image. There's a delay—a few seconds worth, but—"

Everyone waited while Toland hit some buttons. Jim looked over at Ali. She had her arms tightly wrapped around herself. It was cold in here, and Jim wondered whether McManus had thought to move a heating unit into the castle.

Things would get real uncomfortable in a few weeks as fall gave way to a New York winter. Cold, slushy and—if you're without heat—deadly.

But then the obvious occurred to Jim.

If we're all still here weeks from now, it won't matter.

Not any of it.

The screen changed to a high contrast black and white. Lindstrom grew excited. "Yes, now I see them." Jim saw Lindstrom lean forward. "Why, there's a whole bunch of them. Look, on that screen, too!"

And Lindstrom was right. Each screen was filled with the black shapes.

Finally Jim spoke.

"What's going on, Dr. McManus?"

McManus smiled. "I don't know, Jim. It's a Pack, as they call themselves. Yes, definitely a hunting pack. And unfortunately, they're coming right here."

Jim heard Ali shiver, and he turned to her.

"Isn't there anything you can do, anything that can stop them?" she asked.

McManus pursed his lips, giving the question full consideration. "No," he answered at last. "We must stay here and hope that they don't find us."

Jim kept his eyes on Ali.

There was a new fear there, right in her eyes, her voice. And again he wondered: what has happened to her?

Toland spoke to the nervous group.

"Odds are they won't find our back entrance, and all the ground-level entrances to the main hall of the Cloisters, through the tapestry hall and the small chapel, are sealed. We can get out but—unless they brought some heavy-duty firepower—they won't get in."

Then Ali said something.

Very quietly, holding everyone's attention effortlessly. "But if they know we're here, if they want us—"

And Jim looked around to make sure that everyone knew what she meant by that.

"If they *know,* they won't stop looking until they find us."

No one said anything. There wasn't, Jim knew, a good answer to what Ali had just said.

McManus cleared his throat. "*If* they know, Ali. But they may just be trying their luck. The city is a very desperate place now. We should just wait." He forced a smile. "Wait and watch."

Jim looked back at the monitors. The images were clearer now, definitely looking like people, flitting here and there.

"Can we have sound?" McManus asked.

Toland nodded. "But I want to keep it low. In case anyone out there might hear," he whispered.

Jim watched Toland turn a dial, and voices, more like bird sounds, crowlike noises, filled the room.

Toland eased back on the volume.

The sounds, the voices, were creepy. Hungry, excited sounds.

To quote the evil witch from Oz, Jim thought, "What a world . . ."

They listened for a few minutes, and the sound made the waiting that much worse.

"Enough," Lindstrom said. "We don't need to hear that."

It was like being the main course at a banquet and hearing the guests chattering about how good the food was going to be.

Right, thought Jim, enough sound . . .

Lindstrom snorted his approval as Toland brought the volume all the way down. "I'm going back to my work," the history professor said. He looked at McManus. "I suggest you get on with your, er, briefing, McManus."

"Yes," McManus smiled. "I suppose you're right . . ."

And the wizened physicist gestured at some folding chairs . . .

* * *

"It's war," McManus said flatly. "And this time the gloves are off . . ."

Dr. Beck, whose expertise was tending the time travellers bodies when they were not occupied, poured some rich herbal tea that filled the cramped lab with an incongruously aromatic aroma.

Dr. Jacob, a taciturn gnome, sat near the back wall, not really part of the group, more of appendage to his wall of controls that operated the great underground tachyon generator.

"Twice now the Iron Men have played with history, and twice we've defeated them. But now they've moved again, decisively. And I'm afraid this is an all or nothing shot . . ."

"Why do you say that?" Ali asked.

"It's the time stream, Alessandra. It's not a ribbon, something you can tie into so many knots. Every alteration—and believe me, what we did were *also* alterations—makes the strands of time grow increasingly chaotic . . . and dangerous."

"Dangerous? How can it be dangerous?" Jim asked.

"Good question," Lindstrom chimed in. "This was something that I didn't understand either."

"It's like this. Every strand of the time stream represents the cause and effect relationships of billions upon billions of sub-atomic events. If the Iron Men alter the stream, they alter a certain number of those events. And then we act to rectify matters, to change time back. Though you can remember everything you did, you're changed, like everything else in the world. But *part* of your consciousness is rooted to what happened before."

McManus walked around the lab as he spoke, looking at the stone walls, as if he could imagine the stream. But Jim knew that McManus, like Ali and himself, had seen the time stream.

Or maybe *felt* it would be a more appropriate word. A great open expanse of light and color, and the sensation of floating, the feeling that you could turn here or there and follow a completely different path.

It was an odd temptation, being in the stream, and continuing along a single path.

A temptation that Jim didn't want to face again.

"But we didn't really rectify things, not completely. A few minor historical events were left out of place, jumbled. And with each use of the Time Transference Device, we multiply the number of discrepancies."

Jim interrupted. "And what about that brochure, from the *Intrepid?* How could that exist?"

"How indeed? I don't know the answer to that, Jim, but it shows how *bad* things have become, how bad they might be. That might only be the beginning of the strange anomalies that could happen."

"And the danger?" Ali asked.

McManus turned to her, a genuine smile on his face. He cares for her deeply, Jim realized. A protégé, yes, but Ali meant something more to him.

"The Iron Men, and our Time Lab have introduced chaos into the time stream. Events that should never have happened, could never happen, *have.* And they proceed to cause millions of other small events that never should have happened. Why, it's almost like a chain reaction. If the Iron Men fail this time, the window of opportunity—in this century at least—will be closed to them."

"And if they, or we . . . did cause that 'chain reaction'?"

Lindstrom came forward, easing himself out of what looked like the only comfortable chair in the lab. "I did the research on that question, Jim. If we push the time stream too much, introduce too many wild cards, we would create what I call the 'flashback effect'— named in honor of—"

McManus interrupted.

"An unfortunate syndrome that affected a whole group of college students who had the misfortune of going to school during the Sixties," McManus explained. As usual, the physicist was showing little patience for Lindstrom's tendency to ramble.

"Flashback? What would happen?"

"Changes would start to ripple back and forth in time, the altered past affecting the future—quite naturally. But then the newly reconstructed future would start sending messages back to the past, which in turn would interact with the other chaotic elements, and—"

"So on and so on, until, well, we don't *know* what might happen," McManus added.

Lindstrom raised a finger. "I do have an idea, though."

Jim saw McManus's face scrunch up in a disapproving scowl as if Lindstrom was about to say too much.

"Just an idea," Lindstrom said, turning away, trudging back to his chair, and his computer.

"I want to hear it," Ali said.

"Yes . . ." Jim said. "If we're to do anything, we deserve to have it all laid out for us."

McManus shook his head. "Professor," he said to Lindstrom derisively.

Lindstrom didn't bother to get up again. "All those changes, accelerating, back and forth, growing in size . . ."

"And what would happen?" Jim pressed.

"It's only an idea," Lindstrom apologized. "But the time stream would become a completely unstable thing. True time would last one final nano-second, and then disappear . . ."

"To be replaced by?" Ali whispered.

Lindstrom turned and smiled at her. "Haven't a clue, my dear Alessandra. Not a clue. I just know it wouldn't be very good for the human race."

"Or," McManus added, "the universe. Which is why we have to stop them this time for good," he said. "We'll all have to go back, you two, Lindstrom, myself . . ."

Dr. Beck shook her head and said, "Ich . . . Elliot . . ."

The woman seemed to stammer.

Almost saying something else.

"No," McManus said. "It's perfectly safe. I returned in fine form last time. There's just *too* much to do."

Jim saw Toland moving around the monitors, looking at one, and then the other. The digital enhancer was off, and the screens glowed an ominous red. Something was bothering the security guard again.

"We all go?" Jim said. "Fine. Let's do it. Anything that gets rid of this mess is worth doing. So what year are we going to . . . what do we have to do . . . ?"

Like a practiced vaudeville team of top bananas, Lindstrom and McManus looked at each other, and then at Jim.

"I can't tell you where we're going, Jim," McManus said. "But you're going to—what's the year, Lindstrom?"

Lindstrom rifled through some printouts on his desk.

"Let's see. Ah, here we are. 534," Lindstrom said. And then he added, almost as an afterthought, "A.D."

Jim's mouth flew open as if he was about to disgorge a ferret. "But I thought the problem was in this century? What's this all about?"

McManus looked discomfited.

"It is, Jim. But there's one small detail that we need to correct. Before we all go on to the year that concerns us . . ."

"What year?" Jim asked, feeling as if he was being shanghaied. I don't mind helping my fellow man, he thought, even the whole universe.

But I *would* like to know the whole story . . .

McManus smiled and shrugged. "I can't tell you that now. It would affect what you have to do back there. But I promise you—as soon as you've wrapped things up in the Sixth Century—everything will become—" he looked at Lindstrom for the proper word—"clear."

Lindstrom didn't seem to agree with the choice of McManus's *bon mot*. But then he turned and nodded happily. "Right, clear as glass, Jimbo. Just," the professor gestured at his damning printouts, "we can't tell you now. You'll understand . . . it all later."

Jim looked at Ali. "Is Ali coming with me this time, is she—?"

McManus shook his head.

"No. She'll wait. We'll all wait. Until you're done."

Jim had to wonder whether they would have to really wait, as if it was real time. Or would it happen instantly since he would be in the past.

My head spins, he thought.

"534," he said. "A.D. Where?"

Lindstrom dug around on his desk, pulling out an atlas.

"Mount Badon, Jim. And, if we have the calendars correct, October 15th." He licked at his lips. "I may be off by a factor of a day or so. But you'll know once you get there. And we'll wait."

"Mt. Badon? What am I going to Mt. Badon for? I never heard of the place."

McManus put his hand on Jim's shoulder.

"Jim, Lindstrom will brief you. But there's not a lot of—" he laughed—"time."

"But why?"

"The Battle of Mt. Badon," Lindstrom said. "You never heard of the Battle of Mt. Badon?"

A faint bell tinkled in Jim's head. And then, a connection.

Jim laughed.

"It's a myth," Jim said. "God, it's nothing but a myth. It's not real. None of it—"

Lindstrom laughed aloud. "Oh, yes, Jim, it is quite real. We know it is." Lindstrom stood up and walked over to Jim. "We know that the king of all the Britains defeated the Saxons at what was called Mount Badon, in what is now eastern France." Lindstrom paused, looking over at Ali. "We know that the leader was King Arthur, that he led his knights from his castle. And we know that the Iron Men changed what happened that day nearly 1500 years ago."

King Arthur, Jim thought. Knights of the Round Table.

A children's story, Jim thought, characters from *Tristan und Isolde,* from *Roman de Brut,* from the *Historia* of Geoffrey of Monmouth. A myth, a fable . . .

He felt Lindstrom looking at him.

And Jim knew that the historian must have damn good evidence that it was real.

"And what am I to do there?"

A pause, much too long. And then McManus squeezed Jim's shoulder.

"Tell us first, Jim, do you know aikido?"

And Jim was about to answer that unexpected question when a high-pitched whistle began to shriek.

"The alarm," McManus whispered.

And all eyes turned to Toland to hear the bad news . . .

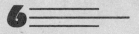

Toland tapped a monitor.

The monitor on the far left.

"They're inside," Toland said, quietly. Then, just to make sure everyone knew what he was talking about . . . "The Pack is inside the Cloisters . . ."

"Okay," McManus said. "Alright. That's still not bad. How did they get in?"

Jim saw Toland shrug. "They must have climbed up to the wall. There's some smashed windows covered only by grates. Wouldn't be too difficult—"

Jim listened. But he also thought:

Aikido? What the hell is McManus talking about?

As if sensing his befuddlement, the physicist turned to him.

"More the reason to hurry, Jim." McManus turned to Dr. Jacob. "Ready, Julian?"

Dr. Jacob nodded.

Then McManus gestured at Toland. "Could you quiet the alarm, Toland? I think we're all quite alert now."

Then, back to Jim. "Dr. Beck will get you ready. I'm afraid, like all of us, you'll have to stay right here in the lab. We don't have the space for a separate room for 'travellers.' "

McManus grabbed Jim's arm, trying to direct him towards a chair near the corner of the lab. And Jim remembered the last time he used the Time Transference Device, how he and Ali broke into the lab because he wanted to do some on-site research about the Beatles, pre-Ringo.

I didn't know I signed on for a full hitch, Jim thought.

He pulled away from McManus's arm.

And said:

"Where's Ali going?"

"I can't tell you. If you know that, if you know what she has to do, it could affect what you must do back there . . ."

"Which is?"

"Lindstrom will brief you on what we think must happen. But remember: be alert to other possibilities. We may not have all the data . . ."

"You may not have all the data . . . God. And now this castle is crawling with flesh-eating crazies. Sometimes, Dr. McManus, I wonder how you remain so unflappable."

McManus smiled at that. "Sometimes so do I."

The doctor grabbed Jim's arm and led him to the chair.

Ali followed. "Don't worry about me, Jim. I'll be fine."

Dr. Beck appeared beside him with a syringe.

"Roll up your sleeve," she said in her best no-nonsense this-is-good-for-you voice. Except Jim knew it wasn't going to be good for him.

She had a moist swab in her other hand. She rubbed his arm, smearing a patch of skin with alcohol. He felt McManus pat his back. Then he felt the swift stab of the needle.

"What is this?" he asked.

"A muscle relaxant," Beck said. "It will make the process easier on your body."

Jim nodded. "And what's this about aikido?"

McManus looked at Beck again.

The Time Lab doctor put down the syringe and pad. Then she turned to Jim. "A five-minute lesson," she said, "in the art of resisting force and using your enemy's momentum."

Jim heard Lindstrom titter, and then cover his laugh with a quick cough.

And for a few remarkable minutes the matronly Dr. Marianne Beck showed Jim four things—just four, she said, so he wouldn't be confused. Then she had him repeat them, even as he began to feel the muscles in his legs start to go all rubbery.

He smiled at the drunken sensation.

"I think I better sit down," Jim said.

"Lindstrom!" McManus said.

And Lindstrom hurried over beside Jim. McManus attached the skull cap that was the key component of the Time Transference Device. Jim knew that his body wouldn't be going anywhere.

But his consciousness would join the stream of tachyons, the incredibly fast stream of sub-atomic particles that made up what we called "time."

Only, his consciousness would be linked to particles going the wrong way.

Like salmon, he thought, fighting their way upstream.

And he had another disturbing thought: has anyone ever travelled that far, nearly 1500 years? Was it possible? And if it wasn't, what would happen to him?

The skull cap, with its wires leading back to Dr. Jacob's control board, was snapped in place.

"Too tight?" Beck asked solicitously.

Jim smiled, feeling like a plucky '60s astronaut about to be fired into outer space strapped inside a decanter-shaped tin can.

With no controls.

Not a bad analogy.

Lindstrom was beside him.

"Here we go, Jim. Listen up. And remember—be alert to any changes that we didn't anticipate."

Ali came beside him and she grabbed his hand. He let her hand close around his. And he looked at her, hoping that some day, somewhere, she would tell him what had happened to her.

He let her squeeze his hand while his fingers just rested against her, enjoying the pressure.

She smiled at him.

A kiss would be too much to hope for, he knew.

Lindstrom started talking.

Jim interrupted.

"I—it's okay if Ali hears all this?"

Lindstrom nodded "Why, certainly. She'll be going in front of you, in terms of time. Knowing what you did, or didn't do, won't affect her at all." Lindstrom paused, and looked up at the ceiling for a moment. "At least I don't think so."

McManus was at Lindstrom's elbow. "We have to get going, Lindstrom."

Lindstrom nodded.

And then—Jim's legs feeling like taffy, like long strands of bubble gum melting on the sidewalk in the hot summer sun—Lindstrom told him about Arthur, his knights, and—oh, yes—the chivalric code . . .

And someone named John Dean.

Ali took a breath and stepped back as McManus gestured at them to move well away from Jim.

Jim raised his fingers from the arm rest and wiggled them, the only goodbye wave he could do with his arms strapped to the chair.

Jim smiled at her, looking amazingly unfazed by the craziness of Lindstrom's story, unfazed by what he was supposed to do. At the near impossibility of it, Ali thought.

I never would have picked Jim for the brave sort, thought Ali. Not the hero type . . .

And she knew that he was terribly troubled by the way she was acting.

By this chill that had claimed her.

She tried to fight it, really tried to shake it off.

She even told herself:

It wasn't real. In those few hours, it didn't happen. It's not real history.

But then she could feel them, feel them around her, *on* her, touching, probing. She heard their voices, the commands, the sudden stinging slaps, the wild cackling that greeted her cries, her tears. And then, when they grew tired of her fighting them, confused by her resistance, they just pulled out some handy rope.

And the real horror began.

And she told herself:

All the showers in the world, all the baths, all the cleaning, and soap, and scrubbing won't *ever* make it go away.

Jim wiggled his fingers.

She'd tell him. Sometime, when this was over.

He smiled at her.

McManus barked at everyone to stand well away, ready to give the signal to Dr. Jacob, ready to take Jim away.

"No," she whispered. And then louder, making sure that they could hear her. "No!"

And she ran to him, her hand trapping his fingers. And then she leaned down to his face, Jim looking goofy under the skull cap, and she said:

"Couldn't let you go without a kiss," she said.

He smiled. His eyes, locked on hers, looked watery.

Equal parts pain and joy.

"Till we meet again," she laughed.

"Till then," he said, smiling back at her.

McManus came to her, and pulled her back.

"Alessandra. Please," he said.

She nodded to Jim and let herself be led back, well away from the chair, well away from the giant, snakelike wires that curled and coiled around the chair, leading back to the generator.

McManus held her.

And then he said:

"Ready."

Ready?

Flynn Lindstrom had to wonder about that. Were they really ready, or was McManus and his Time Lab over his head?

A Mets fan, Lindstrom thought of an apt analogy.

It's a full count, bottom of the ninth, and—once again—we have to come from behind.

And Lindstrom looked at McManus, holding Ali tightly, giving Jacob the signal to send Jim further back than anyone has travelled thus far.

And what was it they had left out of their little briefing, Lindstrom thought?

Oh, lots of things.

Lots. But, as Lindstrom watched McManus, there was something else that bothered him.

It wasn't completely new.

This concern he had about McManus.

No, he never felt completely comfortable with him, not once he made sure that the old Time Lab was swept clean of any spirits.

Fortunately, Lindstrom had a few wonderful Cabernets and Fume's now hidden in the Cloisters . . . so many wonderful hiding places.

But there was this worry that gnawed at Lindstrom.

A question about McManus. And a fear.

How did McManus know that the Time Transference Device would work that far back in time? Dr.

Jacob didn't seem at all assured that it would work. But McManus blithely waved his concern away.

As if he knew.

Knew . . . that it would work.

And that's when this odd fear began to grow in Lindstrom. If McManus knew that it would work, what else did McManus know, what other secrets did he have?

What is McManus up to, Lindstrom wondered.

And am I playing for the right team?

Lindstrom wondered . . .

He heard the tachyon generator whine, the underground accelerator sending a stream of particles into the wall unit behind Jacob.

Do I really know what is going on here?

I hope to God I do . . .

The sensation wasn't exactly familiar.

No, Jim thought, It's probably like the second time you do a free-fall out of an airplane, plummeting a thousand feet before madly grabbing at the handy rip cord, praying that it works.

The sensation wasn't exactly old hat.

But he did remember the tingling that now coursed through his body, how everything, McManus, Lindstrom, the machine, the noises, Ali—

(She kissed me! he thought)

All of it faded into a gossamer fog. Jim felt himself trying to breathe in the fog and then was only dimly aware that he no longer had a mouth, no body with lungs to breathe with.

He was out.

Between bodies, so to speak.

And this trip, he watched the vast time stream, the shimmering network of particles, flowing like a rapids as he joined it, moved with it.

But then he felt himself turn, and—if he was seeing this, not just feeling it—he watched himself moving back, gliding over the stream, making tiny ripples and waves rush past him.

He directed his—what, his consciousness?—to look left, and then right.

And he saw thousands of other ribbony bands, stretching as far as he could see, crossing together, weaving together, and Jim couldn't imagine the size of this net, the extent of the warp and woof of time.

It seemed longer this time.

A longer time travelling in this vapor.

But not as long as could be, he knew, seeing just how far the strands extended in all directions, left, right, up and down . . .

Forever.

Yes, he thought. Time would be a bad thing to lose . . .

He felt something.

Or was it a smell?

But he had no body, no nose. He couldn't feel anything, could he? But the stream darkened, turning wine-red.

No. It wasn't changing. But he was, his consciousness was changing . . .

This time he got to experience it. He could be aware.

Until . . .

Yes. He heard something.

A grunt. Again.

The sound came from within him.

The ribbons of time disappeared.

He looked down.

Jim could *see*.

A blackish metal mesh, reflecting a dull light to his eyes. He tasted salty sweat dripping off his upper lip, onto his lower lip. His tongue snaked out, tasting the salt. The bristles of a beard, a mustache.

He took another step—not his decision.

Another grunt.
And he was *there*.
Someone said something to him.
And—at first—it didn't sound like English.

Like deep end when an end of month. Or even the
last time in toaught around it then.
That too have used group, east, but to ear as about

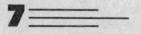

7

Jim looked down at what he was wearing.

He saw, and felt, the thick layer of blackish mesh, heavy metal armor covering his body. He took another step. And grunted. He looked up, seeing the world through a narrow slit.

I'm wearing a helmet, he thought.

How convenient . . .

"Fae, gaon til dae dropt?"

Yes, Jim thought, still sucking at his own rivulets of sweat. Someone was definitely talking to him. No problem, he thought. So what if I don't understand him?

At least not yet.

Because that will change.

It always does.

Just have to be a bit *patient*.

The man spoke again, and Jim looked around for the voice uttering the strange words.

(It's Old English, Jim thought. Or probably something even earlier, something even more primitive, from before the Normans took over the good old United Kingdom and made everyone speak French, forever screwing up the English language.)

Jim waited for understanding, for the words to make sense.

Like they did when he had to speak German, the last time he bounced around in time.

That had happened pretty fast. Not to get alarmed. But the last time he travelled to a foreign land, in a foreign body, language had kicked in almost instantly . . . just as soon as he arrived in Hamburg in 1961 to meet the Beatles . . .

His foot caught in something, trapping it. With difficulty, he swiveled his head left and right. The dull metal of his helmet scratched at his neck. And he groaned again, under all this tremendous weight.

God, he thought, how many pounds am I carrying here—one-hundred, one hundred-twenty-five? I can barely move.

He tried to dislodge his foot from where it was snagged.

But he had to stop and look down to even see his foot, clothed in a mesh of metal links, lodged into a crevice between two rocks. He saw a flower, something like a black-eyed susan, blowing in the steady wind that rushed off the hill.

I'm climbing up, Jim thought. That makes things a lot worse. And—

I'm holding something. I have gloves on, one side with the handy mesh, the other a very stiff leather. What am I holding? he wondered.

The gloves were so heavy Jim could barely keep holding his hand closed tight, grasping—

He squeezed his hand.

And pinned by his trapped foot, he tried turning around, to see—

He heard a clattering behind him. Then, a sound that he remembered from those moments when he zapped past *Gunsmoke,* endlessly repeating on the Family Channel.

An impatient whinny.

He was holding a horse.

"Gae, on," the voice said again, the *lingua franca*

sounding like a mix of war-movie German and tipsy leprechaun.

Little did the Anglo-Saxons know that, when they invaded England, they'd help create what would become the planet's number-one language.

It just wasn't there yet . . .

And neither am I, Jim thought. Neither am I . . .

He heard more voices and still the internal translator, the subconscious host mind, wasn't rising to the occasion. This could get very bad, Jim thought, if something doesn't happen soon.

As if in agreement, his horse snorted.

First things first, he thought.

Jim tried to dislodge his stuck foot by pulling it straight back, like a cork. It popped out. But then the momentum sent him stumbling backwards. His armor—what did they make this stuff out of, lead?— gave him enough of a push that he let go of his horse while he tumbled back onto the rocks down the hillside.

He crashed backwards, feeling as if he was about to tumble over Niagara Falls in a tin can.

He heard the crash and rattle as he landed. The sun glinted through the opening of his facepiece, blinding him with an unearthly brilliance. Damn, the air was so incredibly clear here, before the industrial age.

Jim heard laughing, oddly reassuring even though he figured out that the laughs were at his expense.

More Anglo-Saxon gibberish, and Jim detected question marks dangling, unanswered, in the air.

They're going to think I'm loony if I don't answer them soon, he thought. And just what did they do to crazy people back in the good old Dark Ages?

He tried moving, wiggling turtlelike, but he succeeded in only making his armor rattle.

He wasn't going anywhere.

There was an eclipse.

Someone stood between him and the sun, a giant, a massive man covered in the heavy blackish mail, but with a crimson cape blowing from the back.

"Doen gae her?" the voice boomed and laughed.

Jim smiled before realizing that there was no point in smiling. Only his eyes were visible.

Why can't I understand what he's saying, Jim thought? What the hell is wrong? And he remembered what McManus had said, about the anomalies, the *Intrepid* brochure, the fact that this time they had all remembered the real past even after time had been changed . . . and how small changes could ripple back and forth, like water sloshing in a basin, growing to chaotic waves.

This time-transference stuff wasn't going smoothly.

The large man standing in front of him extended an arm.

He was still laughing, still sending a steady stream of proto-English flying at him.

Please, Jim thought, whatever must happen inside the brain of my host, please let it happen.

Fast . . .

Jim reached out his hand.

The other man pulled hard on him. Jim started coming up, like a flagpole being raised.

Then Jim was upright. The other—what, knight?—smacked his back.

(Though Jim had to wonder . . . he didn't look like the storybook image of a knight. The armor was just a rough mesh, more like chunks of metal. It looked like a link fence pulled tight.)

"Gae on, broder," the knight laughed.

Jim brought his hand up. His head was sopping wet from the sweat. He reached up for his helmet, hoping it wasn't fastened tight with latches of the intricacy of a Chinese puzzle.

But the helmet slid up easily—save for a tiny sucking sound as the helmet's ring passed his skull.

The air felt wonderful.

Jim's rescuer smiled at him.

And spoke.

In words that Jim—at last—understood perfectly.

Ali chewed at her lip and waited.

For a few moments, it was as if Jim had merely fallen asleep. One second he was waving at her, smiling, wiggling his fingers, and the next he looked like a small boy tuckered out by too much play.

But then Dr. Beck came and held Jim's wrist while she checked his pulse with a stethoscope. Even though all of Jim's life signs were being monitored, even though Ali could look at a side wall and see how many times Jim was breathing a minute, how many times his heart was beating, she knew that Beck wanted to make sure that she wasn't missing something.

Ali turned. McManus and Lindstrom bustled about. Lindstrom flicked noisily through his pages of scan paper. Dr. Jacob hovered near the controls of the tachyon generator.

And—for the moment—Ali felt forgotten.

Until McManus looked over and smiled at her.

"Well, Ali, now that Jim is launched we can proceed with phase two."

She nodded. Toland walked over to McManus and tapped his shoulder.

"Fine," she heard McManus, smiling up at her.

He's worried, she thought. No it's worse than that. The old man is scared. In fact, it may be the first time that Ali had seen him scared since this "war" began.

And if *he's* scared, how should I feel?

She waited to hear what Lindstrom and McManus couldn't tell Jim, the real focal point for the Iron

Men's activity . . . the point in time that they had changed to bring their strong police state to power.

And as soon as she thought about that, she felt a disturbing tingle. All this, just because some KGB officers didn't like the way Glasnost turned out? They just want to bring back the old days, the dreams of an invincible Soviet Union burying the rest of the world . . . ?

That was *disturbing* . . .

Disturbing, because—standing here, looking at this ugly new world—it didn't make sense.

Not at all.

"Alessandra," McManus said. "You're ready? Good. I'm afraid Dr. Lindstrom will have to take much more time with you." McManus made a hollow laugh.

Ali nodded.

McManus cleared his throat and said, "Dr. Lindstrom?"

Lindstrom didn't move.

"Dr. Lindstrom," McManus repeated.

Lindstrom surfaced from his stacks of print out.

"Bloody awful mess, completely—" Lindstrom slammed his fist down on the stack. "I tell you, McManus, this time it's all too much. I don't know—"

McManus smiled. Then—an odd gesture—she saw the scientist finger the back of his neck. He looked pained, or discomfited by something. Arthritis perhaps? or—

Ali saw Dr. Beck look over as if she too saw the gesture. McManus wasn't a strong man. This could all be too much for him . . .

"Lindstrom," McManus said a bit hoarsely. "Please, give Alessandra the background she needs."

Lindstrom took a deep noisy breath. He gestured at Ali to come over. She walked to his small wood table—probably lifted from one of the museum's offices. And Lindstrom, who seemed on the verge of yelling at her, looked up and said:

"Well, Alessandra what do you know of Japanese?"

Ali laughed.

While Lindstrom's smile faded.

"Poor Sir Gawain, is the heat addling your poor head?" The knight laughed. "Best keep your helmet off, at least until we can see the damned Merovingian castle."

Jim nodded.

Appreciating that he had permission to keep his metallic head-sauna off.

And Jim turned around.

The hill was filled with twenty, maybe thirty grim-looking warriors looking like primitive knights. Except they were not wearing the sleek armor that Jim remembered seeing in the Metropolitan Museum's wonderful hall of armor.

A few seemed to have only leathery garments with bulky helmets. Others were covered in the thick mesh of mail.

Jim turned to face the man who had picked him off the ground.

"Come, Gawain. You are ready to fight?"

For a second Jim thought that the knight standing in front of him wanted to go a round. Jim licked his lips. But then the big knight turned and gestured at the crest of the hill.

"Over there lies the castle . . . and my lady in distress . . ."

Jim smiled.

"Yes." he said—

Wondering what should come next.

A voice shouted from the top of the hill.

The big knight turned.

Jim saw the scabbard of his sword swing, making a heavy, slow arc. It was a big sword, real big . . .

Good enough to slice a man in two with one blow.

How do I know that, Jim thought. How the hell do I know that?

Just as quickly, he knew the answer.

Because I've *seen* it. I've seen this man unsheathe it, swing it over his head, and, with a barbaric cry, cut through the air and—

The voice yelled again from the crest of the hill.

Saying a word that made gooseflesh sprout on Jim's borrowed, overheated flesh.

"Lord Arthur! Sire!"

The voice rang from the top of the hill. And again:

"My Lord Arthur! The dogs of Dagobert come!"

The smile vanished from the man's face. Jim saw the king's hand slide to the hilt of his sword.

Excalibur.

Or a reasonable facsimile.

Jim turned to see the other warriors hurrying up the hill. Arthur turned to him and said, "Now the heartless curs will taste the metal of Arthur of Camelot."

Jim nodded as Arthur waved to the others. Sure, and Jim thought: that's exactly what I have to prevent.

King Arthur is just too itchy to hack away.

And he doesn't know that he's being set up.

Jim closed his eyes. He heard the rattle of the pack horses—it was too early for mounted knights. That technology was still centuries away. The horses carried food, spare swords and maces, perhaps a ham bone to gnaw.

Jim picked up the bridle to his pack horse and once again began trudging up the hill, pulling the horse and the incredibly heavy coating of mail . . .

Wondering what Ali might be doing.

* * *

"The situtation changes every few minutes, Alessandra." Lindstrom shrugged. "I'm doing the best I can to stay on top of it. But—" he eyed McManus standing close to her elbow—"this time I'm less than optimistic."

"Just proceed, Lindstrom. The sooner she's there, the better."

"It's the same bloody year, Ali," Lindstrom said. "The same year as the *first* time they started playing with time. Perhaps they thought that all they're mucking about in the same year would somehow interact."

"We have no evidence of that, Dr. Lindstrom," McManus said in a schoolmarmish tone.

"Right. Then tell me, Dr. McManus, why are they dabbling with this bloody date, this month? Only weeks after they tried to steal all the priceless art that Herr Goering had secreted away . . . ?

McManus shrugged. Ali looked over at the physicist. As he spoke, she saw him wince, and again—there it was!—he touched his neck.

The old man's in trouble.

"It's obvious, my dear Flynn. What other year decided more about the fate of the world than 1941? I'm just surprised that they didn't figure out how to do something with Hitler's ill-fated Russian excursion."

Lindstrom laughed, a sardonic sound that chilled Ali.

"That will be for next time. Just wait . . ." he growled.

Ali touched the big man's shoulder, gently trying to calm him down. Just behind Lindstrom she could see Jim, sitting in his chair. She watched his chest rise and fall, a smooth, gentle rhythm, as if he didn't have a care in the world.

Except she knew that Jim had entered an even more alien world than the era of Big Band music,

Joe DiMaggio, and world domination. Stranger, and more dangerous—

"What's the exact date I'm being sent to, Dr. Lindstrom?" she asked.

"December 6th, Alessandra. Or the 5th, depending on which side of the dateline you're on."

For a second, no light bulbs went on in Ali's head. But then the obvious connection was there.

Lindstrom pulled out a heavy atlas, and flipped the book open noisily to a page marked with a stack of papers.

It was a map of an island.

She read the name, a familiar name. "Oahu," she said. Then smiling. "Hawaii. I've always wanted to go to Hawaii."

Lindstrom nodded at her sternly, sans amusement. "Sure, Alessandra. Well, I'm afraid you don't get to go there this time, either." Lindstrom turned the page and Ali immediately recognized the new map, a familiar city.

Washington, D.C.

"I'm not sure that you'd want to be there, at Pearl Harbor . . . not on December 7th, 1941. Besides—" he outlined a section of Washington with a thick, black marker, "you're needed here. Study this well, my dear. We wouldn't want you getting lost, now would we? Not on such a special day . . ."

Ali looked at the map.

"And listen up, young lady, so you know what has to really happen on the Day of Infamy . . . and pray to God that I'm right."

8 ═══════════════

Ali felt the chill in the room.

McManus stepped away, as if upset by Lindstrom's words.

We're not exactly together on this one, she thought.

Lindstrom quickly reviewed what really happened at Pearl Harbor. No, he said, Roosevelt *didn't* know that the island was going to be attacked. But yes, an alert had been sent to all the Pacific bases warning of imminent action by the Japanese.

"But they expected the Japanese to hit the Phillipines, Singapore, Wake, Guam, anywhere, except Pearl."

McManus cleared his throat from behind Lindstrom.

"Do hurry, Professor Lindstrom. There is a question of synchronizing things here. I'd hate—"

"Yes, yes," Lindstrom turned. "She'll do a lot better if she knows the background, McManus."

Ali tapped his shoulder again.

"Go on," she whispered.

"Except for two things, everything that could go wrong for our side, did. Radar picked up the attack, but it was discounted. Our planes were bunched together on the airstrips." Lindstrom snorted. "To protect them against saboteurs."

"Please," McManus said. "Less editorializing. We must get moving."

Lindstrom took no notice of McManus.

"You mentioned two good things?" Ali said.

"Besides the fact that Pearl finally got us into the war—the single most important event in the history of mankind—we had two lucky breaks." Lindstrom jabbed a pudgy finger onto the page, pointing at an area below an island, Ford Island.

"All of our carriers were at sea. With our carriers left intact, America lived to fight again. At Midway, the tide would turn."

"And the other break?"

"Admiral Nagumo, the cautious commander on the carrier *Akagi*, looked at the American losses after the second wave and decided to call it a day."

"Hadn't they done enough damage?"

Lindstrom shook his head. "No. There was still the dry docks, and the tremendous fuel reserves, billions of gallons of fuel, the gas farm tanks filled to bursting. If they had been wiped out, Pearl would have become useless. A completely unprepared America would have been fighting from California, having ceded the Pacific to the Greater East-Asian Co-Prosperity Sphere . . ."

"The what?"

Lindstrom laughed. "Before Nintendo, Japan had the Co-Prosperity Sphere, my dear Alessandra. It was Japan's attempt to put the Pacific under one corporate umbrella, so to speak."

"And these are the things that the Iron Men are changing?"

"Oh, no," Lindstrom said. "These are only some of them, the ones you need to now about know. Just like Jim, there's only so much we can tell you . . . and so much that will have to be left for later."

"Later?"

McManus slid between them, a bony finger up to

his lips signalling Lindstrom that their little tête-à-tête was over.

"Later," McManus reiterated.

Lindstrom took a breath.

"Here's what you are to do, Alessandra . . . try to do." He looked up at her, his eyes tired, overwhelmed.

Ali sensed Toland watching his monitors, pacing, holding his rifle close.

It's only a matter of time till they get in here, Ali thought. Then it's all over. The battle for time will have been won by the bad guys.

"Go on," she whispered.

His big, burly hand closed over hers.

And as Ali listened, she studied the maps of Washington, of Oahu, imagining a balmy December night before the world went to hell . . .

Jim pulled his horse, wheezing noisily behind him. Up the hill, clambering over loose rock and stunted bushes.

Until he could see the castle.

Which was a big disappointment.

It didn't look like any castle out of Prince Valiant or some Fifties Technicolor epic with Tony Curtis.

It had a timber roof, and the castle walls were made out of a combination of fieldstone and wood posts. And there, rising from the center, Jim saw a wooden tower, nearly as high as the hill.

Jim stood on the crest, the full force of the late morning wind blowing in his face, cooling his body weighed down by his armor.

And he tried to remember what he learned about this era . . . about the Merovingian knights . . .

He knew that they had controlled most of Germany and France, ruling what was called the "Frankish" empire—Aquitaine, Burgundy, Paris, as well as Austrasia and Neustrasia.

They brought a new art to the world—an abstract, nonrepresentational art—well before the arabesques of the Moslem Moors appeared.

Jim looked at the tower.

And he remembered it.

I've seen a painting of that, he thought. No, not a painting, a tapestry. At the top, there's a bell tower, something else the Merovingian designer excelled at.

Someone nudged him.

Jim spun around.

"Not so terrible looking, is it Gawain?"

The knight stood next to him and the ripe odor of metal and perspiration mixed dizzily with the gusts of air.

Jim smiled at the other knight.

Yet another stalwart from the Round Table, he reminded himself. Yes, sports fans, one of the Round Table . . .

Jim looked at him. The warrior had dark blue eyes and black bushy eyebrows set in a face that smiled easily.

"Yes, quite a prize," Jim said, looking at him, searching for a name—

And then it was there.

Unbelievable . . .

"Lancelot . . ."

Lancelot patted Jim's shoulder. "We have a good day for a battle," Lancelot said.

But Jim barely heard him, thinking of the myth, the legend, of Lancelot, and Arthur, and Guinivere. His final battle with Galahad. Legends to fuel countless generations, to inspire, to move.

And that was just it, Jim thought.

That's why I'm here.

He smiled to himself.

To make sure that John Dean gets it right.

Lancelot's eyes narrowed, as if he saw that Jim had just gotten lost in some meandering.

"Come, I think it's time," Lancelot said, and he strode on down the slope, his pack horse rattling noisily as he led him down the hill.

Jim sniffed at the air.

Jim took a step, then another, following the line of knights down the hill, thinking:

I'm the only one who knows what's really happening here.

I'm the only one who can stop what's about to happen.

The event that could, among other things, save Richard Nixon's ass.

Jim laughed at this.

And wouldn't old tricky Dick be surprised to learn that the fate of his presidency depends on my getting to that tower before anyone else . . .

Especially Arthur.

And Jim hoped that four moves of aikido would be enough to keep his head from being severed from his body.

He looked up. There was movement among the ramparts of the small castle's walls.

This wasn't any sneak attack.

No sir, because that wasn't how they did it in these formative days of chivalry.

And—almost instinctively—Jim touched the hilt of his sword.

Lindstrom patted Ali's hand.

And Ali smiled at him. The historian seemed more agitated than normal. Probably, she thought, because this time he was going to be travelling too.

Lindstrom wasn't the adventurous sort.

She saw McManus consulting with Dr. Jacob at the controls to the generator. Then McManus turned to her. "We're all set here, Ali."

Dr. Beck spoke from behind her.

"Everything's fine, Elliot."

Lindstrom leaned close to her.

An odd gesture. Lindstrom was so close to her so that no one else could hear. His brows squinted, giving his face an exaggerated look of concern.

"Be careful," Lindstrom whispered.

She smiled at him. "Don't worry," she said, smiling. "I always—"

Lindstrom put up a hand. "No, Alessandra. You must understand that things are—" Lindstrom paused, and Ali saw him look over his shoulder as if nervous that the others might be listening.

"Things are different this time," he said.

And suddenly she felt scared. She heard Dr. Beck say, "You may start, Elliot."

Lindstrom's face was still in front of her. Ali thought of the strange anomalies, the fact that they all remembered other histories, other pasts. And she thought of that house, the guards standing over her, stripping out of their clothes, often with the splatters of blood barely dry. Coming to her . . .

There's something else going on here.

Something that Lindstrom doesn't want the others to hear.

He backed away. And McManus was there smiling, like the family dentist about to start drilling for oil on some jumbo back molars.

Dr. Jacob came up and whispered something to McManus. "Yes," he said to the dwarf-sized man. "Fine." Then back to Ali. "Very good," he smiled. "We're all set, Alessandra."

She heard the high-pitch whine of the tachyon generator. Its scream seemed so much louder now that it was she who sat in the hot seat.

I've done this twice, she thought. Why am I so nervous? What's the big deal?

McManus's smile broadened in response to her anxiety.

The whine jumped a frequency or two as if straining to inject Ali into the time stream.

Alessandra had a thought.

A cowardly, craven thought. I don't care, she thought . . . I don't care what happens to history, to time. I don't care—

I just don't want to do this.

But the thick straps pinning her arms to the chair were evidence that such thoughts were worse than idle.

They were futile.

She made her fingers stretch out and then close around the arms of the chair. She heard Jim, sleeping just behind her. And for a second she smiled at the thought. The whole lab will be filled with sleeping bodies, everyone except for Dr. Jacob and Dr. Beck.

Like bears hibernating through the winter.

Then she thought of those sounds, those animal-like people prowling inside the Cloisters, rummaging through the small chapels, fingering the spots that use to hold display cases, searching, hungry—

"What's wrong?" Dr. Beck. "Alessandra, what's wrong?"

"All set," McManus announced. Then, "Five, four, three—"

Ali could picture the Pack, the human animals, hungry for food, for meat, of any kind. Finding a way in here, breaking in. Pouncing on their sleeping bodies.

Ali gripped the arms of her chair even harder. Squeezing tight until her knuckles looked a burnished white.

"One," McManus said.

She looked from Beck, to McManus, to—

Lindstrom.

Thinking: what is he worried about? what is scaring Lindstrom?

She saw McManus open his mouth, ready to say, "Zero . . ."

The generator whined in her ear, an electronic scream.

Surely they hear that, she thought. Surely those animals outside hear it?

But then she wasn't there.

What is Arthur going to do, Jim wondered? Walk up to the front door and knock? Arthur and his band didn't seem to be carrying any siege equipment.

But, as they neared the castle, a surprising thing happened.

The wood doors opened. Jim saw warriors wearing silvery helmets, tapered to a smooth point.

The Merovingian knights resembled the Coneheads.

They wore a combination of mesh and leather, but also Romanesque capes that trailed to the ground.

They're opening the gates! Jim saw.

Why in the world would they do that?

One knight came out wearing a crimson cape that glowed with a richness missing from the other warrior's more drab garb.

He unsheathed his sword. And damn, if that sword didn't look as big as he was.

Jim saw Lancelot standing a few yards ahead and he pulled abreast of him, nearly stumbling over the stones.

"Who is that?" Jim asked.

Lancelot didn't look at him.

"Dagobert," Lancelot said. Jim looked at the knight's face, grim, set. Judging from Lancelot's expression, whatever was ahead wouldn't be too pleasant.

He looked up at the tower.

That's where it will really take place, Jim knew.

I can't get distracted, I can't be stopped. Have to get there, before—

Jim heard a sound, a primal, blood-curdling scream. Then he heard sound, the smooth, sliding sound of metal and leather. And Jim watched Arthur bellow at Dagobert as he unsheathed his sword.

The blade flew into the air as if it was powered, as if it could fly through the air.

We're getting near slice and dice time, Jim thought.

And he knew why this Dagobert—a king, Jim wondered, or just one of the Frankish lords?—came out to greet Arthur.

He's been challenged. And there was only one way you answer a challenge. You open your doors and face your enemy.

God, isn't chivalry wonderful?

Another sound. And Lancelot unsheathed his weapon, with that same slippery sound. Jim looked at Lancelot's sword, as tall as a parking meter. It glowed with a burnished rosy color in the morning sun. A trick of light, Jim speculated . . . ?

Or was Lancelot's sword covered with a thin sheen of blood.

Lancelot went to his horse and removed an oval shield emblazoned with a crest with three lions. Then the knight turned to Jim.

"Best to ready yourself, Gawain."

Jim nodded. I'm supposed to pull out my sword. After all, Gawain probably was no slouch in the sword department. In fact, by the time Gawain met the Green Knight he'd have a reputation as both a fighter and a womanizer.

What no one knew here was that, before Lancelot, Gawain had dipped his middle-aged wick in—

Another bellow, another blood-curdling scream. Jim at last knew the meaning of that expression. He could feel the lumps moving through his frazzled veins. Arthur swung Excalibur through the air.

"Men of the Round Table!" he screamed.

No one moved.

"Prepare to avenge our Lady Guinivere's honor!"

Arthur led his men forward. And Jim had to wonder—

Is this the point the word *cuckold* enters the dictionary?

Am I crazy, Ali thought, or is there some—God!—pain this time. Her chest felt as if someone had kicked her there. She seemed to be gasping at the air.

Even though there was no air to gasp.

For one terrible moment she had no recollection—*nada*—of where she was going, what she had to do. All she knew was that she was travelling along the time stream, going . . . somewhere.

Then it was there, in her mind—the background, the information, enough of it, anyway, so that she wouldn't feel at a total loss when she arrived.

She smiled,

When she felt something cool and slippery run along her back, as if she had a body.

She turned—

Or seemed to.

She saw different streams, the colored swirls rushing this way and that. But she also saw something that she had never seen before.

Great blackish lines ran along with a river of colored light. She stared at them, fascinated. I've never seen them before, she wondered. And:

What could they be?

What in this world could they be?

She thought of the cold, clammy feeling.

It was one of them, she realized. It touched me.

Somehow. Even though I have no body. No head. No eyes. No lungs.

Right now I'm a whole lot of nothing.

But maybe, when I get to Oz, the wizard will have a new body for me.

She kept watching the blackish swirls, moving snakelike, chaotic, jumping around.

She thought of Lindstrom's fear, his warning—

She thought of a word he had used.

Chaos. We're tilting closer to chaos, he had said.

She looked at the swirls.

Chaos.

Ali turned away. And in that moment she suddenly flashed on what it was that had Lindstrom scared.

Something that he couldn't have said in the Time Lab.

But then Ali felt heat, and warm air, and the tangy bite of salt in her nostrils.

While the taste of something lemon and sweet lingered on her tongue . . .

Lindstrom watched him.

Go on. You old lying bastard, Lindstrom thought. Go ahead, do it again. I'm watching you. Go ahead . . .

McManus stood beside Dr. Jacob, looking at the read-out from the generator.

Go ahead, Lindstrom thought. Do it again.

McManus's head fluttered in the air in front of him, gesturing at the dials. Lindstrom looked over to Beck who was tending Ali, just wheeled into position next to Jim. Was she part of it, too, Lindstrom thought?

I don't know who the hell to trust.

Maybe with Jim and Alessandra gone, there was no one.

Go on . . . Lindstrom thought. Do it one more

time. So I know for sure, so I can confront you, you wizened old bastard.

Go ahead.

McManus's right hand floated in the air.

And rested for a second. Then, oh yes, the physicist pulled it back, up to his head, and further, around to the back of his neck.

Now . . . thought Lindstrom.

Now!

Lindstrom hurried to McManus as fast as he could, his own hand reaching up to intercept the scientist. McManus's fingers came to rest near his collar, pressing down.

And Lindstrom grabbed his wrist.

McManus spun around, a startled expression on his face. No, Lindstrom thought, *more* than startled, angry, scared—

"Whatever are you doing, Lindstrom? What in the world is wrong with you?"

Lindstrom kept his hand closed tight around McManus's wrist, freezing it there.

Lindstrom saw Beck and Jacob look over, concerned. In the sudden silence, he heard his own breathing and then, from beyond the soundproof walls of the subterranean lab, he heard other sounds. The Pack, skittering around like rats, nudging this way and that . . .

"Let go, Lindstrom! What's got into you?"

And in that instant, Lindstrom knew that he was right, that McManus was hiding something. Lindstrom forced McManus's hand down, lower. But he didn't let go. Lindstrom knew he was overweight, and he had certainly spent too many years sampling the best the vineyards of Burgundy could offer.

But I have a grip like a bear, he knew.

He didn't let go of McManus.

Instead, he came close, still pinching the other man's wrists tightly, real close and whispered:

"You and I have something to talk about Elliot."

McManus's eyes fluttered up, feigning shock, Lindstrom guessed. There were too many secrets here. But Lindstrom kept him fixed with his eyes, his bushy eyebrows.

I'm on to you . . . he hoped his face said.

And then McManus took a breath. The physicist smiled. He nodded at Beck and Jacob.

"It's okay," McManus said. "Go on with your work—"

Then back to Lindstrom, his face grim, cadaverlike.

Lindstrom matched him glare-for-glare.

"Perhaps we *should* talk," McManus said.

Lindstrom favored him with a big smile. "Precisely my sentiments," he said.

McManus looked down to his wrist.

Then back to Lindstrom.

And, reluctantly, Lindstrom released McManus and walked with him to the far corner of the lab.

Dagobert's cone-headed knights arrayed themselves outside the castle walls.

And Jim did some quick counting.

There are more of them . . . than us.

And he tried to tell himself. No problem. This is Arthur, the ancient king of myth and legend. With his crackerjack men of the Round Table.

What we lack in numbers, we'll more than make up for in skill.

Jim tried to unsheathe his sword.

Time to join the party. But the heavy, cumbersome weapon didn't seem to want to come out.

Another of Arthur's warriors looked over, confused by Jim's antics, then concerned.

"Why are you drawing your sword so awkwardly?" the knight said. Jim smiled, hoping that he could avoid an answer. And he watched one of

Arthur's knights pull his weapon, grabbing the hilt, and then pulling it up and away from his body.

Got it, thought Jim. And he quickly removed the weapon.

And even before it sprung free, Jim felt its dull weight in his hands. It has to be a two-handed weapon, Jim thought. No doubt about it.

But, when he looked around he saw everyone else was holding their swords aloft with one arm and the clumsy-looking shields in the other.

Jim tried it. The blade wobbled, as if he was balancing a vaulting pole.

There's a trick to this.

He closed his eyes.

Trust the force, Luke, he told himself.

Or—in this case—trust that Gawain's sword-handling skill will bubble to the surface. He took a breath, and then he felt it. A different way of grabbing the sword, using the whole arm, making the sword an extension of the arm.

Jim opened his eyes.

The two groups of warriors were moving towards each other.

Simple as that.

No Roman phalanx, no wedge-shaped maneuvers.

Mano-a-mano, plain and simple.

And—at that moment—it didn't look like Arthur and his mighty men of the Round Table would live to create so much as a footnote in the annals of legendary heroes.

Jim thought of turning around and running, hiding until it was all over and the Time Lab yanked him off to location number two—wherever that was going to be.

But this had to be done.

He took a breath. He went to his pack horse and untied his shield.

Why am I breathing so hard, he wondered?

Like the other knights, he let his horse's bridle slip through his fingers.

He took a few quick steps to catch up with the line of men, their swords out, all of them breathing heavily from the weight of their mail, the sword, the difficulty of moving over the rocky rubble.

While Dagobert and his cone-heads, twice as strong, waited patiently outside the gates of the castle.

Guarding their treasure, Lady Guinivere, who—at this very moment—was probably having a good old time up in the classic Merovingian bell tower.

Because if McManus and Lindstrom were right, she was up there alright.

Most likely without a stitch on . . .

2════════

Jim still had to struggle with his blade but, by God, at last he was holding it with one hand. Now he could only hear the footsteps of Arthur and his men, marching grimly towards the awaiting soldiers.

And Jim was struck with this odd thought.

This is not a King Arthur that people back in the twentieth century would recognize.

No, this was the dawn of the Middle Ages, a very primitive dawn at that. Ye olde knights of the Round Table barely look like knights. There was something almost Viking in their appearance. But all the stories, the tales, agree on one thing. From the epic Welsh poem, *Gododdin* to Wace's *Roman de Brut*, they all agree on one thing.

Arthur was a fierce warrior.

Jim started to hear a low mumbling.

As if the warriors were talking to each other, grunting.

Jim looked at them, but they had their eyes focussed on what lay before them.

The grunting, the muttering grew. It was unnerving, Jim thought, downright spooky. Weird stuff . . .

Louder still, until Jim had an idea what it might be.

It's some kind of ritual, something to get them psyched before the battle.

Jim let his concentration waver, and his sword dipped to the ground, the finely edged tip nearly brushing the dirt. He nearly dropped his shield.

Jim grunted, at first to just join with the others. But then he found the sounds—dark, primitive and brutal, coming naturally—as the ancient Celtic words rolled off his tongue.

"I will kill . . . I will kill my enemy. Today he dies at the point of my sword. Today, my enemy's blood will cover the barren soil . . . this day, I kill . . ."

Nice bit of doggerel, Jim thought. A variation on the time-honored "go team."

Closer, until Jim could see the enemy's eyes watching through the narrow slits of their cone-shaped helmets. And he thought he saw stark fear staring out through those slits.

There was movement among Dagobert's men.

And here was another bit of the Arthurian legend that didn't jibe with fact, Jim thought. Arthur became the romantic leader of his island nation, a mythical king who defended its shores against the Saxon invaders.

But Arthur's exploits romping through Western Europe were far less well-known.

That wasn't the problem that Jim had to deal with.

No . . . there was a damsel.

And despite Arthur's protestations, she wasn't in distress.

Not at the moment.

Dagobert's men raised their swords. Then they started bellowing back at Arthur's advancing force. The sound was a brilliant clarion call that echoed off the slope of the hill.

Jim looked to his side and caught Arthur raise his sword—a signal—and his men followed. Jim felt the sweat running off his body, dripping inside his mesh armor.

Dagobert's force was only fifteen yards away. Then ten yards away. And then, a mere five yards away.

Each line faced the other. Arthur's knights advanced, shield in one hand, sword in the other. Dagobert's men were arrayed to face them, their helmets just visible from behind their shields.

There was a final scream.

A sound that Jim thought was answered from behind him, some bird, a crow, laughing at all the noise.

And—in a blurry fraction of a second—the battle was joined . . .

Lindstrom pulled McManus into the corner. He was aware that Doctors Beck and Jacob were both watching, concerned by his strange behavior.

Let them watch, he thought.

Just as long as they don't hear.

Not until I know whose side they're on.

"I'd like to know just what you—" McManus started to say.

But Lindstrom raised a finger and leaned close to the gaunt scientist.

"Let me tell you what *I* know. And then—" Lindstrom forced himself to grin, thinking: I have to scare this guy. I have to make him think that I might be capable of anything.

That is, if I don't get the goddamned truth.

Lindstrom rubbed at his beard.

I need a shower, he thought. A trim.

He glared at McManus. What do I really know about him, he wondered? I know he sought me out for this project . . . that he needed someone with my background in history.

My *scope,* as McManus put it.

And now, Lindstrom had a sick feeling in his stomach.

"Here's what I know—" Lindstrom began. "I

know that you suggested moving the lab well before we knew that the—'' Lindstrom gestured to the outside world—''nonsense outside was going to happen.''

''But my dear Flynn,'' McManus said, effectively feigning confusion, ''you yourself found the first discrepancy, the tip of the iceberg, so to speak . . . that small glitch about Watergate and Arthurian legend.''

Lindstrom raised his voice, now not giving a damn if Beck and Jacob were listening. Hell, they were probably involved with McManus.

Yes, they might very well be as guilty as he was.

''That,'' Lindstrom said flatly, ''was small. Minuscule. Our history is probably filled with all sorts of glitches now, tiny tears in the fabric of time and events. We'll never be able to repair them all.''

McManus made a face, agreeing but still pressing his point. ''True, but it *was* a curious development. One that warranted further study. And when I—''

Lindstrom, using his size, his great bearish hands, poked McManus in the stomach. ''Yes, that's what I want to hear, Dr. McManus. How that small problem led to this big move, hiding the Time Lab in the Cloisters . . .''

''Well—''

''But before you answer, there are other things I want to bring up. Before you answer.'' Lindstrom smiled, ''Just to be sure that there are no discrepancies.''

McManus waited.

''This time, McManus, everything is different. This time you seem to be *anticipating* the moves of the Iron Men, as if you knew what they were up to.''

McManus's eyes narrowed, and Lindstrom noted a chilling glint of recognition there. The old boy knows I'm onto something here.

The question, Lindstrom asked himself, is: what am I on to?

"You know too much, McManus. More than we should have. For the first time, you needed me only to confirm actual historical events. You seem to have the blueprint that the Iron Men are following. And that's what gave me my idea."

McManus's lips were tightly pursed. Lindstrom licked his own lips and—instinctively—he pulled away from McManus a bit.

"You see . . . I wondered: how could the Iron Men affect change, how could they get everything they wanted—and make absolutely sure that we did nothing to interfere?"

"I don't know. How could they do that?"

"Infiltrate the Time Lab, Doctor McManus. Use their Time Transference Device to take over one of us. No great leap to the past would be required, just a matter of minutes." Lindstrom raised his hand and pointed at McManus's bony skull. "Get in here, and they would have nothing to worry about."

Lindstrom waited.

For McManus to defend himself, for him to explode, for *some* kind of reaction.

And McManus smiled, a broad grin, followed by a laugh. "My dear Flynn, that is absolutely the most marvelous theory that I've heard in a long time." Another shallow laugh. "Absolutely marvelous." McManus shook his head, and then he let his smile melt.

Lindstrom steadied himself, waiting for the monster to erupt from McManus's chest. The air was thick with the most horrible suspense.

Lindstrom felt as if he had lost control of the show.

"A very interesting theory, Flynn. One we best be on guard against in the future . . ." The smile rebloomed on McManus's face. "Except, we won't have to worry about me in that regard."

Lindstrom heard steps from behind him. Beck, and Jacob, stepping close.

Probably with meat cleavers in their hands, he thought. They're all spies for the Iron Men. And I can kiss history as I knew it goodbye.

"There's one other thing, McManus," Lindstrom said.

McManus made a moue of surprise, mocking him. But Lindstrom saw that the physicist was disturbed. I'm definitely onto something here, Lindstrom thought.

"I've been watching you, carefully. Ever since I began to wonder what you were up to. And I saw you do something, something that confused me . . ."

"Go on."

Lindstrom cleared his throat. "I saw you reach back—like this." Lindstrom demonstrated. "Reach back and touch your neck. Just at the top of the spinal column."

McManus's face registered more interest.

"When you thought that no one was looking. You just touched it, as if checking that something was secure, in place—"

The historian waited for McManus to interrupt. And when he didn't . . .

"I came close to you, close enough to see that there was something there, something dull, flesh-colored—unnoticeable if you didn't know it was there. But I saw that you had something stuck in your neck."

Dr. Marianne Beck was suddenly there, beside Lindstrom, and Lindstrom jumped when he became aware of her. He turned from her—checking that she wasn't holding either a syringe or a meat cleaver over his head—and then quickly turned back to McManus.

Who hadn't moved but only stood there, watching Lindstrom as if intrigued by developments.

"So I put together the whole package, McManus. First, you are not what you seem. You are one of them, one of the fabled Iron Men. And you know what they are trying to do. Somehow, maybe through a communicator buried in your neck, you are being kept abreast of what they are doing."

Dr. Julian Jacob came beside Lindstrom, and Lindstrom saw that, with Beck, the three of them had McManus cornered.

And for a second the little tableau reminded him of something.

An old television show.

He racked his memory, trying to remember.

He saw it in black and white.

Then, the mists of time cleared. He heard Rod Serling's voice, saw him walking down a small street in Anytown, U.S.A., telling us that, today, the monsters were due on Mulberry Street . . .

And by the end of the show we knew who the real monsters were.

Our own hate, our own fear. The monster that lives in the human soul.

Not quite ready to emerge from the cave.

Lindstrom shrugged the thought off.

This is not like this. This is different.

I have evidence . . .

McManus nodded. And Lindstrom watched him look from Beck, to Jacob, and finally at Lindstrom.

He nodded, appreciatively.

"Well done, Lindstrom. Good detective work, as they say." McManus raised a hand.

The other three nearly jumped away, startled.

McManus smiled. He reached around to the back of his neck. Lindstrom heard a small popping sound, the clicking noise you make when you pop a battery out of a walkman.

McManus held up a small, circular device. "This is, indeed, a communicator of sorts. But it doesn't work quite the way that you imagine, my dear Flynn. You see, this small chip contains a chip and a micro-transmitter so that I can access any information from our main computer."

McManus paused as if the import of his information should have been immediately obvious.

"It's like this. This chip can alert me to each change in the time stream. What's happened, and what must be done to counter it. It's taken me a while to make it, especially without you being aware. But it works quite well now."

"So you are one of them," Lindstrom whispered.

McManus shook his head. "Hardly. Though you are right about two things." He paused, and Lindstrom thought that the old bastard was enjoying this. "First, you don't understand what is actually happening here. Mind you, I was planning on telling you—at some suitable point, perhaps when it was all over. This—er—complicates things considerably. You are right, Lindstrom. I can anticipate what the Iron Men are doing. I can do that because there are *no* Iron Men."

Lindstrom felt his breath catch in his throat.

His hand raised involuntarily, as if he wished he could reach out and grab a snifter of his finest Brandy and douse his brain with a heady alcoholic shock.

"No . . . Iron . . . Men . . ." he repeated.

"No. I mean, there are a group of KGB hardliners who call themselves 'Iron Men.' And there is another Time Transference device in good old Soviet Georgia. But that was mere cover, a ruse. Designed to confuse me—at first—and then to protect their activities."

"The time bandits aren't from the K.G.B.?"

McManus laughed. "No. Not at all."

Dr. Jacob, the master of the tachyon flow—a man

who rarely showed any interest in anything but controlling that flow—took a step forward.

"Then where are they from?" Jacob asked.

And McManus fixed Dr. Jacob with his small, grey eyes. "Oh. I would have guessed that you would have figured that out by now. Especially Dr. Lindstrom . . ."

"Go on," Lindstrom said quietly.

McManus turned to Jacob, then to Dr. Beck—whose face was impassive, unsurprised. "Why they're from the future, of course. Didn't want you to know. But—well—there it is."

"The future," Dr. Jacob said in a voice filled with hushed wonder.

Lindstrom shook his head.

Asking a question that—he feared—he already knew the answer to.

"And the reason that you know what they are up to . . . ?" Lindstrom said.

"Why, that should be obvious," McManus said. He looked from Lindstrom to Jacob. "You see it now, don't you?"

No one said anything.

"I'm from the future, too . . ."

10

"More tea, Mr. Manly?"

With a disturbing suddenness, the mists cleared.

And Ali looked at the woman sitting across from her. She was thirty-ish, had great waves of auburn hair shaped into waves. A too-small black hat with an olive green feather sat incongruously on her head.

Ali looked down at her own place setting, down at an empty tea cup.

More tea.

Mr. Manly?

She looked at her arms, at the gray gabardine suit jacket she was wearing, the sleeves a tad too long, the pin stripes just about too far apart. There were dark hairs at her wrists.

She ran a quick check on her body, just sitting there.

"No?" the woman sitting across from her said.

Ali looked up. Her brief physical tour had brought two novel sensations. First, she was suddenly aware of having no breasts. Their weight just wasn't there. Instead, there was a blaring striped tie large enough to double as a tablecloth.

And farther down, there was a sensation of something new.

Something that, for curiosity's sake, would bear closer examination later.

Marvelous, she thought. It's one thing to travel through time and be someone else. *But to become another sex.*

Well, that was marvelous.

"Yes," she said, quickly wondering if her voice had the proper masculine heft. In her mind's ear, she practiced speaking, hearing the words resonate.

Ali looked at the woman across from her.

If Lindstrom was right, this was Lucy K. Barron, secretary to Senator Burton K. Wheeler of Montana. And she had just delivered some bad news.

Burton K. Wheeler was *not* going to supply Manly, a *Chicago Tribune* reporter, with a secret plan called Rainbow Five.

The *Chicago Tribune wouldn't* run a banner headline in tomorrow morning's edition.

The December 6th edition.

Giant, inch-high letters that read:

F.D.R.'S WAR PLANS!

Funny, you'd think that was a good thing, stopping such a giant leak, such a publishing coup by the non-interventionists, the America Firsters, the Lindbergian ostriches who hoped that Europe and Hitler would just go away.

Funny . . .

You'd think that was good.

But the publication of FDR's plans, Rainbow Five, was absolutely vital to the outcome of the war.

McManus and Lindstrom had both said this:

Nothing else was as important, Ali. Not Midway. Not D-Day. Not the Manhattan Project.

Nothing.

And here was this woman, a Big Band-era Fawn Hall telling her—

No, telling *him,* Ali corrected herself, that Senator Wheeler wasn't going to fork over the plans.

I've got to find out why, she thought. In just a few

hours. And then convince Wheeler to change his mind. While he was still in Washington, D.C.

Lucy Barron looked at her watch then pushed her chair back, ready to leave.

Ali reached out a hand. She marvelled at its size, the definition of the veins on its back, the coating of dark hairs near the wrist.

This is too much, she thought.

"Wait," Ali said, her voice a low gravel. And she was curious what Chesly Manly, the man who broke the Rainbow Five story, looked like.

"I really should get back," Lucy Barron said.

Ali nodded.

Then, searching for something Ali hoped would seem like male charm, she said, "Just a few more minutes. I *would* like another cup of tea."

Lucy Barron looked around the room, the rich, subdued splendor of the Park Grill.

Damn, Ali thought, they got the time wrong. I should have arrived at the *beginning* of this assignation. Instead, all the talking is done and the Rainbow Five plans look as if they are gone forever.

Ali quickly poured some more tea.

"Would you like another cup?" Ali asked the Senator's aide.

Barron shook her head.

She's nervous being here, Ali thought. Not unreasonable, she guessed. It must seem a bit like espionage to her.

Even though the United States wasn't at war.

Not yet.

Ali searched for the Sweet and Low. She was about to wave for the waiter, to request some, when she caught herself.

It was a few decades early for the little pink packets.

"Anything wrong?" Barron said.

Ali smiled. "No." What the hell. She opened a packet of sugar and emptied it into her tea.

"I'd like to ask you one more question," Ali said—not knowing how many questions the frustrated Manly must have already asked. He must have been mighty upset. One day he thinks he's going to break the story of his life. The next, it's snatched away from him.

And even Chesly Manly didn't know how important it was.

"What happened to Senator Wheeler? Who got to him?"

Lucy K. Barron stiffened, and Ali knew that this was territory that they had been over before.

"I've already told you, Mr. Manly. Senator Wheeler has simply determined that it wouldn't be in the nation's best interest to reveal—"

This is getting us nowhere, Ali knew.

I don't have time to play a Forties-era film noir detective.

Ali put her tea cup down.

And—at the same time—she felt an unusual fullness in her bladder.

His *bladder*.

"You know as well as I do that someone got to Senator Wheeler, Miss Barron. Someone scared him." Ali leaned close to the woman with her Robin Hood hat. "But, with what I know, it's already news and—"

Ali tried to gauge how far she could go with the next step.

"And I can go to my paper with what I have already . . . 'Montana Senator Plays Footsie with Secret War Plans' . . ."

"You wouldn't!"

"Try me."

What a tough guy, Ali thought.

Miss Barron looked genuinely upset. What was

probably supposed to be a simple, civilized meeting—albeit a disappointing one—had just turned nasty.

Good, thought Ali.

"What do you want?" Barron said quietly.

The waiter appeared and started clearing away the small silver tea server, and then the cups—

Ali looked up at him. "If you don't mind," she growled.

The waiter backed off as if stung.

I kind of like this, Ali thought.

"This is all I want," Ali said. "I want to meet with Senator Wheeler—"

"That's impossible," Barron interrupted. "He's in committee meetings all afternoon and then has a dinner at the British Embassy and—"

Ali raised a hand. "Fifteen minutes. To let him hear what I have to say. That's all. Otherwise, I go to the *Chicago Tribune* with the sordid story of our dealings so far."

Barron looked left and right, as if seeking a way out of the trap that Ali had just sprung.

Then Barron licked her lips coated with thick lipstick.

"Alright," she said. "I will talk to him. But I don't—"

"There's a bar—" Ali recalled the name of the small cocktail lounge given her by Lindstrom. It was a place the history professor used to frequent when he was at Georgetown, he said. Nice and quiet . . . Ali dug a pen out of Manley's suit coat and wrote the name and address on the inside of a matchbook from the pile in the center of the table.

The dining room was filled with a bluish smoke.

Of course, she thought. This was before cancer and cigarettes.

"I'll be there at five o'clock," Ali said. Enough

time for the story to make the morning edition. "Tell Senator Wheeler that it's in his interest to be there."

Lucy Barron got up, none too steadily. And Ali felt a bit guilty about being so hard on her.

But then she shook her head at that thought.

As if anything else mattered in the slightest.

She looked up at Barron. "And thank you, Miss Barron."

The senator's aide nodded, turned, and walked out of the dining room.

And, without knowing why, Ali felt like a cigar.

But first—nature was calling.

Jim tried to stay with the others.

But Arthur's knights didn't seem to be struggling at all under the weight of their mesh, their swords and shields.

Jim saw that they all had their helmets on. So he put his on even though it felt as if he was poaching his head.

The two groups of warriors faced each other, the air filled with the primal cries of opposing clans led by wily chieftains.

And that's what Arthur was. History called him a king, though Jim knew that it wasn't quite right.

There was something dark and ancient about Arthur's position.

These men aren't that far removed from caves and hunting giant Mastodons.

Arthur was their chieftain, the greatest fighter among them. And—

Strange though . . .

Where is Merlin?

Is there a Merlin?

If there's a Gawain, and a Lancelot, and a Galahad, then surely there's a Merlin the Magician.

Hell, maybe there's even magic. And dragons.

All sorts of neat stuff.

Jim nearly tripped over a stone that he didn't see.

"Steady," Lancelot said.

"Right," Jim said.

The bellowing echoed inside his helmet. His sword was a dead weight in his hands.

The line of Dagobert's men stretched out in front of him. They waited.

Arthur's men stopped.

"I come," Arthur said, his voice carrying easily on the open plain, "to avenge the dishonor done to my good queen Guinevere, to reclaim my Lady!"

Dagobert's men had their helmets down, covering their mouths.

Good thing, Jim thought.

That way nobody could see if they were smirking.

It was a stand-off, a duel at high noon, both sides waiting for the other to blink.

And suddenly Arthur turned to his men and bellowed out, "For Lady Guinevere!"

In that instant, Jim was left two steps behind as the clank of heavy swords grew to a deafening din.

Jim took a breath. Held his sword high.

And walked into the fray.

"Sit down," McManus said, pointing at a chair. "You too, Dr. Jacob, Toland, er, Dr. Beck . . . might as well tell everyone at once."

Lindstrom sat down noisily, keeping an eye on McManus. He still didn't trust the man, still wasn't sure what was going on. And he thought: this is getting too bloody confusing for me. It was alright when I felt as if I were controlling events.

Now I feel like a puppet. A pawn.

Doctors Beck and Jacob pulled up straight-backed chairs close to Lindstrom. Toland stood to the side.

McManus, Lindstrom saw, also remained standing.

"Good," he smiled. "Now, I do have to rush

through all of this. I'm afraid we're already running behind schedule.''

Lindstrom grunted.

"But yes," McManus said quickly. "It is time that all the cards were placed on the table.'' He shook his head. "I really should have explained all this earlier.''

Lindstrom looked up. "McManus—do get on with it.''

"Right. Well, let me start by telling you a few things about the future—'' He held up a palm. "But only a few. You see, it wouldn't do for you to know too much.''

"You can start by telling us what year you're from," Lindstrom said.

"Ah, the year. Well, this body is from here and now—but I guess you figured that out.''

Lindstrom laughed derisively. "You mean that there really is a Dr. McManus?''

McManus's face registered shocked umbrage. "Of course, one of your era's finest particle physicists. Not up to speed as far as we're concerned, but still a damned fine scientist.''

Dr. Beck cleared her throat. She's been extremely quiet, Lindstrom thought. Too quiet. Perhaps her attachment to McManus was more than professional. Question is: which Dr. McManus was she attracted to?

"Dr. McManus," Toland said quietly. "Whatever you're name is . . . where is the real McManus?''

"Good question," McManus beamed. "Bits of his consciousness are right here, of course.'' The physicist pointed a finger at his head. "You all know how the Time Transference Process works. But since I was going to be taking up residency for an extended period of time, it was important that I didn't bury my host's consciousness for such a long time. There might be unforeseen complications, for him—and perhaps for me.''

''So—where is he?'' Lindstrom asked.

McManus smiled. ''He's in the future. Getting advanced training in areas of particle physics that he only *dreamed* about. I very much doubt that he'll want to come back. Except, of course he must. I'm already pushing the limits of the envelope by my long stay.''

Lindstrom nodded. Trying to pretend that he was absorbing all this, that it all made sense. When, in fact, Lindstrom wondered which was crazier—the world outside, or the nuttiness of McManus.

''You were about to tell us the year . . .'' Lindstrom said.

McManus's smile faded. ''Yes, I was.'' Lindstrom saw the scientist look at Jacob and Beck.

As if he was gauging how much shock their system could take.

''Yes . . .'' McManus said. Then, after a breath, ''2852.'' McManus looked up. ''It was summer when I left. The 'Dome Season' on Earth, as we call it.''

''On Earth?''

McManus raised a finger in rebuke. ''Remember: there are some things I cannot tell you. It would be far too dangerous.''

Lindstrom looked over at Dr. Beck, expecting to see a mirror image of his own shocked face.

But there was no reaction.

''2852 . . .'' Dr. Jacob whispered. ''I can't believe it.''

''Oh, believe it,'' McManus said. ''It must be a relief to hear that our species gets to live that long, eh?''

Jacob nodded.

McManus turned to Lindstrom. ''But you see, that's the problem. And I can tell you only so much.

But there have been conflicts—not wars exactly, but terrible battles fought in the colonies, and even on Earth. The battle has even been waged on a biological level, fought with special microbes developed that could imprint information from someone's brain, recording it. Other microbes could be programed, like hunter-killers, to seek out someone and kill them.''

Lindstrom harrumphed. ''I'm glad to see that the better side of human nature has not gone away, McManus. But what does this have to do with us?''

''By the twenty-sixth century, genetic engineering became an every-day fact of life. But having such tremendous control led to terrible abuses, human monsters with phenomenal I.Q.s, soulless creatures who lusted for power or wealth. And physical marvels who almost seemed like new species. The Combined Governments finally acted to control the engineers.

''But the renegade engineers went underground. They perfected their genetic work, and became total masters of the DNA code. They could field a mutant army of extraordinary intellectual and physical powers—powers that bordered on the miraculous.''

Lindstrom grunted. ''Makes what's outside seem not so bad.''

McManus laughed hollowly. ''You're only too right, Professor Lindstrom. The future became a dark place where the genetic engineers could be found in every strata of society, undercover, trying to control the world while the Security Service tried to discover the hidden labs, the cells, the great subterranean holding pens where mutants were bred and kept.''

McManus took a breath. ''Eventually it became a war between one species—humans—against something else, something lurching towards an abomination. I mean, consider the possibilities, Dr.

Lindstrom . . . imagine having the entire genetic code to play with: strength, size, color, intelligence, even sexual orientation and interest. For some, it was too much to resist.''

Lindstrom scratched his beard. A pawn, he thought, a puppet. I'm a minor player in a story that won't happen for another 800 years.

The historian cleared his throat. "I don't see how that effects us. Why all this about the Iron Men then, the cover of using the KGB?''

McManus smiled. "Good question. But to—''

He stopped.

At first Lindstrom thought that he had forgotten his train of thought.

But then Lindstrom heard it.

Sounds. From outside the lab.

Noises of the Pack. Hunting, sniffing around. Hungry human animals.

The sounds were close.

"Dr. McManus, do you think—'' Jacob started to say.

McManus glared at him. "Quiet,'' he whispered. "They're close. Trying to find a way to us.''

Lindstrom shifted uneasily in his seat. He heard scratching, then some grunting. The entrance to the lab was hidden, down one of the many secret passageways. And even then, the metal door was bolted. Still, there might be another way in.

So he sat there, listening, waiting for the Pack to go away—or find a way in.

Waiting for McManus to finish his story.

11 ═══════

I *could* go to my hotel, thought Ali.

She looked into her pocket and saw that she had a key for an establishment called The Hermitage, which sounded pretty nice.

Maybe take a shower.

Soap down the old body hair, scrub those arm pits. Walk around the room in a manly kind of way, with the old family jewels swinging in the wind.

Shave.

Wouldn't it be great?

She had to admit that this *was* fun.

It sure had to be easier than what Jim was facing. But she had faith that nothing bad would happen to him. We've been lucky so far, she thought. And that luck would continue.

Had to continue.

But instead of looking for the hotel, she decided to walk around Washington.

In this, the last days of peace.

Before the world changed forever.

She had to force herself to stop staring at the clothes, the women with their Minnie Mouse high heels and pleated jackets with wide, pointy lapels. And men wearing suits big enough for two, with pants legs that rustled in the wind like sails.

Every car was a vintage masterpiece, tear-drop

Lincolns and Chevrolets. Black was the most prevalent color. And nearly every car had a running-board. And they seemed to go *so* slow.

Ali knew Washington, from trips with her father, long weekends when her dad took her on jaunts to the nation's capital. And when he had some high-level business deal, she was free to wander the city.

The trips ended the day Mom died.

There were no more trips after that.

She lost her mother that day. And she lost her father.

So she walked past the Capitol, then over, towards the great plaza leading to the Washington Monument. She'd like to see that.

But, at the corner, she passed a movie theater, the rich aroma of popcorn, sticky soda, and bon-bons erupting from inside the dark cavern. The marquee listed Joan Fontaine and Cary Grant. Then, in big letters . . .

Suspicion.

Not a word about Hitchcock. These were the days before the cinematic auteur, she thought.

She paused a moment, in the warm romantic breeze gusting from inside the theater, and looked at the tinted lobby cards. The classic cars in the photo matched those on the street.

Life imitating art.

She looked at the ticket booth. A young woman inside, her hair carved into a flamboyant bouffant, smiled.

With interest, Ali imagined.

Ali nodded, noncommittally.

It was 50 cents to go in.

A genuine bargain. Ali looked at her watch. Just enough time—if she didn't care about catching the movie from the beginning. She always heard that it wasn't such a big deal back in the good old days. No one worried about which show to catch, or waiting in lines. People drifted in, and then out, piecing the story together as they went along.

Ali dig out her wallet and walked up to the booth. "One, please," Ali said.

The woman hit a button and a ticket snaked out of a silvery trap door. The name of the theater was on the yellow ticket.

The Diplomat.

The woman smiled, her red lips and hair nearly frightening.

Ali did not risk another smile.

(Though she had to wonder what would happen if she was here a while . . . long enough for Chesly Manly's, er, natural biology to take over.)

Ali picked up the ticket and walked into the theater to see Hitch's latest . . .

The first blow hit Jim from the side.

I didn't even see it coming, he thought. I didn't even know that the fucking blade was slicing right near my head.

Fortunately he had kept moving, so the attacking blade slid off his helmet and down his front, right into his shield.

Jim turned.

All he could see of the man fighting him were eyes.

Two black dots in a sea of white. Jim could see the red veins crisscrossing the bastard's eyes.

Looks like he had a rough night last night.

And who knows? Jim thought. Maybe I did, too.

Maybe I had a bad time of it, too.

The attacker's blade slid to the ground.

Jim's own sword was suspended above his head. And it was clear what he was supposed to do, what he had to do.

But he didn't move.

The attacker's eyes, dark and feral, looked up. He was grunting, talking to himself.

Probably an occupational hazard when fighting a nice melee with long sword and shield.

The attacker quickly brought his blade up, aiming right for Jim's midsection.

Jim tried to think of an appropriate aikido move from the meager four that the unlikely Dr. Beck had showed him.

But that's all he had time for. To think. The blade was moving much faster than he was.

Then there was clank, metal against metal. More grunts, and someone yelling at his ear, trying to be heard through the covering of the helmet.

"What in Our Lord's name are you doing?"

It wasn't Lancelot, but some other knight.

Jim awkwardly slammed down his blade, barely blocking the up-thrust of the attacker.

"I—"

But before Jim could launch his explanation—

Suggesting things like I'm not really supposed to be here, and it wouldn't be right for me to kill anyone . . . and I really just have to bypass this whole thing, you see, because Guinevere—

He heard a mushy sound.

He looked at his attacker's midsection. Jim's savior had brought his blade up and driven it home, right into the poor warrior's gut . . . either slicing through the mail or finding an open space between the warrior's chest-armor piece and his jockstraplike codpiece.

The blood literally exploded out of the hole, and ran down the length of the sword.

Jim's protector removed his blade, and the wounded knight fell to the dirt.

He was still muttering, talking now to the sand, the rocks.

Jim's protector—who was it . . . which knight?—clapped Jim on the back.

"Now, protect yourself, Gawain. Lest the ladies lose one of the favorite champions."

Then Jim was alone.

And another one of Dagobert's knights was coming towards him, waving his sword around his head like a madman.

And Jim knew that aikido wouldn't protect him.

I've got this giant sword for a reason. And I better use it . . .

McManus cocked his head.

No one seemed to be breathing. Lindstrom heard the sounds, the scratching, digging noises. Like rats trying to get at a secret cache of cheese.

He had gooseflesh on his arms. Toland walked over to McManus, his heavy rifle unslung.

He whispered.

"Do you want me to go out and find them . . . try to scare them away . . . ?"

"No," McManus whispered back. "If there are too many of them, you'd be . . . overwhelmed. We'd best just—"

He looked back to Lindstrom.

"Wait."

Lindstrom licked his lips. The gooseflesh didn't melt away. The sounds stayed there, growing in volume, seeming closer, until he realized that it was just his fevered imagination.

I'm just imagining it.

That's all.

And he tried to imagine, instead, what the rest of McManus's story might be.

How much stranger could it get, he wondered?

But, as Al Jolson might have advised him, he hadn't heard anything yet . . .

* * *

Ali thought that she knew how the movie turned out. Cary Grant was *not* really going to try to murder Joan Fontaine. It was all in her head. But then, half way through the movie, Ali started to doubt that memory. In fact, she wondered whether she could remember at all how *Suspicion* turned out.

And by that point, she was convinced that Cary Grant *was* a killer.

When the film was over, Ali felt as if she had just seen the film for the first time, just like the rest of the audience. That's why Hitchcock is so damn good, she thought. He gets inside your head and plays with doubt, over and over, teasingly, until you don't know who or what to believe.

There's been no one like him. Certainly none of the new-age Hollywood wunderkinds. Nobody.

She left the theater, the rich, sweet smell of the interior of the movie palace giving way to a late-fall, damp December afternoon.

She still had time, looking at Chesly Manly's watch. But she thought she'd get to the bar early. Maybe have a drink.

And what would Manly imbibe? And as soon as she thought of the question, an answer was there, some urgent message from inside the reporter's repressed psyche: *send gin martini fast.*

Ali felt a furry burr on her tongue, an anticipatory tingle as she thought of freezing cold gin cut with just a hint of vermouth.

She crossed Independence Avenue, making her way to the Carlton Lounge. A light mist began to fall, and the sky turned dark early, as the clouds gobbled up what was left of the afternoon sun.

The red neon of the lounge's sign was the lone beacon on this quiet block. The capital was quiet on a Saturday. A few cars went by, their engines sounding loud and powerful, in these last few days before gas rationing.

Ali reached the sign and she saw that the bar was a basement operation. She stepped down, and opened a heavy glass door. More smells, this time the aroma of alcohol and spilled drinks hung in the air. She could almost feel the romantic assignations arranged here, feel the breaking waves of those affairs coming to a crashing halt in some back booth.

A bartender looked up, dressed like a pristine butcher, polishing a glass. His bald dome head reflected the yellow light of the rows of booze behind him.

Ali smiled.

"Evening, Mr. Manly," the bartender said.

He knows me, Ali thought. But she felt no name emerging from Manly's mind. So she smiled and said, heartily, "Evening." Then she pointed to the back. "Got a nice quiet table? I'll be meeting someone . . ."

The bartender signalled to a young kid dressed in a red suit. Ali smiled at the bartender and started to follow the kid. But the bartender came close to him, and asked, "How's the wife and kids?"

Ali turned, and broadened his grin.

"Couldn't be better," she said, without missing a beat.

The bartender tapped the surface of the bar. A totemistic act meant to ward off evil, Ali assumed. She then hurried to catch up with the young waiter.

He directed Ali to a booth and then waited while she sat.

The young waiter flipped open a book to take her order.

"A gin martini," Ali said, marvelling at how easily the words rolled off her tongue.

Then she was alone. It was too early for a dinner crowd, if this place served any food. There was no one back here. But then it was Saturday. She guessed Washington was a lonely city on weekends.

It was quiet. Just the sound of ice hitting a shaker somewhere in the distance. A few muffled voices. But then, from the gloom, from a pair of small, definitely not-hi-fi speakers, there was music.

Big band music. She listened a moment. It was Glenn Miller. Some peaceful, beautiful melody that came out of the trombones like a lullaby.

The waiter appeared with her drink. Crystal clear, and ice cold. Ali nodded. And then she picked it up. She hadn't, in her own life, ever drank anything this strong. She liked a nice Cabernet, or Pouilly Fume. But a martini?

She took a sip.

For the first second it was like drinking liquid crazy glue. Airplane fuel.

She thought her tongue would curl up and just die. Then it rolled down her throat, leaving a burning trail that she thought would sear her.

She took a breath of air after that sip was finished, and it felt as if she was inhaling a breath mint.

She felt a small buzz in her brain. Somewhere, back inside, she got a signal.

This is good, the signal said.

So she took another sip.

The music played.

She looked at her watch. She was early, by a good fifteen minutes.

She thought about Rainbow Five. And what she had to do . . .

Jim was getting the hang of it. Or rather, Gawain was sending some much-needed messages about self-defense circa 590 A.D. After all, if the consciousness of the host is still in there—and McManus didn't know what really happened to it—it might respond to a sudden surge of adrenaline. Like now.

The knight Jim faced was on the short side. But he had massive arms, big, meaty, pork-roasts fore-arms. And he was out-swinging Jim two-to-one.

But Jim was feinting and dodging effectively.

Too effectively. It's not me who's doing this, Jim thought.

Another one of the Dagobert's knights came over to join in the fun. Great, Jim thought, now I have two of them to deal with. So, while he tried to catch one swipe with his shield, he tried to block the other knight's sword with his own blade. So far, there didn't seem to be any opportunity to do any damage.

Around him, a different story was going on.

Arthur's knights were winning. They must be brilliant swordsmen. Here they were, outnumbered, and they were spilling Frankish blood all over the yellow dirt.

The groans, then the screams, filled the air. Jim heard the crows answer, cawing at the goodies that awaited them.

And Jim knew this:

I can't do this much longer.

I may be getting a bit of subliminal help from Gawain, but that was it.

Sooner or later, I'm going to lose this game.

As if to hammer that point home, one his opponents, the recent arrival, brought his sword up in a maneuver that drove his blade in, and then under Jim's shield.

And Jim felt his shield being pulled away from his hands. He locked on.

But the other knight had the advantage. He whipped his sword back and Jim felt his shield being ripped from Gawain's powerful hands.

Then, distracted, Jim didn't see the attack by the other knight. The blade smashed into Jim's side. The blow knocked the wind out of him. Jim waited for the terrible sting of metal digging into his skin, making puree out of his entrails.

But the mesh had absorbed most of the blow.

"Shit," Jim said.

In Modern English, he realized. And the knight that just ripped off his sword let his eyes go wide.

"Never heard the King's fucking English before, you bandy-legged moron?" Jim shouted.

The warriors seemed to freeze.

They must think I'm working some black magic on them, mumbling some powerful spells.

It gave Jim enough of a break—just enough. He screamed, a rebel yell that would have done him proud on the streets of Brooklyn. And he swung his sword around. One knight quickly leaped back. The other tried to raise his round shield.

Too slowly.

Jim's blade caught him just above a bit of mesh at his chest, between his helmet and the metal webbing.

For a second, Jim thought that the man's armor would absorb the blow. But the mesh seemed to be pushed along with the blow. Jim heard the man's guttural grunt as the mesh, and then the blade, dug into his throat.

The next few seconds were in slow motion.

Slow motion, Jim thought. Like the time he smashed his first car, a used Mustang, on the icy Northway while heading to Montreal. Time slows, and you know that you'll remember this forever.

Forever . . .

The man's grunt was replaced with a high-pitched scream. A tearing sound. Then the blood erupted from the man's throat, shooting out like a geyser.

Jim heard a laugh.

I'm laughing, he thought. I'm laughing because he's dead, and I'm not. Now isn't that just too damn funny?

Too. Damn. Funny.

The knight fell forward, nearly colliding into Jim.

There were other screams, other moans, as the ground outside the castle became filled with the bodies of men who had awakened to a beautiful morning but wouldn't live to see the sunset.

The second knight backed away.

Jim fixed him with his eyes.

"You're next, Waldo," he said in English.

More black magic mumbo-jumbo.

The knight backed away.

Remembering another engagement.

Jim took a step. Another step. This time stepping over the dead body, still bubbling, the blood percolating onto the ground.

Another.

The castle gate was open. More of Dagobert's men were coming out. Things didn't look so good. And the rule was, Jim guessed, everyone stand and fight.

Part of the emerging code.

The chivalric code, Jim thought.

Now to be crushed before it even was born.

Because of Guinevere.

The gate was open.

Jim knew he should turn his attention to other knights. Arthur would wonder why he didn't.

But that's not what I'm here for, Jim thought.

I have a more pressing matter to deal with . . .

And he walked, as quickly as he could, his blade hanging down, marking the dirt with a rusty-red trail.

Jim thought he heard voices calling to him, wondering where he was going.

But Jim didn't even turn around.

12 ═══════

Lt. Commander Mitsuo Fuchida sat down at the chair.

And he waited.

On the small table, in this, Admiral Chichi Nagumo's private cabin, there were just two glasses. Filled, Fuchida guessed, with sake. But Admiral Nagumo had his back to him, looking at the map of the island, and the squiggly lines showing the route to be followed by all the planes. Some lines were black and solid . . . others were dotted. A third was red. The three waves, Fuchida knew. They had been over this many times.

Then why this meeting, he wondered?

What else was there to say?

Hai, Nagumo was an old man. Some of Fuchida's pilots would say too old. But he had Admiral Yamamoto's complete faith.

There must be no questioning of Admiral Nagumo.

Finally, Nagumo turned.

"I worry," the admiral said quietly, "about the airplanes . . . the three bases . . ."

Yes, Fuchida thought. Perhaps you do. But more than that, something else afflicts Nagumo's *seishin* . . . his spirit. Is he scared, this night before we strike this great blow against America? Does he believe, like so many others, that they will prove too powerful?

Nagumo sat down.

His hand, brown and veined, as if carved from a fine, sturdy wood, closed around his glass.

Fuchida looked the admiral in the eyes.

"Soo desuka?" he said, worrying at the sound of it as the words escaped his mouth. He would not permit himself to be impolite.

But the question implied something, hinted at some inner fear. *Soo desuka?*

Indeed . . . is that so?

Nagumo looked up.

His eyes looked fiery for a moment, his lips pursed, as if holding back angry words. But Fuchida watched the man's face relax.

A smile was there, not a real smile, but something to put Fuchida at ease.

"We cannot hit all three air bases at once. There will always be the chance that the Americans will be able to get planes into the air . . ."

Fuchida heard the words trail off. If the Americans got fighters into the air, they'd be able to meet the Japanese force. But even worse, they might get to the carriers, to Nagumo's *Akagi*.

The surprise attack could turn out to be a deadly fiasco for the empire.

Fuchida nodded solemnly, to let Nagumo know that he understood, his fear, his concern. Commander Genda's plan was brilliant. *Madman* Genda, who said this great attack was "not impossible."

And now it was here, only a day away.

And Fuchida answered the best way that he could. With a story.

"When I was a boy," Fuchida said, "my mother would let me play in the garden, by myself. And I loved to explore the garden, lifting up stones, examining the insects that scurried about. And every-day, when I lifted a certain stone there were always these insects that scurried about, so startled to see me, once again, uncovering their home, their hiding place.''

Fuchida paused.

''No matter how many times I did that, it was always the same. And even then, a small boy, I realized that the insects were not smart enough to imagine this thing happening, this incredible thing.'' Fuchida studied Nagumo's face. ''They slept on, just as they always would . . .''

Admiral Nagumo nodded. Then he smiled. ''Yes.'' His hand brought his glass of sake up.

''To sleeping insects,'' the admiral said.

Fuchida, a day away from leading this great attack, grabbed his glass. He raised it to Nagumo.

They took their sips together, eyes locked on each other, the bond of comrades in this great adventure for the empire.

While Fuchida wondered at his own story.

Wondered about the insects . . .

Lindstrom heard Toland click something on his gun.

Something to make it ready, Lindstrom guessed. The sounds seemed to be all around them. Voices mumbling, dully passing along information to each other. Then steps, running here and there, through the castle.

This is great, absolutely wonderful, thought Lindstrom. His bowels felt like jelly in anticipation of the human wolves breaking in and feasting on them.

''Perhaps,'' Lindstrom said, ''we should get out of here. There's still—''

McManus raised a finger, signalling him to be quiet.

Toland walked close to one wall, tilting his head

to listen. Could Toland stop them, Lindstrom wondered? Did he have enough firepower?

How long can we stay holed-up in here, waiting for them?

Lindstrom rubbed at his mouth. Suddenly, he was dry. His lung was a parched wind tunnel.

The voices faded. The steps ran away.

Toland walked around the walls.

His steps echoed in the small underground lab. Nobody said anything. Lindstrom heard his own breathing.

They waited. And then Toland turned and said quietly, "I think that they're gone."

"They might be waiting for us," Lindstrom said, too quickly, revealing his panic. "They might be waiting to hear some noise."

McManus stood up. "Could very well be, Professor. But we have a lot to do. And I'm afraid that we're running out of real time. We must get moving—human cannibals, or no."

Lindstrom nodded.

McManus walked over to the tachyon generator, pulling along Dr. Jacob with him.

And Lindstrom remembered the questions that had been left unanswered.

He got up and followed McManus, who was checking the dials, the settings.

"But why here, McManus, why now?"

McManus didn't answer for a moment, but then turned and said, "Oh, yes. I hadn't quite finished. Just give me a moment here."

Lindstrom waited while Dr. Jacob prepared the generator, fidgeting about the machine as though it was some demanding, electronic lover. McManus pointed at a row of dials, shook his head, and then pointed again.

Was there something wrong, Lindstrom wondered? Or was it just a normal shake-down for the machine. It all made sense now, this piece of incredible hardware. Yes, it came from the future, where McManus said that he also came from.

If he was telling the truth.

And that was a possibility I have to be aware of, Lindstrom thought. Must hold onto that idea. If he's from the future, anything is possible.

Finally, McManus turned and looked at him.

"Why here?" McManus said. "And why now? It has to do, my dear Lindstrom, with *detection*. The Time Transference Device has existed—in my century—for over fifty years. But it was immediately recognized to be a dangerous device. Certain rules and regulations were promulgated regarding its use. For any scientist, it was nearly impossible to get that permission. And, when granted, time transference was to be used for observation only."

"But these others, these genetic fanatics, they—"

McManus nodded. "They were held to the same strictures. You see, any travel through time could easily be located. It leaves a trail through the time stream of high-speed particles. Anyone using an unlicensed machine for unauthorized travel could easily be located . . ." McManus smiled and took a breath.

"Except during this century. Due to the amount of nuclear explosions, the tests, both underground and above-ground, there is a cloud of radioactive particles that acts like a blotch on the twentieth century . . . like interference . . ."

Lindstrom shook his head. "But that shouldn't affect earlier years, should it?"

McManus made a grimace, as if the physics was almost too simple to understand.

Lindstrom frowned back. So shoot me, I'm a historian.

"Some of the particles released in a nuclear explosion

travel at the same high speed as the tachyons. And they travel forward and back in the time stream. We know that any trails are ruined for a good fifty years in either direction. After that, we can again locate someone using the transference device."

"Then that explains why the, er, renegades from your time have been using this century, especially the wars."

"Of course," McManus said.

McManus turned back to the machine as if the discussion was closed.

Lindstrom tapped his shoulder, feeling like a small boy getting the attention of his parent.

"You haven't told me two things, McManus. And—I'm afraid—I can't continue without that information."

"Very well," McManus said. "What is it?"

"You haven't told me where I'm to go. And just who it is we are fighting, what they hope to accomplish . . ."

"Yes," McManus said, sounding weary, Lindstrom thought. "*You* will have to penetrate the Third Reich, my dear Flynn. I would have thought that you figured that one out."

McManus shrugged.

"And as for who we're fighting, you remember Chau, the North Vietnamese General, who tried to introduce some novel techniques of hostage-taking years before their time?"

"Yes, he was one of the Iron Men, one of the KGB—"

McManus laughed. "No. Hardly. This Chau is, in fact, from the future. He is the mastermind of everything that's happening here." McManus turned and looked at Lindstrom, an amused smile on his face.

"And—it so happens—he is my brother . . ."

* * *

Ali looked up from her half-finished martini and saw a man watching her.

He had wire-frame glasses, and thin white hair, with a monkish bald spot on his head. He stood there, studying Chesly Manly.

Ali looked up and said, "Senator Wheeler?"

And Burton K. Wheeler, hat in hand, a trench coat over his arm, walked over and took a seat.

"I don't like—" he started to say, but then the waiter was there, ready to take his order.

"Would you like something to drink, Senator—?"

Wheeler shook his head, and then said, "Er, a cup of coffee, please." Wheeler dug out a cigarette and lit up.

"Another martini, sir?" the waiter asked Ali.

She shook her head. Though, she had to admit, the idea didn't seem entirely without merit.

"Thank you for coming, Senator," Ali said quickly. Wheeler looked anything but happy.

The senator looked round, making sure that they were alone. Then he looked back to Ali, his eyes glowing with anger. "I don't like being summoned, Mr. Manly. I've changed my mind, and that is that."

Ali nodded.

Knowing that something happened.

Somebody got to Wheeler.

Because—as of yesterday—Wheeler had been prepared to give Chesly Manly, and the *Chicago Tribune,* the biggest scoop of his career.

On December 6th, the *Tribune* was supposed to publish the contents of Rainbow Five, F.D.R.'s secret war plans.

And Wheeler—an America-Firster, a senator from the Big Sky state who opposed American boys fighting Europe's war—would blow the whistle on warmongering FDR.

Which, as it turned out, was exactly what had to happen.

The leak was no leak at all . . .

Ali leaned across the table, aware that Manly was an imposing figure.

"Why the change, Senator? You were all set to turn over the documents. What changed your mind?"

The waiter appeared with a cup of coffee, a small creamer and a bowl of sugar.

Wheeler waited. Then he leaned across the table too, so that he could whisper just inches from Manly's face.

"Do you know where this leak came from?" Wheeler asked.

Ali knew it came from General Albert C. Wedemeyer. And Wedemeyer caught hell for the leak.

But he was only the messenger boy.

"No," Ali lied. "I don't."

Wheeler harummphed. "And you never will. But I'll tell you this—" Wheeler stuck a pudgy finger in Ali's face.

"It came right out of the War Department, from the highest sources. Roosevelt plans on plowing under every fourth American boy. And there are people close to him who want to stop the warmonger."

"Really . . ." Ali said. "So, why won't you give us the plans. That will help, won't it?"

Wheeler pulled back. "I—I thought so. You know, Americans don't want this war. It's none of our business." He waved his hands in the air again. "It's the Easterners, the money interests, the—" Wheeler waved his hand in the air, leaving an unspoken innuendo dancing sickly around the cloud of cigarette smoke.

"I agree," Ali said, stringing the senator along. "So what happened? Why won't you give us Rainbow?"

"I'll tell you." Wheeler folded his hands in front of him. "I'll tell you. Someone else came forward, someone who I never would have expected to be . . .

one of us. Turns out, he's a big admirer of Lindberg. He's willing to do anything to stop Roosevelt. But this, he told me, would be rank disloyalty. If war came, this story would tell the enemy everything about our plans.''

Wheeler licked his lips, and Ali saw that Wheeler felt as if he was in over his head.

"I can't do it. It's too dangerous.''

I need a name, Ali thought. More than getting Rainbow Five from Wheeler, I need that name.

But, she thought, first things first.

"So you fell for it?'' Ali said. She smiled, and then laughed, a man's laugh, rich, full, and, she hoped, a bit derisive.

"Fell for what?'' Wheeler said.

"The trick. They scammed you,'' she said, immediately wondering whether the word "scam'' was in use circa 1941. "Somehow they learned that you were going to expose the plan and stop the war propaganda machine dead in its tracks . . .''

Ali thought of the cartoon that would accompany the *Tribune* headline . . . good, solid, blue-collar workers, farmers, miners, each wearing the name of a state, huddle by a trench looking up at the outline of the nation's Capitol. A cloud hangs over Congress. The words "War Propaganda'' can be read.

The *Tribune's* message was clear. Washington was out to make war, no matter what.

"But he—he told me that it was a security leak, dangerous—''

Ali pounded the table, a strong gesture, but it certainly got Wheeler's attention. "A security leak? Senator, are we at war?''

"No . . . but—''

"And with your help, maybe we won't be pushed into this war. *If* you aren't intimidated by one of Roosevelt's henchmen.''

Ali checked Wheeler's eyes, to make sure that she

wasn't overplaying her hand. Wheeler's eyes widened. He moved uneasily in his chair.

God, she thought, I went too far, He's going to leave. And that will be that. It will be all over.

But Wheeler looked up, ready to hear more.

Just like the thousands who flocked to rallies to hear Lindberg argue that this was a war being forced down the country's throat. They want a way out . . . no matter what the cost.

"It wasn't one of F.D.R.'s henchmen . . ."

"No. You were duped, Senator. They found out about the leak—just in time. And you've been cleverly bullied into sitting on it. Security? Hell, they just need more time to get us into the war. But you— you can help stop that."

Wheeler took a sip of his coffee. Black. A bleak drink for a bleak man . . . in a bleak situation.

"Tell me who it was, Senator. Tell me and I'll prove to you that you've been had."

Wheeler shifted uncomfortably in his seat. Another sip.

Come on, Ali thought. Come on. Just the name. I've only one day . . . and I have to have the name.

"I don't think I can. In fact," Wheeler said, "I can't give you the plan. It's just too—"

Ali cut him off. Time to use some techniques pioneered by the *60 Minutes* newsteam. "Okay. We'll run with what we have," she said. "My paper has enough for a story, and your name to back it up. We can still have a page one story. 'FDR's Secret War Plans Buried by Senator.' "

Wheeler looked up as if his lips had been scalded by the cup.

"You wouldn't!"

Admittedly, it was a bit early for such jugular journalism, Ali thought. But it seemed to be having the proper effect.

"If I don't get the plans, we run with the other story. My editor had already agreed."

Hope he doesn't check that one, she thought. But she knew how violently the Hearst-owned *Tribune* opposed Roosevelt. Now you're trapped, she wanted to say.

But Wheeler seemed aware of that fact.

Nobody said anything for a minute. Wheeler played with his coffee cup.

The waiter came by, hovered for a second, but a look from Ali scared him away.

Then Wheeler spoke, very quietly.

"Very well, I'll give you the plan, this Rainbow Five." He looked up. "And may God have mercy on your soul, Mr. Manly . . . and your goddamned paper."

Score one for our side, Ali thought.

Ali smiled. "Don't worry, Senator. But there is one other thing. Who tried to stop you?"

Wheeler's eyes narrowed.

"You don't need to know that. Why do you need to know who that is?"

"Because he might feed us false information. We have to know who we can trust in the War Department . . . and who we can't."

"I don't know—"

"You don't want a war, do you, Senator?"

She thought that he wouldn't answer, that she'd have to find out the name some other way.

But then Wheeler cleared his throat, and told her.

And it was worse than she imagined . . .

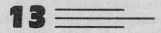

13

More of Dagobert's knights rushed out and—for a precious few moments—the gate was open.

And Jim strode clumsily past people: Women in drab cloth dresses with white skull caps. Wives waiting for husbands. Mothers waiting for sons.

Just as soon as the battle is over, dear.

A few old men watched Jim. Old knights, living out a few years free of armor before dying.

There's no one to stop me, Jim thought.

He turned and looked back over his shoulder. Some of Dagobert's soldiers were hurrying to close the gate. There was no portcullis, just this large wooden door, a giant's door, swinging shut slowly.

But then Arthur's men were there, and the battle spilled into the castle itself.

No one tried to stop Jim.

As he kept marching to the tower.

Every step felt like agony, the terrible dead weight of the armor trying to drag him down to the ground. His feet slid leadenly across the dusty dirt of the courtyard.

He approached the entrance to the tower, a rough wooden structure with inch-long splinters bristling off the side of the wood.

I'd expect a guard here, he thought. Someone to stop me from getting to the treasure.

But apparently Dagobert's confidence level was at a low point. Obviously he had pulled all his knights out to face that famed Chieftain, Arthur. After all, Dagobert had something that Arthur wanted back.

Arthur's very own queen, the fair Guinevere.

Only Jim knew that he had to get to her before Arthur did.

He pulled open the squeaky door to the tower. The hinges seemed misaligned, and the door groaned as it cantilevered open at an odd angle. Once inside, he saw that only a single torch lit the curving staircase. It barely outlined the buckling planks of the steps leading up.

Jim heard noises behind him, the fighting raging noisily in the courtyard. Dagobert's men must have fallen back.

And though his muscles ached with every step, Jim pushed himself to hurry, climbing as best he could in his armor, feeling the sheen of sweat building inside his armor.

The light of one torch was left behind and there was a long gap before the faint flickering of the next torch appeared, catching the dull glow of his mail, the hilt of his sword sheathed beside him.

Higher he climbed, taking care not to trip, to tumble down, perhaps to roll all the way back down. A metal-covered Sisyphus hurrying on an errand of myth and legend.

God, he thought, my legs ache. I can barely move.

More steps, and it grew brighter. Torches flickered nearby. He reached a landing, breathing hard, gulping at the air.

Jim stood on a landing and there was a door ahead of him.

That's where she'll be, he thought. If Lindstrom is right, Guinevere is inside that chamber.

More sounds, now from below, and Jim knew that he had only a few precious minutes.

He reached for the door, expecting it to be bolted. He grabbed the latch and pulled the door open.

He smelled something sweet in the air. Sweet and alluring. Through the slit in his helmet, he saw the room, the wall aglow with torches, a rich, red carpet on the wood floor. A table filled with fruits, a metal flask that surely held a sweet wine.

From the entrance, he saw the bed.

And—just visible—a bare foot, a trim ankle . . . leading up to—

Jim could see no more.

From here, that is. And though he wondered whether he should show more caution, the sound of the knights below, Arthur's knights, made him hurry in.

The word "blunder" would occur to him in a few moments.

He stepped into the room.

Seeing—at first—the buff naked Guinevere. How horrible, one might think . . . such a great lady, stripped down to the altogether, sprawled out on this bed with sumptuous bedclothes.

A fistful of grapes in her hand and a drunken smile splattered across her face.

Because Guinevere was, in fact, plastered.

"My—my lady," Jim stammered wondering if he'd have enough time.

She laughed again, and rolled on the bed, exposing what Chaucer might call her "downy nether regions."

Guinevere was beautiful. She also was, considering the times, one hell of a party girl. She was liberated a good 1400 years before it became fashionable.

Jim took a step closer to her.

A fatal error.

He heard the wood groan behind him. A step, he realized. There's someone behind me. And when he turned—too late to do anything—he saw this big knight outfitted in the uniform of Dagobert's men, but adorned with a fine cape.

It had to be, Jim thought . . . Dagobert himself.

Letting his men do the dirty work while he dallied with Arthur's lady fair.

This is it, Jim thought. The death of courtly love. The still-birth of the chivalric code.

In those last few seconds, Jim recalled Lindstrom's fevered explanations of why this absurd event was so damned important.

It's a sideshow, Lindstrom told him. But the Iron Men needed certain concepts of loyalty, and trust, and duty to one's country to be tossed into the trash heap of history.

It was almost hidden, this event. Until John Dean's infamous appearance before the Senate Select Committee on Watergate was suddenly changed.

Dean was supposed to reveal the machinations of Tricky Dick in the White House. Nixon was scrambling to protect his bully boys and preserve his White House.

Dean blew the whistle.

But then, it changed. Lindstrom picked up this ripple in history. Dean didn't do anything, according to the records. And Nixon continued as president.

There was no honor, no loyalty to country. The power of abstract loyalties and values went out the window. Situational loyalty took over.

And Dean's transformation was only a clue to the larger changes in history, changes that Lindstrom couldn't tell Jim about.

Not until this problem was solved.

Here. With a drunken, very beautiful Guinevere.

Except Jim knew that he had just walked into a trap.

He tried turning around, tried getting his sword out. All actions that took forever.

While the knight, this Dagobert, raised his sword above his head, ready to slice Jim in two.

"Can you pull him?" Lindstrom said.

McManus shook his head. "No. It's too close. If I yank Jim now we might very well interrupt him just as he was about to straighten out fair Guinevere."

Lindstrom nodded. He was scared. Though the others had all used the Time Transference Device successfully, he was nervous. After all, Lindstrom thought, what's the state of my heart? Can I stand the strain?

But deeper than that, he had to admit his real fear.

Can I do what I have to do?

I'm no hero, he thought. I'd much prefer reading my books, writing my papers.

McManus walked over to him. "I'll have to wait . . . at least another ten minutes. By then, Jim will have succeeded—"

"Or he will have had his head cut off," Lindstrom added.

And the history professor had to admit that there was something else that worried him. Something closer . . .

The ones outside, prowling the castle.

What if they get in, while I'm asleep in this chair, my mind stuck on the past? He imagined them creeping close to his body, poking him, feeling if he was still warm, alive.

And such a plump morsel as well.

Their lips would smack and their teeth grind in anticipation.

"Let's get on with it, McManus," Lindstrom said.

There would just be Dr. Beck and Jacob left, who, with Toland, would have to hold down the fort . . .

And bring everybody back.

"Yes," McManus said. "We're all set here. I just—"

McManus was studying something by Beck's corner of the lab, watching the monitors.

"What is it?" Lindstrom asked.

"Getting some readings for Jim . . . something that's affecting his body here, pulse rate, respiration. Doctor Beck, how, er, alarming is this?"

Beck took a quick, almost cursory look at the monitor and then announced:

"He's in distress."

Lindstrom scratched at his beard. *Get me out of here,* he wanted to scream. Just undo the straps and pop me the hell out of this seat. Let's just say the Iron Men won, okay? The monsters from the future won, and let's be done with it . . .

"Terminal?" McManus asked.

Beck didn't bother looking back at the screen. She shook her head. "No. It doesn't appear so. Not yet, at any rate."

"Good. Then let's get Professor Lindstrom off, shall we?"

Lindstrom was too rattled to even grin at McManus's inept choice of words. Too late, he thought. I'm here. And, in a few minutes, I'll be stuck *there.*

He heard the whine of the tachyon generator increase. Dr. Jacob whispered something to McManus. "I'm ready," he said.

McManus came up to Lindstrom and, in a gesture that seemed entirely out of character, he touched Lindstrom's hand.

"Good luck, Flynn. We're really up against it this time. All hands on deck, so to speak. But take care of yourself."

Lindstrom nodded. Then, feeling McManus's eyes on him, watching him, studying him, Lindstrom turned away and grunted. "Don't worry about me, McManus. Just make sure that you get me the hell back here—whether we succeed or not."

McManus laughed. "Who knows? You might like visiting the Forties, Lindstrom."

Lindstrom looked back at him. "Yes, and I'll probably have a ball playing in the Third Reich. It's a bloody dream come true."

McManus laughed.

Lindstrom wondered what kind a fool he was to put his trust in this man from the future who could be as crazy as a loon.

But Jacob's high-speed particle generator drowned out his thoughts with an incessant whine that grew to a most painful intensity.

Before it vanished . . .

There was no phone in Ali's hotel room. Though the room was clean and presentable, without too many cigarette burns on the furniture or the carpet, there was no telephone. And—even more disturbing—no tv.

So, she had to go down to a booth in the lobby, and call the *Chicago Tribune* collect.

She had a list of names on a sheet of paper, hoping that they were the right names, that she shouldn't be calling someone else with the story. And she had her story, written down on hotel stationery.

After a long wait, the operator finally announced that the call had been accepted and the scratchy long-distance line hissed in Ali's ear.

And she waited for Tom Burns, national editor of the *Tribune* to come on the line.

"Ches," he said. "Where are you? Damn, I've been holding page one for an hour now. We expected your call this afternoon. What's going on?"

"Senator Wheeler got cold feet," Ali said.

"Damn—what the—"

"But I got him to cooperate. I applied a bit of pressure."

"Terrific, Ches. Let's have it, then. No. Wait a second. Let me get a copy boy on the other line."

A pause. Ali heard the editor call out a name.

"Billy. Pick up."

A click, and the line went even noisier.

"All set?" Ali said.

I'm tired, she thought, thinking about her room upstairs. I've got to rest, get some sleep. And then tomorrow—

She didn't really need the story. Not at all. It was the name that she needed.

Yeah, tomorrow is the hard part.

"Okay . . . okay. Ches, we're all set here. Any idea of the headline before we begin?"

"Sure do," she said. "How's this: F.D.R.s WAR PLANS!"

"Wonderful," Burns said. And Ali could imagine the editor rubbing his journalistic hands together in glee. The *Tribune* was no fan of the New Deal and F.D.R.

And here they were playing right into his hands.

"Great, Ches. We'll set the headline in two-inch letters. It will be the story of the year."

Wrong about that, Ali thought.

Absolutely wrong.

"Okay," she said, "let's get started."

"Shoot."

"Now set this in ten-point block letters . . . 'Goal is 10 Million Armed Men; Half to Fight in A.E.F.' "

Burns whistled, a shrill sound that broke up on the primitive line.

"Now, set this in five point, maybe smaller . . . 'Proposes Land Drive by July 1, 1943, to Smash Nazis; President Told of Equipment Shortage.' "

"God. They even have a date. Jeeez, Ches, what the hell are we doing here?"

Ali felt a tremor of concern in Burn's voice. She moved quickly to squelch it. "Don't worry, Tom.

We're not at war, not yet. But it might all happen if we don't run with this story.''

''Okay, okay. Go on.''

''Here's the text of the story . . .'' Ali had the first three paragraphs, the crucial paragraphs of Manly's actual story nearly memorized. Always was a quick study, she thought. The rest she had the general outline for. Historically, the stories would be identical.

She had arrived knowing the story. But she needed a source, someone that the paper could confirm it with. With Wheeler back on track, that part was taken care of . . .

Though, when Manly snapped back into place, he might wonder what had happened.

''Ready . . . here goes . . . 'Washington D.C., December 5—A confidential report prepared by the joint army and navy high command by direction of President Roosevelt'—are you with me, Tom?''

''I've got two copy boys taking it down.''

Ali took a breath.

The leak was reopened.

It was important. Maybe vital. But it was nothing compared to the other stuff that had to happen.

Ali flipped through the scrawled pages of the story, guessing at words too illegible to read, but getting the essentials right. She thought of Jim.

And—in a melancholic way appropriate to the misty era—she wondered what he was doing this evening . . .

14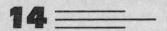

Jim's hand, actually Gawain's powerful hand, locked on the hilt of his sword.

And locked it was.

Whether the gooey, bloody streaks that coated the blade glued it to its sheathe, or Jim was just too weak, the sword didn't budge.

Until—while grunting, panicking, his view of the world restricted to the few open inches of his helmet's visor—he realized that even if the sword popped out immediately it would be too late to assist him.

Dagobert screamed at him, the sound of a Papa Bear protecting the lair of its new mate.

Guinevere was still laughing.

Her virtue certainly didn't need any protecting, that was for sure. But that's not what this adventure was about.

And while Jim would have liked to close his eyes, and tap his heels together to get back home, all he needed to do was think about home, the way it was now, how the world had turned into a dark, ugly thing.

That's all he needed to think about. And he knew that what he was doing here was important.

Dagobert skillfully brought his blade down, and

Jim saw over three feet of metal coolly arching toward him.

He had, he guessed, about a second to do something.

He decided to use one of the four movements of aikido, as demonstrated by Dr. Beck.

Move, but don't move, she had said.

In this case, that meant feinting to the left.

Which he did.

Disappear for your enemy.

Which meant, falling to the floor, and rolling.

And expecting all the time that he'd get snagged by the blade, Jim moved as fast as he could, mumbling to himself, "Please, please, please—"

Talking to a God that he only consulted at the worst, and often last, possible moment.

Amazingly, the blade missed.

The feint startled Dagobert, who instinctively adjusted his sword. That slowed his swing, Jim guessed—jumping into a giddy post-game analysis. Then his quick crumble to the ground made Jim vanish from Dagobert's limited view.

Except the game wasn't over.

He looked up at Dagobert, who was peering left and right, searching for a vanished Jim.

It was only seconds before Dagobert would see him again, and drive his sword home. Jim, meanwhile, lay on the floor, almost weighed to the ground by his armor.

He spied a lone grape lying on the floor. A reminder of the normal sporting activity that transpired in these chambers.

Jim looked up.

Just as Dagobert looked down.

Dagobert growled and brought up his sword. And Jim rolled to the door, a painful process as the twisted mail chewed at him as he rolled.

He heard Dagobert follow. Jim quickly knocked off his helmet.

I need to be able to see. Even if I do lose my head.

Then Jim got himself off the ground, onto his knees, then standing, as Dagobert charged him.

The next part was easy.

The third aikido maneuver.

Cribbed from the matadors of Seville.

Slide and guide . . .

Jim moved to the side. As Dagobert plunged oafishly past him, Jim gave him an added push, out the door. He heard the noisy rattle and clank as Dagobert tumbled down the stairs.

There were noisy grunts, Frankish curses that linguists would probably find interesting to study. And then a flurry of excited yells as Arthur's men, heading this way, found a surprise bouncing towards them.

But Jim had no time to enjoy his victory.

He ran over to a drunken Guinevere, still laughing as if this was one of the lost Lucy episodes. Ricky and Fred dressed up as knights for Halloween.

"Get dressed," he said.

She giggled.

Jim tried a more direct statement.

"Your husband is coming home."

The giggles stopped. A hopeful sign, Jim thought. "He will slice your slender body in two, my lady. Just as soon as he figures out how much you have been enjoying your visit with Dagobert and his men."

Guinevere—born before her time—made a sad moue. Then—was Jim imagining this?—there was the beginnings of a sly grin growing on her face. An invitation . . . for the present?

For the future?

What a lady . . .

But she had a role to play in the establishment of courtly love, for the whole chivalric code that would get us through most of the twentieth century, until the nasty days of Michael Milken, Neil Bush, and the rest of Ronny Reagan's raiders.

Ethics be damned! Full speed ahead.

Guinevere was an ideal that had to be preserved.

Hard to believe as it was.

Jim tossed her gown to her.

Then she spoke. A lovely voice, sweet, beautiful. One that Jim wouldn't mind whispering in his ear on a summer's afternoon as they drank wine, or mead, or whatever gave you a buzz in this century.

He heard steps.

Guinevere pulled on her dress.

"I will kneel," Jim said. "And you will tell Arthur how I protected you from Dagobert's frustrated rage, how you fought off his advances these past days. He will look in your eyes—the old fool—and believe in your virtue."

Guinevere turned somber, solemn. "I do love my Lord Arthur," she said quietly.

And looking at Lady G's blue eyes, her pale, alabaster skin, damned if Jim didn't believe her.

And he thought, if I believe her, then Arthur sure as hell will.

Guinevere straightened her gown.

Jim kneeled.

Arthur burst through the door.

"My Lady Guinevere," he yelled.

Guinevere bowed. "My Lord Arthur," she said. The birds and the butterflies blushed at the sweetness of it.

Jim fought back a smirk.

"This good knight, your Gawain, saved me from a last violent assault on my virtue."

"Sire, Lady Guinevere praises me too much."

Arthur walked past Jim.

And Jim could still hear the clash and clatter of a few random fights outside. Mopping up.

Jim felt Arthur's sword tap his shoulder. "Rise, Gawain, and hear my thanks for your noble deed."

Pretty noble, Jim thought. I got her dressed and I got the man killed who could, er, impugn her virtue.

Hopefully, Guinevere would be safe until she and Lancelot started playing hide the salami under the willow tree.

Jim stood up.

The sounds of the swords banging, the yells, grew faint. As if I have cotton in my ears, he thought.

Arthur grabbed his shoulders. "My good knight, Gawain," he said.

But the words echoed in Jim's ears, as if they had been shouted into a long dark tunnel. And Jim knew that his visit to the early Middle Ages was over.

And he had a long time to wonder where he would show up next.

Admiral Husband S. Kimmel didn't like to think of himself as a *cautious* man. But, as he always told his wife, the historian may remember the great generals, the great admirals and their victories; but an army or a navy lives or dies by the careful planning, the *caution* of its unsung heroes.

He got up from his desk, a rich Hawaiian teak that he wished he could bring home with him when this tour was finished. He got up and walked to the window.

And there they were. The carriers.

The *Enterprise*. The *Lexington*.

They were back now.

And he wasn't too sure how he felt about it.

Kimmel pushed aside the curtains and looked out the window. It was perfectly clear, another gorgeous day in paradise. The sun, high in the sky, glinted off the water of the bay. And he saw his fleet, the great

Pacific fleet of the United States at anchor off Ford Island.

Crewmen walking on the battleships *Tennessee, Oklahoma,* the *Arizona,* the *Nevada.* He felt secure looking at the great battleships, lined up, so powerful and strong. A mighty force, made even mightier when so close together.

He pushed more of the curtain aside. To his right, he saw the rows of destroyers and minesweepers, and past them the submarines.

He shook his head.

The Japanese would have to be crazy to start a war with America. Pearl was a mighty fortress, and if war came it would send this mighty fleet against the Japanese Empire.

He looked left.

At the recent arrivals, plumes of steam still billowing from the cooling engines of the carriers.

Caution, he thought . . .

And though it wasn't his order to bring them back, he felt more secure with the two additional ships.

The *Lexington.* The *Enterprise.* They're safer here than at sea, or at Midway.

The door behind him opened.

He turned to see his personal aide, a bright-eyed ensign.

"Yes, Brian."

"Sir, your car is here . . . for your luncheon appointment with General Short."

Kimmel smiled.

Saturday should be a day off. But with this blasted alert it was best he review the island's response to an attack in the Pacific with the army's man, Short. It wouldn't be so bad. There was a small restaurant just outside Pearl City that served a wonderful mahi mahi.

Kimmel picked up his hat. "Thank you, Brian."

And he uncovered the telegram that had arrived yesterday from Washington.

He looked at the name on it, the block letters . . . Admiral Stark. He didn't much care for Admiral Stark.

But then Stark made no secret of his disdain for Kimmel. Kimmel picked up the message. It should be destroyed.

But for now, he just stuck it in his pocket.

Already, he could taste the succulent dolphinfish.

Good seafood . . . just another bonus of this assignment.

He hurried to his car.

Ali woke up in the middle of the night. She was having a dream.

No, a *nightmare*.

She was in a strange town, dressed in ragged clothes. And everyone was looking at her, staring at her. They pointed and sneered until she knew, *knew* that they would kill her.

And that's when she came to the bodies.

Crumpled in a great pile. First, there were just a few. A few bodies dressed in ragged clothes, arms and legs akimbo, looking like marionettes who had their strings cut.

Then, she looked up. There were more bodies, an even greater pile, and beyond more and more, until she saw a mountain of bodies.

All dead.

And at that moment, when she had that thought, she saw that some were still moving. A finger twitching here. A knee flailing away, struggling to escape the press of bodies.

She saw people she knew in that pile, on that mountain. McManus. Lindstrom. Jim. One eye looking at her. Blinking, the last few moments before his death.

Her father. Jack Moreau. Jack the Pirate. The man who she thought would never die. A man who, when she was a little girl, seemed invulnerable. Until that day Ali's mom died.

She lost two parents that day.

And she thought this, in her nightmare.

They're waiting for me. I'm next. This is a world of dead bodies. A planet of the dead. And I'm next.

She woke up.

With a strange, animal-like cry escaping from her throat. Only it wasn't her throat. It was a man's throat. Chesly Manly's throat. She felt the sweat on her brow, the bedsheets sticking to her skin. The rooms dark except for a thin crack of light from the hall slicing in.

There were voices out there. People laughing, drunk, stumbling, crashing into her dream.

Ali took stock.

She remembered where she was, who she was—thinking: this could get pretty schizophrenic.

And then she was aware of something else.

Her male appendage was as hard as rock.

At the same time she felt an incredible fullness in her bladder.

She reached down and touched herself, thinking, this is damned uncomfortable. Does this happen to guys every night?

It was like a directional arrow pointing the way she should go.

Up, and out of bed.

She got up. Manly had been thoughtful enough to pack warm pjs and cozy slippers. Still, the room was cold. A dark and bleak place at what had to be some ungodly hour of the night.

She walked to the bathroom.

Flicked the light on.

A rumpled Manly squinted back from the mirror,

bleary-eyed with a field of stubble running across the planes of his cheeks, on down his neck.

Ali waited, feeling the erection deflate. I think it will be easier to pee if I let the swelling go down, nurse . . . And she grinned at the absurdity of this.

It was crazy.

Then, looking at her dopey, sleepy smile from this man she didn't even know, Ali thought of what was ahead.

The man she had to see tomorrow.

To find out whether Senator Wheeler was right.

Whether the man who tried to stop him was one of the Iron Men.

Because if he was—

She heard more laughing. The rattle of a key in a door. A man and a woman. The woman giggled.

It might be noisy for a while, she guessed.

And just how damn hard is this going to be, she asked herself? How hard is it going to be to get to see Admiral Stark, to question him, to—

She rubbed her eyes.

She was still very tired.

As Scarlet said, I'll think about that tomorrow.

And at last she was ready to answer nature's pressing call . . .

Lt. Commander Mitsuo Fuchida felt the sea even under the great weight of the *Akagi*. The sea felt rougher than before, and he wondered if the weather was taking a bad turn.

Omishiroi, hai?

Amusing, yes . . .

To have done all this planning just to have the weather, some clouds, a bit of rain, bring the great surprise to an end.

And Fuchida saw the worry in Admiral Nagumo's face today. His terrible fear that he might do something wrong and lose his own honor, and that of the Empire.

Fuchida did not worry about such things. The predictions were for good weather. Not great, but good. And Fuchida had no fear that the Americans wouldn't be surprised.

He knelt down and pulled a small footlocker out from under his bunk.

It was unlocked and he opened it quickly.

It was filled with personal things, a photograph of his family, his mother, his father, his two sisters. A book of prayers given to him by his teacher at flight school, just before he left for Osaka.

Fuchida never said the prayers.

He dug down through a pile of other things, letters from friends, a few letters from Miyaki, rich with her perfume and poetry. And deeper until, he came to the shirt.

He pulled it out.

It was dull red. Dyed to match the color of dried blood.

He spread it out on top of the rough blanket on his bunk.

He'd wear the shirt so that everyone could see it under his uniform.

He'd wear it so that no one would know if he got hit.

It's just Fuchida, they would say, wearing his lucky red shirt. Banzai, Commander Fuchida!

Because nothing must prevent him from leading each wave of the attack until the Americans' great base in the Pacific is nothing but a burning blotch on the beautiful Hawaiian island.

The war must begin tomorrow, Fuchida thought. Begin, and end.

Then pushing aside his shirt, Fuchida sat down and picked up some of the letters, to read them again and lose himself in thoughts of Nippon . . .

15

"So," the voice barked brusquely, "what do you think? Tell me."

Lindstrom thought that he must have gone blind. Everything's so bloody *dark*.

And he thought of that stupid joke.

It went:

I can't see! I can't see.

Well, open your eyes idiot.

Which is what Lindstrom did. He opened his eyes and saw that he could see just fine.

And hear.

"Come, come, Joseph. I can't rely on old von Ribbentrop's opinion. *Everyone's* a good fellow to him, everyone can be trusted."

The man laughed.

Lindstrom was looking around the room. A huge expanse of shining wood. The room smelled of fresh paint, or was it some other stench. He was at a table, a map of—he looked down. Yes, Eastern Europe . . . and Mother Russia. Little flags dotted the map. Little swastikas and little hammer-and-sickles.

War games.

And Lindstrom turned to the voice. And he looked at the man, the brown suit-cum-uniform, the arm band . . . the mustache of Der Fuehrer, Adolph Hitler.

Lindstrom's jaw dropped.

He felt as if he couldn't breathe.

Hitler's arms were folded, self-satisfied, staring at the map as if he could make all those little flags jump and move with merely a flick of his eyebrows.

Which was probably true.

Hitler turned to Lindstrom.

And Lindstrom wondered why, when he arrived, he heard everything, *understood it* as if they were speaking English. I thought that there was this delay, that one second you hear the native tongue . . . and the next it's all neatly translated for you.

"I don't have all day, Paul Joseph, don't get lost in other . . . distractions."

A tiny smirk crossed the fuehrer's face.

And Lindstrom thought. Here he is, the most-hated man in the twentieth century, bar none. Why I could reach out, grab his throat and spare the world the damned madness of his war.

But McManus had warned him about giving in to such a temptation. History, true history, must not be tampered with. There's no telling what the repercussions might be. And—for now—Lindstrom had to believe him.

Hitler, looking almost too young to be conquering the world, waved a finger in Goebbels's face.

"If I can't get the truth from you—hah—who can I?"

That was another thing.

Why the hell do I have to be Goebbels? he had asked McManus. Surely there was *someone* else who could do what had to be done. Admiral Raeder perhaps, Field Marshall von Runstedt, anyone but please, not the slimy propaganda monster of the Third Reich.

But the facts seemed pretty clear.

In these crucial days, Goebbels had Hitler's ear more than anyone else.

"I'm sorry," Lindstrom said. He smiled, even in the face of Adolph's wagging digit. Then he said, with difficulty, "Mein Fuehrer. But I was lost . . . in contemplation of—"

Lindstrom gestured at the map.

And with that small gesture, he felt a sharp pain, somewhere near his hip.

"The Eastern Front."

Hitler's eyes narrowed, a scolding squint that made his face look almost comical. Mel Brooks as Der Fuehrer. Or Dick Shawn in *The Producers,* playing AH as a whining hepcat.

Wailing . . .

Man, I'm losing the war.

But this was no charade. This maniac was the genuine article.

Hitler stuck out his lips as if he had just digested a fatty piece of sausage that was giving his lower intestinal tract difficulty.

He waved his hand. A gesture familiar from newsreel footage, Leni Rifenstahl's documentaries.

"Ah, you're probably thinking about one of your show girls, Goebbels. The Japanese . . . tell me! Do you believe the ambassador?"

Have to be careful here, Lindstrom thought.

Real careful. Can't say too much. But I have to keep Hitler interested, keep him piqued.

Until I find out who else he's talking with.

Lindstrom looked back at the map. "It may all change, my Fuehrer. If the Japanese start war with America, it could be very dangerous for us . . ." Lindstrom grabbed the edge of the table. "But it might also give us a wonderful opportunity."

"Yes . . ." Hitler said, apparently liking the sound of what he was hearing.

"The Japanese, like us, are prepared for war. They have a powerful navy, a wonderful air force. And their army will die to the last man for the emperor."

"But . . . ?"

This has to come out right. Keep the pot boiling, McManus had said. Just stir up those war fires.

"The East is bogged down, my Fuehrer. Your generals won't admit that. And I can keep the public in the dark. But here, looking at the map—you and I—we know the truth. We need a breakthrough, a surprise—"

At the word "surprise," Hitler slapped his right fist into the palm of his hand.

"Yes, a surprise. Something new that will rock the world." He swung his arm at the map as if summoning a wave to wash over Eastern Europe and the Soviet Union. "Something to fire up my generals, to make them seize Moscow, and bring the Russians crashing to their knees!"

Lindstrom nodded. This is pretty disgusting, he thought. Imagine . . . *Goebbels*. The Propaganda Minister for the Third Reich. A scrawny hate machine. And he's somewhere in here, inside this mind.

It's enough to make one sick.

"And Ambassador Oshima?" Hitler asked.

Lindstrom had prepared an answer to this question.

"He's telling you what he knows, what *he* believes. But events have passed his level. He'll be the last to know if the Japanese move. And I say, move they will. And we must be prepared to capitalize on it."

Hitler refolded his arms and went back to the contemplation of the map, to looking down at his Eastern Campaign slowly, which was becoming entrapped by the Russian Winter.

The Germans are great fighters, Lindstrom thought. Brilliant composers. Good clock makers. But damn, couldn't they look at what happened to Napoleon and learn something?

"Yes. I'll think over your . . . counsel. You may

leave, Joseph. We'll talk tomorrow. After your morning broadcast.''

Lindstrom, with a revolting ease, clicked his heels together and saluted. The pain jabbed at his hip again.

Then he turned to leave the room. Wondering: where am I supposed to go? What should I do? He limped out, feeling the drag of Goebbels' bad leg pulling at him.

And here was a man who condemned undesirables, banishing the weak to the gas ovens.

Lindstrom looked down at his watch.

It was nearly six.

Six A.M., if things went right, Adolph will turn in for the night. And what the hell shall I do, Lindstrom wondered.

He opened the door, grabbing one of the shiny polished handles.

A young S.S. oberstleutnant stood at attention.

''Your car is waiting, Reich Minister Goebbels.''

Lindstrom nodded. And I guess someone will know where to take me. Probably home, to Frau Goebbels, and all the little Goebbels . . .

But on that point he was completely wrong.

The woman called Dr. Beck covered his hand with her own.

''Why didn't you tell them?'' Dr. Beck stood close to him and he could read the concern in her face. It might have been a mistake, he thought, the two of us coming back like this, together. A mistake.

''Because,'' he sighed, ''they wouldn't understand. Professor Lindstrom already knows too much, in my opinion. It can only be distracting. If he knew you were from the future too . . . well, it might all be too much.''

She patted his hand. McManus's hand. My hand is not so old, not so gnarled . . .

"You know that isn't the only thing I'm worried about."

He turned and looked up at her.

He saw Toland walking around the lab, listening for any sounds, any sign that they were in danger from invaders from the outside. And Dr. Jacob was getting the Transference Device ready for the last element in his great plan.

"No. What are you worried about?"

"You know, you didn't tell me . . . they can't all come back."

McManus smiled. "Oh, you figured that out?"

Beck nodded. "I spoke to Dr. Jacob. He confirmed what I suspected . . . what you were keeping from me. It's true, isn't it?"

"Yes, it's true. More of my manipulation, I suppose. Necessary manipulation. No. Everyone can't come back. One person will have to be . . . left behind. But that will prove to be an academic question, anyhow."

He saw her chew at her lip, and he wondered how much he should confess to her. Their cell had insisted that she go. She *was* the most qualified, the one person who could help him the most. His arguments against her—strictly personal—fell on deaf ears. Personal relationships had no role in the battle.

"You might die . . ." she said.

"Any one of us might die," he said. "We might all die. If only one of us makes it back here, I'd be very happy. If not, you'll know whether we succeeded . . . or not."

He tried turning away. But she held him, her eyes going watery. Amazing, he thought. She was no beauty now, in this body of a middle-aged woman doctor. No beauty at all. But somehow, she was still there for me. Just the way I suppose I'm there for her. Our spirits shine through.

And there was something he hadn't even told her.

As the length of their transference increased, as bits of McManus's real personality assert themselves, it was growing increasingly hard to function. Surely, she must feel it too, as bits and pieces of the real Dr. Beck emerge. It was especially bad at night. Even now he could feel the battle inside his mind to retain control.

Now he would leave this body again.

I'm pushing it, he knew.

One way or the other, our time is nearly up.

"Come back," she whispered. "Don't leave me alone here."

He nodded. "I'll come back."

His voice sounded insincere.

He tried again. "I'll come back." He smiled. "Just to make sure that *you* get back."

Her tears came then, that battle lost. She leaned close to him, her cheeks pressing close to him. Then, she planted kisses on him, showering him with wet kisses that mingled with her tears.

"Please, please, Yos—" he started to say her name.

But he caught himself.

Best not to upset Toland, Jacob. Not when we're so close to the end, to—

Victory?

Of that he wasn't sure.

She whispered in his ear.

"I love you," she said. He felt her lips moving.

He waited until she pulled away, rubbing at her eyes, her cheeks all blotchy. Then, softly, barely audible, he answered her.

"I love you, too."

Meaning it.

This is goodbye, he thought. What are the odds? What are the chances I'll be back here? That any of us will be back here? We're an army now. And an army takes casualties . . .

"Ready, Dr. McManus." Dr. Jacob turned away from his machine, apparently not noticing their scene.

Like the engineer who stokes the fires of a battle-ship, oblivious to the bombs ripping great holes in the hull, Dr. Jacob works on, keeping it all running.

Funny thing, he understands so little of the real process. It's all hardware and magic to him.

That's understandable.

"Ready," McManus said. Then, clearing his throat, louder. "Ready."

Once more into the breach.

He smiled at that.

Like leading some ill-fated charge against superior forces . . . at Gallipoli, through the Ardennes.

It was brave, crazy, maybe hopeless.

But, in its own way, wonderful.

His wife didn't let go of his hand.

He looked at her, at his hand, making a frown.

"I'll be back," he said, smiling.

She pulled away.

And he hoped that he hadn't just lied.

"Look, here's what I think."

Jim heard a man speaking, then—right there—he saw his face, just inches away. The smell was of too many beers and a lit cigarette dangling from the hand draped around Jim's shoulder.

"What *I* think is that we walk over to the table, sit down—real nice—and talk to the young ladies." He gave Jim's shoulder a squeeze. "Hey, even army nurses get horny."

It was then that Jim realized that his companion, a naval lieutenant, wasn't sailing with an intact rudder.

The music sounded lush and wonderful. Someone was singing: "Bewitched . . . bothered and bewildered . . . am I."

There was red, white, and blue bunting flying from the metal beams of the high ceiling. The room looked like a hall you might use for a wedding. But— he looked up and around—

Jim saw that it was a hangar. An airplane hangar. Decorated for a party, a dance—

He looked at his watch.

10:30.

Okay, I know what time it is. Now, what the fuck year is it?

Goddamn McManus and Lindstrom. Why didn't they tell me where I would end up? What the hell am I supposed to do here?

He thought of their words . . . meant to placate him, only driving him more crazy.

"One anomaly at a time, Jim. We can't let your actions in the past be influenced by a future yet to be changed."

Jim shook his head.

"So, whadya say?"

He looked at his companion, his arm draped over him. The smell of second-hand smoke biting. Jim guessed he was a lieutenant. And he saw a name, above a bunch of ribbons on his jacket pocket.

Lt. Murphy. And, from the sound of his accent, Murphy hailed from Brooklyn.

Those old movies didn't lie. There really were guys from Flatbush in the war, and they really *did* sound like that.

"Whadya say?"

Jim turned and saw the two nurses and he caught them looking back at them. I guess we're not too repulsive, he thought.

And I guess there's nothing better to do.

Until I find out what year this the hell is.

"Okay," he said.

"Great, Tad. You wait. These girls are going to love you . . ."

And Murphy led Jim across the floor, past a maze of couples slow-dancing, to the table with the nurses.

The singer's voice was shrill, but sweet over the speakers.

It's the Forties, Jim thought. The Forties. World War II time . . .

"Excuse me, ladies, but my friend, Lieutenant Gorman and I were jus' wondering, that is if you have no plans, if you wouldn't like some company?"

The nurses—their starched uniforms looking just a bit small, especially in crucial areas—turned to each other.

"Sure," one of them said. She was blonde. Her hair was set into a smooth wave that caught the glare from the lights on the roof of the ceiling.

The other nurse, a brunette, said nothing.

Murphy grabbed a chair from a nearby table and planted himself right next to the blonde. He smiled at Jim and gestured at the other girl,

Jim smiled at her and she smiled back.

The song ended. A scattering of applause. The band picked up the tempo a bit.

The horns blared out.

Dah-dah-dah-dah.

One of the trumpets cracked the last note.

Jim pulled over a chair and sat down.

"So, I'm Lieutenant Johnny Murphy, and this here is my best buddy, a farm boy from the midwest, Tad Gorman." Murphy nodded, holding back the really good stuff a second. "We're naval pilots," he grinned. He leaned across the table, grinning. "And if those Japanese start something, we're going to kick their butts. Ain't that right, Tad?"

Jim nodded.

The brunette watched him.

Murphy, the master of ceremonies, moved on to get the names of the girls while Jim looked from the brunette to the windows. There were some lights outside.

And he could see trees.

Palm trees.

I know where I am, Jim thought.

Not Kansas.

Not Berlin. Or Saigon.

God. I think I know where I am.

It's the Forties. Before World War II.

Just before . . .

What's the date . . . what's the goddamned date?
He saw the brunette—her name was Helen, she looked like a "Helen"—studying him. I'm weirding out.

He wanted to explain.

Happens to me all the time. Yeah, everytime I jump around in time I get all screwed up. Just a little side-effect.

It's before the war. And this, sports fans, is Hawaii. The blessed isle of Oahu.

"Hey," Jim said. Tapping his new friend's arm. But Murphy already had his trademarked arm draped around the blonde's shoulder. Telling her his life story. Jim tapped Murphy's arm harder.

"Hey, where are we?"

Murphy turned around. He looked annoyed. "What? What the heck do you mean?"

Jim pressed on. He grinned. Let him think that I'm drunk. Let him think anything.

"Where the hell are we?"

"Hey, Tad. Take it easy. We're at the Ford Island Naval Air Field. What's the matter with you? The air commander's annual bash. What's the problem? Too many brewskis?"

Jim smiled quickly.

"Just forgot," he said.

"Sure." Murphy rolled his eyes, and floated back to his blonde.

The brunette was looking a bit nervous.

Jim smiled at her. He listened to the song.

"Pardon me boy . . . but is that the Chattanooga Choo-Choo?"

"Hey, let's dance," Murphy said to his blonde. She smiled and Murphy led her away from the table.

Jim felt the brunette, Helen, studying him. My turn, Jim thought. He took a breath. Then, he said:

"Want to dance?" At least it would beat sitting here.

Helen looked around, apparently considering other options . . .

"Okay," she said, without any enthusiasm.

Jim led her to the center of the floor.

He pulled her close and quickly discovered that she was waiting for him to lead in a bouncy two-step that was beyond his ken. He pulled her close, and bounced around.

"Nice song," he said, searching for small talk.

"It's number one back in the States."

Back in the States . . .

He waited a few more seconds before asking her, as offhand as he could, just what the date was . . .

Yeah, it's so easy to lose track of the date.

Her answer was no surprise.

No surprise . . . and that was funny, he thought. Considering what's ahead.

Because surprise would be the word of the day in about another thirty-two hours.

Everyone would be surprised.

Almost everyone. And when Jim considered the terrible curse that was now his, what he'd have to live through, he knew why McManus never told him.

He understood. And he forgave him.

Though he wished he had just a clue as to what he might have to do.

The song ended. Helen disappeared. To powder her nose. Or ditch the strange navy pilot.

Which, all things considered, was probably a good thing.

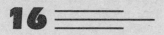

16

Lindstrom was under the sheet, under the black satin sheet that slid against his—dear, God!—naked skin.

There's not much I can do, he thought. Now is there?

He heard a voice sing out, calling from the kitchen of this ornate apartment on Friedrichstrasse.

"Liebschen . . . Josef . . . some tea—?"

Lindstrom pulled the sheet down so he could look, in the cold, clear light of midday.

Midday, and still in bed! How decadent.

And worse. It was December 6th. And, for America, the war was just hours away.

I have to get to the Propaganda Ministry, he thought. Get the telexs. I must see the fuehrer.

The voice was closer.

The blinds were drawn, and there was just a single lamp on, casting a soft, funereal light over the sumptuous apartment. The bedroom was heavy with a musky smell that only reminded Lindstrom of his activity at dawn.

He saw her.

She was blonde.

A natural blonde, from the looks of things, dressed only in a sheerest black nightgown that billowed about her as she walked to the bed. A full-figured young lady. Generous proportions.

One of Goebbels' actresses, a plaything. His hobby . . .

She threw herself onto Lindstrom, pressing her not unpleasant flesh against Goebbels' body.

Lindstrom felt her breasts mashing into his chest. She looked up at him.

"Why are you so very quiet?" she said, her voice waiflike, whining. "I think my Josef is not himself . . . I think that maybe he's getting a bit—"

He felt her hand fumbling under the satin sheets, rooting around, and then locking on the propaganda minister's not-so-privates.

Lindstrom was about to yell out, to ask the young lady to *please, stop!* This is simply not appropriate, he thought. Even if I am saving history.

But the actress's hands proved too deft, too knowing.

She smiled, broadly. The cat ready to eat the canary.

And Lindstrom had to admit there was one plus to all this. The brandy was superb.

And—he thought—I suppose another hour in bed won't hurt anything.

The phone rang.

Ali picked it up.

"Good morning, Mr. Manly. This is the front desk . . ."

Ali was about to ask the front desk why the hell someone was calling for a Mr. Manly, waking her up at—

She looked at the watch on her wrist. Seeing—at first—the dark hairs on her arm. It was 8:30.

"Right," Ali said. The first sound of that deep, sonorous voice surprised her. "Thank you."

She threw off the bedclothes.

She sat there a second, longing for a remote control to summon Willard Scott's goofy face blocking a weather map or Bryant Gumbel trying to talk turkey with whatever politico was desperate for some coast-to-coast PR.

No remote. No TV.

Not even a radio.

The rug felt cold and she thought of taking a shower. Soap down this big old hairy body.

There had been times when she wished she was a man. It seemed easier for men. How great it would be to relieve yourself standing up. Such a practical advantage . . . men have so much less baggage to deal with.

But now—living out the dream—she wasn't so sure.

This was like going into the body of some creature just a bit lower on the evolutionary scale. Not a complete drop, say, down to ape class.

But definitely a drop.

A shower, she decided. Then on to the War Department.

She stood up.

It was Saturday. December 6th.

The story would come out today.

A few days late. But it would be there.

In the morning edition of the *Tribune*. And the afternoon editions of everything else.

But the hard part was still ahead.

I have to get to Senator Wheeler's contact, the man who tried to kill the story . . . Admiral Stark. Find out what else he did.

And stop him.

Somehow.

Ali trudged to the tiny bathroom, outfitted with tile and antique plumbing. She stripped off her pajamas and stepped into the stall, still marveling at the novel apparatus dangling between her legs.

She turned on the water, as hot as she could stand it.

I may need this body, she thought. Before this day is out, I'll need this body.

Ali tried not to let herself think about something. She tried not to think that she might die in this body.

She soaped herself down, letting the water run off her head, down her body, wonderfully hot.

And all the time, the unwanted thought, the terrifying fear, was there . . .

There were great bells, Big Ben, giant chimes, ringing in his head. The floor slipped away at weird angles. The lights were lasers etching tiny painful lines in his eyes, right into his brain.

No doubt about it, Jim thought.

I'm hung-over.

He heard water running. He looked down at the metal sink, and—for a second—he thought it was inviting him to throw up.

Jim groaned.

"Too much guava juice, Tad, my boy?"

Someone was talking to him, the voice shocking in its loudness, its dizzying volume, echoing in the latrine.

I just had a few beers, Jim thought. Just a few beers. Sitting there, trying to deal with this thing.

He splashed some water on his face, cold, rich with the smell of a long trip through the pipes. Then he took the bowl and brush and started whipping up a lather. The motion made him feel sea-sick.

He saw a white froth appear at the lip of the bowl and dabbed some of the cream on his face.

I'm shaving.

Then someone patted his shoulder. His friend, this bumptious Naval Lieutenant, Johnny Murphy.

"You okay, good buddy?"

Jim nodded. "Just great." He looked out the window, a black patch. It was still night, and they were up damn early.

Murphy laughed. "Just give me a ten second warning if you're going to upchuck, okay pal?"

Jim wished that he hadn't said that word. Some words could summon the very events they named.

I only had a few beers, Jim thought. How could I have gotten so smashed?

Then he understood. Obviously old Tad Gorman had been hitting it pretty hard before Jim took up residence. Then Jim went ahead and blithely had some more beers.

Jim grabbed the razor, an old Gillette blade contraption that looked mighty dangerous in his shaky hands.

He started shaving.

And he thought:

I've got to find out why I'm here. What connection does this lieutenant have to Pearl Harbor, to the attack. What am I supposed to do?

Use my intuition?

Or maybe someone will magically appear. Lindstrom. McManus.

Maybe Ali.

He thought about her. Funny, we're always more than just far away. We're separated by space, and time, and even bodies.

He brought the razor up.

Keeps our relationship young.

"We've got a scouting flight at 0700, kid, so don't cool your heels too long." Murphy slapped his back again and then turned to walk out.

How did I luck out, Jim thought? How did I get such an asshole for a friend?

"Course, you may not want too much in the way of breakfast, eh, tiger?" Murphy laughed.

Too damn funny.

Jim felt his stomach tighten.

He grabbed the rim of the small metal sink.

Big wave coming, captain. All hands below deck . . .

But the squall passed. And Jim went back to his face.

A scouting flight. 0700. God, I'm a pilot. That helps. Now there was only one question.

How the hell do you fly an airplane?

Mitsuo Fuchida hadn't been able to sleep, and he got out of his bunk when the ship was still quiet, in the hour before dawn.

He felt the sea rolling beneath the great carrier *Akagi,* as if every swell carried with it the fate of their great mission.

And that got him thinking about the clouds, the few clouds coming together, making a dark grey canopy that would make the attack impossible.

And then what?

Would we wait, sitting at sea, a few hundred miles north of Oahu, and wait for the weather to clear?

Would Yamamoto call off the attack, almost relieved at that fate, that the spirits of our ancestors had intervened?

Fuchida got dressed and left his cabin, leaving the troubling thoughts.

He followed one of the main stairwells down to the first deck, down to the rows of zeros. The wings were folded. They could sleep, the planes, looking so powerful, even like this.

Some pilots were about, looking at their planes, checking things.

They couldn't sleep either.

A few noticed him . . .

They saluted.

But Fuchida, never one for the formality of the military, smiled and said, *"Aisatsu!"*

Other crewmen looked up and returned his word of greeting.

And then they went back to their planes, checking fuel lines, the movement of their flaps, the bombing gear, the torpedo attachments, the ammunition for their guns.

The excitement of it all, quiet and hushed, was almost too much.

We must begin . . . and end the war tomorrow, Fuchida thought.

We must destroy the American fleet in the Pacific. In one amazing battle.

But as he walked past the rows of planes, things haunted him, things that could turn the dream into a nightmare.

Fuchida had no doubt that they would surprise the Americans.

But the weather could stop us.

Only fools would attack in bad weather.

And there was another thing . . .

Fuchida reached the end of the deck, right next to one of the great elevators that brought the planes up.

What if the American carriers aren't there?

What if they're not at Pearl Harbor?

He shook his head, an idle thought. Of course they'll be there.

They are there now. And what would make the Americans remove them on a sleepy Saturday morning?

He smiled to himself.

Nothing. Absolutely nothing.

And Fuchida continued his walk through the carrier *Akagi*.

Lindstrom left his paramour's nest feeling rather sullied. He would have liked to have blamed the fine brandy. But he knew that he was, er, moved by the fraulein's not inconsiderable physical charms.

Some of the things she did Lindstrom found positively shocking. It's a damn good thing we won that war, he thought.

Damn good.

His aide, the Teutonic oberstleutnant, was waiting outside the actresses' door when he emerged.

"Good afternoon, Reich Minister," the young Nazi said, clicking his heels together.

Lindstrom nodded. He wanted to give the helpful fellow a bit of advice.

Get out of Berlin before 1945. Head to the Rhineland, Fritz. Give yourself up to the Americans.

Lindstrom walked down the hall, his aide following at a respectful two paces behind.

He pushed open the metal doors, gilded to resemble a burnished gold. His car waited across the street. He saw his driver hop out and sharply salute.

Lindstrom didn't bother to raise his hand.

There were people on the street, well dressed, with furs and expensive suits. The sacrifices of war hadn't hit this well-heeled neighborhood. For them, the Nazi economic miracle was alive and well.

The door was held open and Lindstrom got into the car.

Strange, he thought, I've got to make this all seem so natural, as if this is the way I live.

The driver shut the door, slid into his seat. Goebbels' aide got in beside him.

"The Propaganda Ministry," Lindstrom said.

And the sleek black limousine pulled away.

"I'm sorry, Mr. Manly—but Admiral Stark is unable to see any members of the press." The young naval officer smiled.

Ali smiled back. She held the newspaper rolled up in her hand.

Here I am, stopped dead at the first ring of the old War Department, Ali thought. And I'm not too sure how to proceed any further.

"Could you please ask the admiral's office whether he might see me? Five minutes . . . that's all I'll need."

I'll try the polite approach first . . .

But the young secretary made his jaw go rigid. "He's seeing *no one* today, Mr. Manly. I suggest that you come back on Monday. I'm sure his office will be able to find some time for an appointment—"

Time to use this body, Ali thought. The voice.

And the power of the free press.

She opened up the newspaper and threw it on the desk.

"Well, maybe you could just do this for me, son. Just this one small thing. Maybe you could ask Admiral Stark's office whether the admiral has seen this morning's *Chicago Tribune,* if he's seen the headline. And then ask him whether he'd like to speak with me . . . before every newspaper from here to Nome wants to talk with me."

Ali gave the lieutenant a few seconds to look at the impressive headline.

F.D.R.'S WAR PLANS!

The lieutenant let his hand drift towards the phone.

"Thank you," Ali said sweetly.

She imagined the craziness going on inside this building, everyone wondering who leaked the story.

And the relief of the White House . . . with Roosevelt finally seeing the story in print.

"Yes, sir," the secretary said into the receiver of the squat black phone. "There's a Mr. Manly here, he wants—no, just Mr. Manly. No other members of the press. Yes, but I thought . . . yes, sir. Yes, sir. Right away, sir."

The secretary hung up the phone.

Ali scooped the paper off the desk.

"Captain Peterson said the admiral will see you."

"Thanks," Ali said. "I thought he might."

Ali waited. When the lieutenant said nothing she asked, "Er, which way?"

"Oh . . . sorry. Down the hall to the right, then

take the first corridor to the left, up the stairs. Admiral Stark's office is in Room 232.''

''Thank you.''

And Ali set off to met the commander-in-chief of the Navy.

If that's who he really was . . .

17

"It's quiet," Toland said.

Dr. Marianne Beck nodded.

But that was just a name, a role I'm playing, a host to my real consciousness . . . she thought. I am a doctor.

But my name is Yoshira Shirato.

Then, fearing that Toland didn't see her nod, she said, "Good."

Her thoughts were on her husband.

Funny. She could see him as this *McManus*, this twentieth-century scientist, and still feel love for him. But she also remembered him as her Ichiro, Ichiro Shirato . . . so intelligent, filled with a brilliant fire.

And it's funny, too, that I've allowed myself to become this Dr. Beck. To see her as part of myself. I know so little about the real Dr. Marianne Beck, just bits and pieces. There's a reserve here, something that has fought against my own feelings for Ichiro.

She smiled at that. But then it wasn't hard to have my passion cool by looking at old Dr. McManus.

She fretted . . .

Will I ever see my Ichiro again?

I couldn't live otherwise . . .

"Nice and quiet," Toland said.

She turned to him, this good man who had helped them out of nothing more than his loyalty to Dr. McManus. *How much of this can he understand? He understands guns and fighting.*

She stood up and walked to the chairs, clustered so close together.

The tachyon generator had four of them back there, more than has ever been attempted before.

"It can be done," Ichiro had said to her. "If we keep the streams separate, if we don't spend too much time . . . it can be done."

But Yoshira wasn't sure.

She didn't like the way Dr. Jacob walked from one end of his generator to the other, tending his machine as if it might explode.

It scared her.

She checked all the sleepers, looking so peaceful, so untroubled. Their chests moving up and down, each one having its own rhythm.

But she lingered at McManus, at her Ichiro.

No, she told herself. *This isn't Ichiro.*

Not now. She smiled. *This is McManus. Back in his own body, pulled from the future. He was asleep.*

Even Dr. Jacob didn't know that we're from the future. And perhaps it was dangerous trusting Lindstrom.

She touched the scientist's chest. Felt it rise and fall.

He will sleep. And if he stirs, I'll give him another injection.

Ironic, she thought. *This time, the story is filled with strange ironies.*

Too much irony . . .

She brought her hand away from the scientist.

A good man? She wondered. *We will never know.*

She just knew that she wouldn't see her husband again until they were reunited in their own time.

After they had changed history forever . . .

* * *

McManus felt the sun on his face. He felt the wonderful heat, the blinding light. He stood at a doorway.

I'm not McManus, he thought. Not anymore.

No. That is over. And yet—he smiled—I'm still not Ichiro.

But—this time—at least I'm Japanese.

He just stood at the doorway and let the sun warm his cheeks. He smelled the sea, not too far away, and the dry grass, the spartina, the phragmites.

He rotated his neck, easing a dull ache.

I must have just awakened.

He brought his hand up to shield his eyes. He cut off the glare of the sun.

He could just see Pearl City to his left and, down the slope to the water, Ford Island, the rows of great battleships.

And he saw them.

He knew he'd be there.

The carriers. The *Lexington*. The *Enterprise*.

Sitting near the Naval Station, right where the maps said they should be.

Except they were supposed to be at sea.

They were supposed to be gone.

Gone.

It was the morning of December 6th.

Tomorrow the planes come.

And the carriers will be here!

He felt a hand touch his back . . .

"Come, Takeo. You promised me a picnic . . ."

He turned and looked at the woman talking to him. She was pretty, a petite Japanese girl wearing a hint of blush, her lips the colors of cherries.

She works in a tea house.

And she knows nothing about me. Hasn't a clue that her boyfriend is a spy for the Japanese Empire.

He just likes to bike and picnic a lot. Oh yes, and

he enjoys birdwatching. Always has his binoculars . . .

She grabbed his hand and pulled him out of the doorway. He saw the shadowy shapes of two bicycles leaning against the house.

The girl held a basket which she strapped to the back of one of the bikes. "Where shall we go?" she giggled.

He made himself smile. "To the hill . . . overlooking the harbor . . ."

He knew where Takeo Yoshikawa did his spying, the innocent picnic atop a hill of grass that rippled in the sea breezes.

The girl squeezed his hand. "Come," she said. "There may be clouds this afternoon . . ."

No, he thought, no clouds. Not really. No rain. The weather was going to be fine.

All weekend.

And Ichiro Shirato, formerly Dr. Elliot McManus, formerly from the twenty-ninth century, grabbed a bike from the side of the house and got on . . .

The sound of clicking heels reverberated through the tiled halls of the Propaganda Ministry. Lindstrom limped towards his office. Clever of me, he thought, asking my aide to go ahead to my office to gather any messages.

At least I'll find the bloody place.

And as he limped along, he thought of that expression: Don't judge anyone unless you walked a mile in their moccasins. Lindstrom pulled along the polio-damaged foot. It was an ugly, twisted thing. And Goebbels, proponent of the master race, was almost dwarf like—barely five feet tall.

I'm doing it. I'm in more than the bastard's moccasins. I'm in his skin.

He saw the rich wood doors ahead, running right up to the ceiling.

He got closer and they magically opened, as if they could sense that he was coming.

More heels clicked together. An attractive woman smiled and raised her hand in the Hitler salute.

Stupid business. Lots of dressing up and secret handshakes. Sad, stupid business.

Someone was at his elbow.

Where's my personal office, Lindstrom wondered. Now isn't this interesting. I can't go any farther until I know where my office is.

He stopped.

"Herr Reich Minister," a black suited SS officer said. "We have those reports on Dachau you wanted prepared."

Lindstrom nodded.

Butchers. Pigs. Let us raise a glass high to the spirit of Deutschland . . .

He took the reports.

They were stories. At the top, in German, he saw the words "Approved for Release, 12/6/41—Ministry of Propaganda." He read a few words:

"The residents at Dachau have been offered every opportunity for self-improvement. Daily classes are available on subjects ranging from foreign languages to modern history. Food preparation is a point of special—"

He stopped reading.

"That one," the officer said, looking over his chief's diminutive shoulder, "is on the opportunities offered at the camps, Herr Minister. And beneath that is a story on the plans for resettlement in the East." The SS man smiled, his white teeth vulpine against the background of his black uniform. "There are some nice photos, there, at the bottom."

Lindstrom nodded. Propaganda. There were good people in Germany. A few risked their lives . . .

their family's lives. As for the rest, they had the balm of the Propaganda Ministry to assuage any guilt that they might feel.

"Good," Lindstrom said. "Put them on my desk, please."

A sudden jolt of pain, someone pinching a nerve. Lindstrom felt a sudden . . . need. Does Goebbels take anything, he wondered? A bit of pain-killer. Something to take the edge off?

Lindstrom watched the path taken by his officer, and he followed.

He followed the SS slug into a sumptuous office. A woman, rather plain compared to the previous evening's companion, stood by an enormous desk, a pad and pencil in hand.

Lindstrom hobbled around to his chair, a giant leather chair that would dwarf Goebbel's body even further. In fact, the whole office was cut on an oversized basis. Compensatory size, Lindstrom thought? A little man with too much power.

He sat down.

"Coffee, Herr Reich Minister?" the secretary asked.

Lindstrom shook his head.

"No. Call the Reich Ministry. Ask for an early appointment with the fuehrer, some time—"

The secretary looked discomfited. Perhaps this was something she didn't do? A painting of Adolph, romantic, heavy with dark, soulful eyes and beatific pomposity, glowered down from the wall, keeping watch on little Josef.

"The fuehrer is usually not available until after eight P.M., herr minister."

Eight. God, is that enough time? Have to lay the groundwork, Lindstrom thought. Eight . . . what the hell time will it be in the states . . . in Hawaii?

He counted back five hours, then five more.

It might be alright.

"Fine. And bring me the news summaries." The secretary looked perplexed. *Perhaps I used the wrong word?* "The reports," Lindstrom pressed on confidently, "from the foreign press."

The woman shot her arm out in a gawky salute, turned and left.

He sat and waited for her.

Feeling the soft leather of the arms of the chair. The desk, so orderly, a place of lies and death.

Death and lies.

She came back.

The secretary walked to his desk and put them down. "There is one there that's has been marked 'urgent,' Herr Minister. From America." The secretary caught herself and backed away.

Lindstrom nodded. He picked it up.

All he needed to see were the first few words.

The *Chicago Tribune*.

Then, underneath, the report was marked, "not a summary."

Important enough to print the whole story.

And Lindstrom read the story, read all about how Roosevelt was going wage a terrible war in Europe. Ten million American boys in an Allied Expeditionary Force.

Way to go, Alessandra! Score one for our team.

He read about all those planes and tanks and ships that American industry could pump out.

Starting in 1943.

Yes, it would all start in 1943.

If Hitler waited that long.

Linstrom smiled to himself. He felt his secretary watching him, confused by his odd behavior.

"Fine . . . thank you . . ." Lindstrom said. *Wishing he knew her name. It will come.* McManus said things like that always popped up in your consciousness.

No. He shook his head. *Not McManus. McManus*

is someone else, someone I don't even know. He really was Ichiro Shirato.

It all felt like losing an old friend.

He looked at the story again.

Yes, Hitler would have to be crazy to wait.

Then Lindstrom had this disturbing, yet obvious thought.

But of course, the man *is* crazy . . .

Ali stood before the desk. The Navy captain looked up, shook his head and—for a second—Ali thought he might spit.

Well, that answered that question . . . they've seen the story.

"I'll see whether the admiral is ready," the captain said, all but snarling. He got up and opened a door behind him. Ali waited.

I could be wrong, she thought. I might not have this right . . .

She dug her hand into the pocket of her jacket.

She felt the metal wire, the four-foot coil she had picked up at the hardware store.

She flexed her fingers.

The door opened.

She jerked her hand out quickly, nearly pulling out the coil of wire.

Someone came to the door with the captain. A man with thinning white hair, dressed in black uniform emblazoned with colored ribbons and stripes. The Navy boss. Admiral Stark.

The admiral didn't talk to him.

Instead, he turned to the captain. "Why don't you take a break, Tom? Grab some lunch."

"Yes, sir," the captain said. And he walked past Ali, creating an unfriendly breeze in his wake.

Then . . .

"Mr. Manly, perhaps you'd like to talk in my office?"

Ali nodded. Her tongue felt unable to speak. It was a dry, lumpish thing. I've got to watch this, she thought. Really watch it . . . because anything can happen.

Anything . . .

Ali walked in. The rug was a rich navy blue. A giant gold anchor was embroidered in the center. There was a portrait of John Paul Jones on the all, another of a masted warship, maybe *Old Ironsides*. A few photos of battleships, a carrier. A small photo of Roosevelt.

The admiral sat down.

He gestured at the seat facing his desk.

"It's your nickel, Mr. Manly . . ."

Ali nodded.

My nickel.

Thinking: what if I'm wrong? This was too damn important to screw up.

Ali cleared her throat. And said:

"Admiral, I know who tried to stop Senator Wheeler from giving my paper the story. I know who did it."

Stark raised his eyebrows. Signalling interest, bemusement?

This is like a gangster movie, she thought. I expect him to whip out a mauser and blow my head off.

Then—a chilling moment—Ali thought of what Stark had just done.

He sent his secretary, the captain, away.

We're alone.

Just the two of us in here, she thought.

How convenient . . .

Then she spoke, aware of how nervous she sounded, how she stammered . . .

"You tried to kill the story . . ."

And Stark grinned.

18

"Okay, Tad. Just check the rear flaps while I run down the instruments."

Jim nodded. The morning sun was brilliant, reflecting off the Ford Island naval airstrip. I have my legs back, he thought. But the damned headache is still here.

Of all days to have a headache.

Jim walked to the rear of the plane.

What I don't know about planes could fill a book.

He fingered the flaps. They gave—too easily it seemed—bending up and down. The Navy plane was a single-engined plane, chunky. Not a fighter. A scouting plane.

Though Jim guessed that there must be guns somewhere.

Johnny Murphy climbed up to the cockpit.

Check the flaps . . .

He touched them again. They moved. If that's what they're supposed to do. He walked to the tail, to the—what is it called? The rudder?

He grabbed it and wiggled it left and right.

"Hey!" Murphy popped out of the cockpit. "What the heck are you doing? I'm trying to check the damn instruments."

Jim smiled up sheepishly. "Sorry . . . brushed against the—"

"Well, just be careful."

Jim nodded. Murphy slid back into the cockpit. And a terrible thought began to grow inside Jim. A fear that not only were they going up in the plane. *But I'll be expected to do something.*

He shook his head.

Tad Gorman, come out if you're inside here. Please . . .

Give me some help.

Just enough so I don't crash the goddam plane.

Then Murphy popped out of the cockpit again. A breeze blew his reddish-brown hair. Jim saw him grin.

"All set here. Let's get her rolling."

Jim walked up to the cockpit. To the handrail. A single footstep.

He grabbed the handrail, stuck his foot in, and pulled himself up.

"Great day for flying, Taddie. Just one thing . . ."

Jim saw his seat, right beside Murphy.

Thank God!

I'm not the pilot.

There was another stick there, a tiny steering wheel.

But Murphy seemed in control. *He's the pilot.*

"If you gotta upchuck, pal, just make sure you stick your puss outside. I got a hot luncheon date, if you know what I mean . . ."

Murphy winked.

Jim smiled.

"Check controls . . ." Murphy said.

Jim waited. Murphy repeated, a bit testily. "Check controls. C'mon . . ."

Jim said, "Check."

"Hey. Do you have your fuel switch on?"

Jim searched the panel filled with so many switches and gauges.

He kept looking. Then he saw the fuel switch. He flicked it on.

"Atta boy. Ready for ignition?"

"Ready."

"Switch on," Murphy said.

Jim guessed he had to respond. He looked for something labeled "ignition." Where's the key? Why doesn't it have a big chunky key like my father's old Camaro?

Finally he saw a small switch.

"Ignition on."

"Here we go," Murphy said. The engines roared to life, a low, throaty growl. Dangerous. No mufflers on this baby.

"Got your ears on?"

Jim looked forward and saw that Murphy had slipped on his headphones. Jim followed suit and—at first—heard nothing but the low hiss of static.

Then Murphy's voice, twice as loud, was right inside his head.

"Ford Tower, this is Navy one-niner apple-betty. Ready for taxi."

The voice came back, distant, scratchy.

"Cleared for taxi, one-niner apple-betty."

And then—*miraculous!*—the plane moved.

"Get ready to check our position, Tad," Murphy said.

Right, Jim thought. Please, begging the real Tad Murphy to let something dribble out. Position, position. What the hell is our position? How do I do that?

No good.

That's our position.

Heading towards bad . . .

"I'll need a heading once we're in the, eh, air."

"Right," Jim said. A heading. Sure. No problem.

He pressed back against the seat. He felt the parachute on his back. That's comforting. Got my trusty parachute on. Now if I only knew where the pull-ring was.

Won't get too much chance to fumble around if I have to drop out of this bird.

" 'Kay," Murphy said. "Here we go."

Jim watched Murphy smoothly taxi onto one of the strips.

"I'm letting you off the hook today, Tad. I'll do most of the work since you've got a bell choir inside your head. You can take the stick tomorrow."

"Thanks," Jim said.

Then Jim looked to his left.

He saw a field of planes. More Navy patrol planes, but also fighters. What were they . . . Mustangs? And they were all bunched up together.

Of course they were.

Jim remembered reading about that. How General Short, the Army Commander, and Admiral Kimmel agreed that the real danger was from saboteurs.

And, yessir, the best protection against saboteurs was to push all the planes cheek to jowl so it would be too damn hard for anyone to fuck around with them.

Except it would be real easy for anyone who wanted to blow them up on the strip. Like dominos, one would go . . . and then the next . . . and the next.

A lone fire extinguisher, looking like a red hot dog cart, stood dopily next to the planes.

"Cleared for take off, one-niner," the tower screeched.

Jim saw a man down the end of the runway waving flags, signalling the plane.

The engine roared even more nastily.

Murphy had the throttle opened.

"Here," he said. "We . . . go."

The plane started rolling, pitifully slow. It will

never fly, Jim thought. Man wasn't meant to fly, and that fact gets proven here, today.

But every few feet the plane picked up speed, faster and faster until the hangars, the parked planes, the squat tower became a blur. There was a bounce, another, and another, and then—

Suddenly . . .

Jim as looking at a sea of blue. Directly over head. Dappled with creamy white clouds.

He wanted to grab something to steady himself. The stick was just there, just in front of him.

No. He shook his head.

He grabbed the edge of his seat.

His stomach clutched.

He tasted something like bile at the back of his throat.

Biting. Acidic.

Higher and higher.

"Hooo-eee," Murphy squealed. "Boy, do I ever love this."

And before Jim could say anything, like "please, stop, take me home, I've had enough, my stomach has had enough," the plane leveled off, and they were cruising out of the southern end of the island, over the ships of the Pacific fleet.

Until the small plane was sandwiched between the brilliant blue-green water and the great sky.

"This will do nicely," Ichiro said. He stopped his bike. The breeze buffeted him. Straddling his bike, he turned around and saw that the girl had pulled alongside him.

He kicked at the stand, but it just dug into the sand and the bike tumbled onto the grass.

"No matter," he said, smiling at the girl.

He went to unpack their simple picnic. He unhooked the basket from his bike and grabbed the rough brown blanket underneath.

"It's so beautiful here," she said.

"Yes . . ."

He felt pain.

In his head. A sharp jab, just on the side of his head, growing, swelling. He winced.

Quickly, he turned away from her.

No, he thought. No.

But the pain built, swelled.

And only one possibility occurred to him. I'm over stressing my system. No one has done this much jumping, not even the Historical Security squads. They never jump from one person then into another, not without a long—a real long—return to their own mind.

The throbbing pain lingered.

"Takeo," the girl said, calling her boyfriend's name.

It's all so schizophrenic, he thought. I'm Ichiro Shirato, not McManus, not this Japanese spy, Takeo Yoshikawa.

I'm Ichiro Shirato, a particle physicist, leader of my cell.

There are hundreds of cells, and together we make up a body.

That's what we say. And this body will stop them, the real Iron Men.

Before they even get started.

Ichiro Shirato. Elliot McManus. And now . . . Takeo Yoshikawa.

"Takeo . . . is there something wrong?"

He felt her hand touch his shoulder. He turned to her slowly, forcing a smile on his face. The pain wouldn't stop. It just kept building.

This is war. And in war there are sacrifices to be made.

"I am fine. Just—" he smiled. "Just a headache."

She brought a delicate hand up to his head, then she caressed his cheek. "Come," she said. "Lie down. I will massage your temples. My fingers can soothe you.''

He smiled again.

''Yes.'' Then Ichiro opened the basket. There was a thermos of saimin, the soup sending up a thin aromatic cloud. And, in wax paper, some dried dolphin-fish. He smelled the tangy oil and salt.

He lay the food down on the blanket.

Then he saw the binoculars, big heavy binoculars. 8x30s, with giant lenses to let in as much light as possible.

He picked them up. He scanned the water.

He saw the carriers, so big—floating cities. There were planes on one ship. He checked the name. The *Lexington.* And next to it, on the *Enterprise,* there were men, tiny ant-men scurrying about, hosing the deck down. The sheen of water glistening on the gray deck.

He looked down at Takeo Yoshikawa's watch.

Nearly 9:30.

By this time tomorrow it will be all over.

All over.

He heard the sound of a plane engine.

An omen . . .

Off in the distance, already at sea. He brought the glasses to his eyes.

A plane, flying out to the Atlantic.

A lone scout plane.

And he thought:

Are you in there? Jim . . . are you in the plane? And will you be able to figure out what has to be done?

And another thought . . .

Will we ever meet again?

The plane banked left, then right again.

And odd maneuver.

But Ichiro felt Tamiyo's hand pulling him down on the blanket.

"Let me make your head feel better," she said.

And he fell to his knees.

At the other end of Oahu, and at the northern tip of the island, Private George Elliot was getting impatient.

He, and his partner, Joseph Lockard, were stranded here until the damned army truck picked them up. They had smoked cigarettes. They had eaten the few sandwiches they brought along. It was getting hot, even here on top of the mountain.

The army's Opana Radar station had been shut down for more than an hour.

Lockard tossed a cigarette into the rocks.

"Call 'im again," he said to Elliot.

Elliot nodded. They had been dropped off here near three A.M.—a god-awful hour. Then they operated the radar station for three hours, getting only two blips, a scouting flight or two, and, later, a private flight, someone taking a flying lesson.

But he only knew it was a private plane since it flew right across the station.

A blip is a blip. How can we tell one from the other?

A little past 7 A.M., Lockard shut down the station, and the swinging metal net stopped moving.

And now they waited.

"Will you get off your duff and give Tyler another call?" Lockard said again.

"Sure," Elliot said. Lockard was senior to him, having been the first assigned to radar duty.

He walked back to the enclosed station. No walls, just a platform and roof to keep the equipment dry. He picked up the phone and waited for the duty officer, Lt. Kermit Tyler to pick up.

"Tyler here; what's up, Opana?"

"Sir," Elliot said. "We're still waiting here. Nobody's come for us. Starting to wonder, you know. Maybe—''

Tyler cut him off. ''Don't worry, Elliot. The army truck's headed your way. Just had a few other chores to run.''

''Right, sir. Er, lieutenant . . . do you want us to keep the radar on . . . since we're here?''

''No. Four to seven, that's all they want it run. We're still getting the hang of the thing, Elliot.''

''Right, sir,'' Elliot said. ''Thank you . . .''

The line went dead.

It wasn't Elliot's job to question anything.

He walked back to Lockard who had a fresh butt in his mouth.

But—Elliot did have a question.

The radar was here to detect the enemy. I mean, we all know that there won't be an attack. There isn't going to be any attack.

How the hell could the Japanese attack Pearl Harbor.

But still—

Why only run the radar for three hours?

Lockard looked up.

''What did Tyler say?''

''The truck's on its way.''

Lockard shook his head. ''Shit. You know we're on our time now, George. Our time. Hope you like sitting on top of a mountain on your free time.''

Lockard looked away.

Elliot also turned and looked, north, right off Kahuku Point.

The sea was choppy. White caps dotted the ocean as far as he could see. And Elliot wondered: what would I see if I went in a straight line, flying across the water, perfectly straight . . .

What would I come to . . . ?

And then he heard the dull, distant rumble of a truck struggling up the hill.

19

The admiral shut the door. Ali felt him behind her, looking at the back of Manly's head.

Damn, she felt vulnerable.

She quickly spun around.

Admiral Stark was right there, staring right at Manly's eyes.

Ali felt a small tug, the claw of a faint undertow gnawing at her feet, eating the sand away from her. Her skin went cold. The room was stuffy, but she felt as if it was filled with ice cold air.

She backed up.

A mistake.

Can't let him see that I'm scared.

Stark flexed his fingers. The gesture of a cheap gangster, a murderer . . .

A ruthless gesture.

Warming up the digits for some delicate work.

"I guess," Stark said at last, the voice unnaturally hushed, ". . . I guess that you feel as if you did something patriotic, releasing that report." Stark took a few steps, moving around to his desk. "Is that it? I guess it all comes under the heading of freedom of speech to you, doesn't it, Mr. Manly?"

Stark looked over.

And Ali felt confused. This response wasn't what she expected.

I expected more fear.

Instead . . .

I'm the one who's scared.

"I guess you felt that the millions of Americans who don't *want* us in this war will thank you and your paper, don't you? And—"

Stark was at his desk. He stopped. He reached down to a drawer and slid it open.

"I guess you simply assumed that the government wouldn't do anything about it."

Ali licked her lips, tasting the hard, rubbery feel of Manly's thin lips. Disconcerting, that—a novel feel to such an intimate body part.

She took a breath. I'm wrong, she thought. I thought that Stark was one of them. But—no. She saw that now. He's obviously not one of the Iron Men. Someone used him. That's it, someone else got to Stark, and got him to stop the story.

She spoke. And Manly's voice cracked a bit.

"Who told you to kill the story, Admiral?"

Stark smiled and shook his head.

The admiral looked up at her.

"The White House, Mr. Manly. The president himself. He said it was national security . . . an executive order . . ."

And then Ali knew.

I was wrong.

Her heart added an extra beat.

He *doesn't* know I'm from the future. Because if he did, if he knew that, he'd understand that I'd damn well know where Rainbow Five came from . . . I'd *know* that Roosevelt himself wanted the story published.

He doesn't know who I am . . .

Or is he just playing with me?

"There are laws," Stark said. "Good laws against espionage, subversion. You and your paper will be very busy in the courts, Mr. Manly."

She heard the drawer open just a bit more.

What is he getting? she wondered.

Ali stood there, thinking . . . I'm wrong. It isn't Stark. There's someone else. Someone else pulling the strings, someone who—

She had an idea.

A gamble.

Her dad always told her that you can't live without taking risks. It's part of life, he said. You have to take your chance when the time comes.

"You called the carriers back," she said.

Stark looked up. And all the bemusement, the arc of his smile, vanished from his face.

His voice was low, even more hushed.

His teeth were set.

As if he had just heard some very bad news.

"What did you just say?"

"You called the carriers back . . . the *Lexington* . . . the *Enterprise*. They were supposed to be on maneuvers, one in Midway, the other at sea. You had them come back."

"That's secret information," Stark said. "How the hell could you know that?"

A glint in his eye. A sparkle. A terrible wariness.

Ali let her hand slip into her coat pocket. Casually—oh, so casually—but each movement felt as if she was waving a flag. Her fingers were numb.

"I know. The carriers are there. And they'll be there tomorrow morning . . ."

Stark's eyes narrowed.

A bit of smile returned.

He said words.

In a language she didn't understand. No. That wasn't quite it. He made sounds that couldn't have been from any language she had ever heard.

He seemed to wait for an answer.

"Forgot the native tongue, slug? Are you so stupid, so backward that you forget the language of the Homeworld?''

Everything seemed wobbily, the room, the floor, her legs. What the hell is going on here, Ali thought?

Homeworld? Native Language?

What is he talking about?

Then he said more words. This time she caught some words, some sounds that were recognizable. But they were odd, not quite English.

And it's not Russian.

She stepped back. The admiral continued, now in English.

''Yes, the carriers are there. And—by next May— the Japanese will hold Pearl Harbor. By September, they will be attacking the West Coast.'' Stark stood up. ''There will be no American war with Hitler because this fat, lazy country will have its hands full fighting the Japanese.''

He stepped away from his desk.

''And things will return to the way they're supposed to be . . .''

Ali shook her head.

''You're crazy. The way things are supposed to be? The Iron Men are screwing up time, you're—''

Stark laughed.

Only now she knew that he wasn't Stark.

''The Iron Men?'' he said. ''Who are the Iron Men? And the way things are supposed to be? What bad history chip have you been using?'' He took another step, away from the desk.

His hands are behind his back, she thought.

He's got something behind his back.

Her right hand fingered the wire in her coat pocket. It felt like a useless coil. The idea had seemed a good one—

But now . . .

''It gets harder to repair history with your—meddling,'' he said. ''We've eliminated nearly all of the cells with Time Transference devices. Maybe there was one, we figured.'' Another step. ''It took us a while to figure out what was happening. That one of you had set up shop at some midpoint, had built another device at a time where we couldn't find it.''

Another step.

Ali backed up.

What's he talking about. Another device? A midpoint?

But as she heard his words, she recognized their truth. It explained so much.

I should have figured it out, she thought. It was right there. The lab, the shielding. The Time Tranference Device. All so clear now—

''You're from the future . . .'' she said.

''As are you.''

She nodded. ''But,'' she was slowly, ''I think that you've come a bit further than I.''

Step.

The man smiled.

''Oh, so you're from the safe-point, eh? What year, 1990, 2000?''

She said nothing.

''No matter. You've been duped. And I suggest that you let me set you straight. Before you go around blundering, doing more damage. But first, tell me the location of your lab. Who's in charge?''

Ali saw the man stop, his hands still behind his back.

He could be right.

Jim and I could have been duped. We could be the ones screwing up time. It would be so easy to trick us. Not hard at all.

Then she thought of the world she left.

A city of cannibals. Packs of humans hunting food. An army of black suits, feeding them and killing them. She thought of the house she was in, how the men took her, used her.

Screw him, she thought.

If that's the *real* future, then I'm throwing my lot with the slugs—whatever the hell they are.

Fuck him.

He saw the change in her eyes.

Stark wasted no time.

He pulled a knife from behind his back.

And her first thought was: how primitive. A knife. And how quiet.

He moved fast.

Ali tried to dodge him. But Chesly Manly's body didn't move so well. She tried to swerve, but Manly's body moved clunkily.

The blade came right at Manly's midsection.

And there was not a chance she could dodge it.

Not a chance.

"Come, come, Josef, don't stand out there like a little school boy, eh? You must have something important to show me. To interrupt an evening with your movie star . . . very important."

Hitler grinned. An engaging smile, a warm smile. You know, Lindstrom thought, if this guy had ended up working in a beer hall he might have been a pretty popular fellow.

Good old Adolph. Boy, can he bullshit with the best of them or what?

Or maybe if he'd gotten into art school and spent his days teaching human anatomy classes and painting pictures of big-eyed schnauzers.

Would have saved the world a lot of pain.

And death. And horror.

"Yes, mein Fuehrer. A very special telex, from the American paper, the *Chicago Tribune*." Lindstrom walked into the oversized office. The appropriately crimson rug was so thick he felt his shoes sinking in it.

"Let me see," Hitler said, digging out a pair of

spectacles. Lindstrom noticed that the fuehrer's hand shook as he fumbled with his glasses. Too little sleep, too many drugs, and not enough tanks.

Boy, dat bad old Russian front was eating up his dreams of conquest.

Hitler nodded at the telex pages, the complete story. He muttered to himself, wordless grumbles. He shook his head. Then, on the last page. "Aha. I told them."

Finally he finished, and Hitler's eyes rolled in his head, Wily Coyote sticking his paw in an electric socket. "Yes! I told them!" His hand arched upward, a great commanding fist, summoning the power of the ancient gods of Valhalla. His voice turned sneering, sarcastic. "No, the Americans won't be satisfied with just *giving* planes and food to England and Russia. Sooner or later, that warmonger Roosevelt, that syphilitic Jew Roosevelt will wage war on us!"

Lindstrom was frozen. Stunned. It was the worst vision from the newsreels, a living nightmare from all the war books he'd ever read. It was like opening the crypt to the mummy and—by God!—having it come to life.

Beyond your wildest dreams . . .

Hitler tossed the pages to the ground.

"My generals say, don't antagonize the Americans. Let them *have* the Atlantic. Let them have Greenland. Let them bring their weapons to Russia by air, by sea. We have friends in America." He turned and looked at Lindstrom with fiery eyes that glowed brighter than any cat's. *"Friends in America!* With an economy that could crush us—" He made a fist and slapped it painfully into the palm of his other hand.

"Yes, mein Fuehrer. I have always thought—"

Hitler waved an accusing finger.

God, this is horrible, thought Lindstrom. *This is*

worse than when Sister Mary Thomas caught me reading comic books in the coat room and decided to play batter-up on my behind.

Much worse.

"You, Josef, have always taken their side. Leave the Americans alone, you said. Let me do my work there, with the Bund, with our friend Lindberg! Does our friend Lindberg know about this? Does the Bund have a plan for stopping—"

Hitler looked around the floor for the discarded pages. He scooped them off the floor and flipped to the first page.

"Yes, how will our friends stop the—ah, here it is—'10 Million Man Expeditionary Force.' " Hitler looked up from the pages. His lips were wet.

Nearly frothing, Lindstrom thought.

And Lindstrom was beginning to worry about his safety.

I don't give a shit if the propaganda minister is killed.

Just as long as it happens after *I've vacated his body.*

"Perhaps it is just propaganda, my Fuehrer. Something to scare us while we suffer on the Eastern Front."

Hitler nodded.

"Yes. Certainly. Except I will . . . not . . . be . . . scared. And there's this, my dear Goebbels. The facts bear out what I always knew, what I always suspected. America is waiting. By 1943, they will have the men, and the ships, and the planes, and weapons to stop our great German army."

Lindstrom sensed his opening.

"But not now."

Hitler looked up. "What? What was that?"

Lindstrom cleared his throat. "Not now, my Fuehrer. If we were to strike now they would be completely, er, unprepared."

Hitler shook his head.

"England . . . Russia . . . and now America. It would be all too much." His shoulder slumped down. He seemed to shrink by half.

Lindstrom took a step closer to the deflated dictator. "Yes, but we can be alert to any opportunity, any chance that might come our way. To wait could be fatal. To strike at a propitious moment could be a masterstroke."

Hitler nodded. His voice turned hollow, distant.

Paging Dr. Morrel! thought Lindstrom.

Give the fuehrer some more amphetamine, please. Let's get his juices running again.

"What moment, Goebbels?"

Now Lindstrom raised a finger, a thin, bony finger, witchlike.

"We must watch the Japanese carefully. The answer may come from them."

Hitler waved the suggestion away.

"Oshima met with von Ribbentrop today. He says that there is no action planned in the East."

Lindstrom nodded. "None that he knows about, mein Fuehrer. But if I was the Japanese High Command, I certainly wouldn't tell *my* ambassador that we were about to wage war."

Hitler arched a dark eyebrow. A bit of life seemed to flow back in the old boy.

"You think that they will start war . . . in Singapore? Indo-China?"

Lindstrom smiled. "Let's just say that I think that their situation has become intolerable. They will act, and we must be ready to act in concert with them."

Hitler nodded.

And Lindstrom had a thought . . .

Why didn't the time bandits jump into Hitler? That would be the perfect position to control events from.

Then he remembered what McManus had said.

The process won't work with the mentally disabled.

In short, you can't enter a crazy person's mind.

Hitler smiled.

"I see—an opportunity, Goebbels. You are right. This information is just what I need to show my generals. I will await the perfect moment, and the event that will say—with no misdirection—now is the time to strike!"

Right, thought Lindstrom.

I'll be right here to give you all the prodding you need.

And unless something goes terribly wrong, you shouldn't have to wait too long.

Hitler walked away, distracted—for a moment—from the terrible reversals of the Eastern Front.

Guess I let myself out, Goebbels thought.

He saluted, clicked his heels, and turned around, leaving the blood red carpet and the master of Europe behind.

"What's our heading, Tad? Will you get on the stick?"

"Right . . ."

Jim looked at a bulb-shaped compass to his right. He unfolded a map showing a great loop that cut east of Pearl for about 100 miles and then curved back.

"Damn. You take the stick and I'll plot our damn course. What did you drink last night, kerosene? Your marbles are gone."

The stick, the plane's small steering wheel wobbled in front of him.

He wants me to take it, Jim thought.

It wobbled a bit more.

"Got it?"

Jim reached out and grabbed the stick. His hands

locked on it and he felt as if he had touched frozen metal with wet hands. I'll never be able to let it go.

"Yes," he croaked.

"Good."

And Jim felt that the plane was under his control.

Don't move, he thought. Must not move, must not do anything. Just hold it nice and steady, nice and steady. See, this isn't so bad. I'm not doing so bad.

He felt a demented grin stretch across his face.

This situation seemed familiar.

I've seen this before. But where?

Murphy reached over his seat and snatched the navigational chart from the small table to Jim's right.

"Too damn hung over to see, eh? What a pecker, Tad. Just hold her steady while I—"

Murphy's words jinxed it. His hands shouldn't have done anything. But just the suggestion that there was *another* possibility, that the plane could do something other than glide smoothly through the thin, gossamer clouds was enough to make it happen.

Or so Jim thought.

The nose of the plane dipped just a bit, just the tiniest bit. I can see more water. More water, because the plane's angle is a bit down.

Which led Jim to take a correcting maneuver.

He pulled back on the stick.

And suddenly all he saw was sky, and Murphy was yelling at him. Jim's back pressed against the seat.

"Damn, Tad. What the hell are you doin'? She's going to stall, you crazy—"

On cue, the engine started sputtering.

"Level off, damn it. More throttle. Give her more juice."

But "level off" become a mirror image of his former manuever. He pushed forward on the stick, and the plane dived down again, much worse this time.

Jim's stomach rumbled. He could see nothing but

ocean now. Murphy was yelling, a frenzied cursing that would easily get him drummed out of the altar boy corps.

Jim looked down.

He felt a warmth spreading at his groin area.

Not understanding that it was a very natural response.

That's what happens when you get scared.

Jim tried pulling up, to the right.

Then, pointed straight down to the blue Pacific, whatever was left in Jim's stomach shot forward, and to the side.

Right at Murphy.

20 ⸺

General Husband S. Kimmel squinted in the sun. Looking up, he saw the ships, his great Pacific fleet catching the light. The dull gray metal almost sparkled on the brilliant blue water.

His driver saluted as Kimmel got in.

I'm off to golf, he thought. A few holes before my lunch with General Short. A business lunch, to discuss the latest hysterics emanating from Washington.

He slid into his car.

The driver shut the door.

Kimmel looked left, the fleet still in view.

A Navy PBY took off from near the Naval Station. A destroyer slowly cruised to the lee of Ford Island.

So many ships, he thought. So many, that there's almost no place to store them.

He started to turn away.

Started to—

But he stopped.

The carriers. For a second, it was as if he hadn't seen them, as if they weren't there.

No. He stopped himself. Not like that at all. It's as if they didn't belong here.

The car's engine started.

It's hot here, he thought. The air is dull and stifling. But Kimmel felt a chill.

The feeling—passed.

He shook his head. Strange feeling, he thought. The pressures of command, he thought, smiling at himself.

The car pulled away, snaking away from his official residence to the Waiawa Golf Course.

Ichiro Shirato stopped his bike and glided to a stop, beside the small candy store.

He looked inside. An old Hawaiian man, all rolls of fat and leathery skin, looked up.

I leave the bike here, he thought.

That's the arrangement. Then I go inside. And if I have news, if Takeo Yoshikawa has news—

He took a breath.

It was difficult posing as McManus, pretending to be some late-twentieth century physicist. But this role as Takeo Yoshikawa was a lot more difficult.

Ichiro walked into the store. A small bell—a quaint touch—rattled noisily at his entrance.

The Hawaiian looked up.

The candy store proprietor wasn't a spy, not really. He was just making a few extra dollars. Ichiro smiled at him and slid onto a stool.

Let's hope the history books are right, he thought.

Let's hope they got the signals correct, after all the principal players were interrogated. "You'd like something?" the man said.

Ichiro nodded.

"I'd like some nice cool guava juice."

The man nodded. It was just a simple order, that's all.

But not so simple.

The man poured a cup of juice into a paper funnel resting in a metal holder. The white paper funnel had the word "Coke" running around it.

Ichiro drank it. Quickly. Damn, I'm so nervous. Got to get my nerves under control, before I go in there. He emptied the cup.

"More?" the man behind the counter asked.

Ichiro shook his head. The store was shadowy, only one thin fluorescent light overhead. There was a small shelf filled with candy. Oh, Henry. M&Ms. Baby Ruth. And, behind him, racks of magazines and comic books, a new creation.

Most of them eventually worth thousands.

It was peace time. The covers were about movie stars, and homes, and a world that didn't want war.

Ichiro got up.

He dug in his pocket and put down ten cents for the drink.

He turned to walk out the door.

He heard the Hawaiian behind him, picking up his dime, his cup, tossing the paper insert away.

Ichiro opened the door and walked out.

The Japanese Embassy was across the street.

And Ichiro knew that the Hawaiian was calling them, letting them know that he was coming, that Takeo Yoshikawa had information.

Ichiro nodded.

Some very disappointing information for Admiral Isorouko Yamamoto.

Fuchida watched the drills.

The torpedo bomber crews sat in a circle while the flight leaders flashed a silhouette.

He stopped and watched one group.

A dark shape flashed. A young pilot raised his hand.

"The *Oklahoma!*" the pilot shouted.

The crew leader nodded.

A good game, Fuchida thought. Keeping them busy, while the last hours trickle away, the last few hours before peace ended and the war came.

And with it, victory for Japan.

Another silhouette was flashed. A hesitation, then

a crewman jumped to his feet. "The *California*," he yelled.

His fellow pilots laughed good-naturedly at him, at his excitement, his exuberance.

The pilot turned red-faced. He looked up and saw Fuchida, and he grew even more embarrassed.

But Fuchida smiled at him. Telling him that it's okay. He waved at the pilots, his pilots. His great aerial army that he will lead into battle.

1941 is nearly over.

1941. The Year of the Snake. It will go into the history books, it will be taught in all the schools. 1941, this most important year for Nippon.

He thought about this attack, the image of a snake. He never doubted the justification for the war, never doubted that Japan was right to want this.

The surprise was important.

Like the way a snake strikes, rising from the marsh, from the grass, uncoiling, leaping at its attacker.

The crew leader flashed another silhouette.

The answer came quickly.

A few of the crewmen answered, shouting out the word . . .

"The *Arizona!*"

Fuchida nodded, and moved on, past the rows of planes and crews.

Ali felt the knife's blade dig into the material of Manly's raincoat, then into his suit jacket. The first touch of metal to skin.

She moaned.

But—at the same time—she arched Manly's lumbering body backwards. And before the blade could dig deep, before it could begin to do some real damage, she grunted and rolled away, falling to the floor.

Stark was committed to his move. Now his blade sliced upwards, clawing ineffectually at the air.

And Ali had a hopeful thought.

As out of shape as Manly is, Admiral Stark is in much worse shape.

Ali crawled to her feet. She felt the opening in her gut. Her hand touched her stomach and she saw the red smear on her fingers.

Get up, she told herself. Move, and get the hell up.

Stark was looking over, his face a horrible grimace.

Why doesn't he call for help, Ali wondered. Why doesn't he scream, get all the help he needs. This place had to be crawling with burly Naval lieutenants.

Ali got on her feet.

I know why.

He's afraid that I'd talk. That they'd hear and— God!—somebody might believe me.

A small fear. But just enough to give me . . .

Ali threw herself against the wall, dodging an awkward blow from Stark.

. . . a window of opportunity.

Her hand, the one with red-tipped fingers, dug in her suitcoat jacket. She pulled out the wire. Nice and strong, the hardware clerk had said—between loud bursts of his gum popping—great for hanging a picture, great for just about anything you need a wire for—

Ali unstrung the thin wire, wishing she had her own body. I can move. I'm agile. This guy is a mess. He smokes, drinks, and sits on his ass way too much.

Stark was coming at her, looking out-of-character, a chorus boy from a Retirement Village production of West Side Story.

He waved the knife in front of her, cutting off an exit route, any room for maneuver.

It looked bad.

Ali wished she could click her heels together. And wish—real hard. I want to go home. Right now.

Stark grinned. He saw the fear in her face.

She held the wire, pulling it taut with Manly's hands.

I'll get one shot, she thought. Just one shot.

And he may get his shot in before me.

She felt the thin trickle of blood wetting the front of her shirt, dripping down her pants.

I can do this, she told herself. It doesn't matter whose body I'm in. I can do this.

Stark took a step.

"You'll never know," he hissed, "what a stupid fool you were."

Trying to distract me. Trying to get my attention away. Poising himself for his move. Knowing that his body is slow, sluggish, that—

She took a breath.

Stark saw the move.

And Ali yelled—

Too loud, Manly's voice low and guttural, sounding as if he had stubbed his toe.

But it had the desired effect. It startled Stark.

Whoever he was. Whatever year he came from, whatever century.

There's no Iron Men? Ali wondered. This is all coming from the future? How come McManus didn't know that? How come McManus didn't tell us?

And this last question.

Before she made her one move, her one shot.

Who the hell is McManus?

She turned the wire sideways. Then—as if she was cutting a slice off a 100-pound block of cheese—she swung her hands and the suspended wire to the right.

Catching Stark's hands. She thought his hands would just slip by. The blade would slip by. And she'd be there, so close to him, exposed.

Waiting for him to stick her. And Ali knew he'd do it over and over. Fast, watching her face contort with each jab.

The wire slid along Stark's forearm, his hands, and—finally—it reached his knife.

It slid up the hilt.

Stark tried to pull it back, away from the wire.

Ali leaned forward a bit.

And the wire caught at the top of the hilt. It caught, and Ali whipped the wire back with all her strength.

Stark's knife flew into the air.

Stark's face looked horror struck. He followed the trajectory of the missing knife.

Not seeing what was coming next, not knowing what was going to happen.

Ali brought the wire up. Manly was a crucial few inches taller than Stark. She brought the wire up, and—before Stark knew what was happening—she wrapped it around his neck.

And pulled tight.

Tighter.

Now Stark turned and looked at her with great fish eyes. Pitiful, bulging, begging her to stop.

His hands grabbed at her neck, trying to fight back.

But from her martial arts training, Ali knew that that wasn't the way to go. He's losing air, blood circulation to the brain. He's getting weaker every second.

Stark should have grabbed at the arms. Try to free his neck.

She watched as Stark realized that, as the fireworks began popping inside his skull, the blackout only seconds away.

He kicked at Ali and caught her in Manly's groin.

Ali gasped. She nearly let go of the wire. But she redoubled the tension. Tight. Tighter.

Until she thought Stark's head must explode.

Then Stark's tongue—a pinkish snake writhing in his mouth—stopped moving. The puffy fish eyes went dead.

She felt a tremendous weight as Stark's body went limp, suspended from the wire.

She let him fall to the ground.

And for a long time—too long— she stood there.

Looking down at him. As if waiting for him to get up to begin the fight again.

A drop of her blood fell onto him.

And she knew that somewhere, sometime, the real Stark was trapped in a strange body, in a strange time.

The big clock ticked. A minute went by. Another.

Until Ali was ready to leave.

Jim didn't want to look. But he had to. He saw creamy curds glued to the side of Murphy's head, and a thin smear threatened to blur the windshield.

He heard Murphy screaming.

And all the time, Jim thought, we're headed straight down.

"Shit. Level her off, Gorman! Pull out. Damn, you got me covered—"

Jim remembered the last time he did something with the plane, a mere seconds ago. He had nearly stalled the aircraft.

Have to do it a bit more gently, that's all. Take it nice and easy.

Jim felt a blessed emptiness in his stomach and a bitter taste on his lips.

He pulled back on the stick.

The airplane screamed.

A terrible moan he remembered from all those neat World War II movies. Just before the plane ditched and exploded in the sea.

Getting cooked in an aircraft was supposed to be real bad.

The absolute worst way to go.

"More, damn it. Pull back!"

The plane hadn't moved. So Jim pulled back hard on the stick, fighting the flaps, the tremendous air pressure holding them flush to the wing, locked into place. He pulled harder.

The scream worsened.

Fortunately, it wasn't so easy to see the ocean anymore. It was a blur. Could be miles away—

Or right in front of us.

"Leggo!" Murphy screamed. "I have the stick. Let it the hell go!"

Jim felt some pull on the stick and—with a breath—he released the stick.

The plane was still screaming, howling at its plunge. But the angle was different. Jim didn't feel his body anymore, just hanging there, straight down, pulling against his seat belt.

He felt the plane begin to level off.

Keep on going, Murphy, he thought.

Save us and I'll see that I never throw up on you again.

More level.

How many feet to the water?

The scream stopped. Once again, Jim heard the noise of the engine. He stared at the stick in front of him, watched it wobble back and forth, as Murphy tried to pull the plane out of its death-defying fall.

He felt his bottom press against the seat. His feet rested on the floor of the cockpit.

It's over, he thought.

We're alive. He did it. We didn't crash.

Jim didn't say anything. And—for a long time— neither did Murphy.

But when the plane was coasting smoothly, as if a

bad dream had just ended, Murphy undid his seat straps.

And he turned around and looked at Jim.

Murphy's face still bore a few telltale smears.

He wasn't smiling.

He looked right at Jim.

And said:

"Thanks, buddy."

21

"I want to go out."

And Dr. Yoshira Ichiro, standing among her sleeping charges, was scared. She wished she could tell them—Dr. Jacob, Toland—her real name. This was not a time for secrets, she thought.

No . . . Ichiro had been very clear about that.

Do not tell them.

Though he didn't say why.

Now Toland stood by the metal door, the hidden door that led to the Cloisters.

And he said that he wanted to open it.

"Why?" she said, hearing the fear in her voice. "They're gone. There's nobody there . . . I don't hear anything."

Toland stood in the shadows, holding his dark weapon tight, close, his friend.

"No," she repeated. "There's no reason to leave. The Pack is gone, they're—"

In the shadows, Toland shook his head.

"I'm not too sure. They might be outside looking for a way to get in. Perhaps there are other ways. Sitting here, listening, we don't know what they're doing." He hefted his weapon. "I want to find out."

She wanted to say, please. Don't go out there. Because then it will just be me. And Dr. Jacob. And what good could he be, a small man who knows about machinery, engineering? Please don't go . . .

"I—"

"If I see anything, I'll come back. If not, I'll make sure everything is secure. I'll check the main gate. But if they know we're here—if they're still trying to get in . . ."

He left the sentence unfinished.

And Dr. Yoshira Shirato could easily imagine what the Pack would do, first to Jacob and herself . . . and then to the others, the sleeping ones.

Then it *really* will be over, she thought.

Because we're the last hope. The last—

She nodded.

Her voice caught in her throat. She cleared it. "Okay. But don't go for long. Professor Lindstrom's due back soon. Then Ich—Dr. McManus. The others. We may have more to do."

Toland nodded. He laughed. "And if they all did what they had to, the Cloisters might suddenly fill with tourists . . ."

She smiled. "At night. I don't—"

Toland turned.

"Leave the door unbolted," he said. Another hint of a laugh. "I may have to return quickly."

She heard the clank as the heavy metal door was unbolted. Toland's steps echoing in a passageway. Then, the bang of the door being slammed shut.

She looked to Dr. Jacob.

He smiled up at her. Sheepishly. Helplessly.

And she felt alone.

Lindstrom was leaving the Reich Chancellery. And he nearly made it to the door when a fat man in a powder blue uniform bushwacked him.

"Josef . . ."

Lindstrom stopped. The fat man literally blocked

his exit. The light was behind the blimplike man, but Lindstrom knew who it was.

Fieldmarshall Hermann Goering, head of the Luftwaffe, art collector, and all-around bon-vivant. Goering's long fingernails radiated a crimson color . . . must be one of Hermann's red days.

"Yes," Lindstrom said. He tried to recall the depth of animosity that existed between Goering and Goebbels. Both were very circumspect in what they recorded in their diaries, always an eye on the future and who might win the "Be-The-Next-Fuehrer" Sweepstakes.

"You were with—" Goering came close—"the fuehrer."

Lindstrom nodded. He looked at his watch. "Yes, we had a chat. Now, if you'll excuse me, I—"

Goering laughed. Though it was night, a steady stream of secretaries and officers walked past them, clicking their heels, saluting while their tête-á-tête went on.

"Oh, I know. You want to get home to your wife, and the kinder. Isn't that so?"

Goering smiled, a bearlike grimace more appropriate for eating one's young.

"Yes. My family—"

Goering draped an arm over Goebbels, and pulled the scrawny Propaganda Minister closer. "Maybe—though first—a visit with your special fraulein, eh? War can be so—enervating."

Goering was leading Lindstrom to the side, away from the flow of night traffic by the Reich Chancellery entrance.

"I was just wondering if you wouldn't share with me your conversation with the fuehrer. I like to be informed. So I can make the best use of the Luftwaffe."

Lindstrom nodded. What would the real Goebbels do? Tell him nothing? Everything? Something in between? It might be best to have Goering on the team—in case Adolph asks for some counsel.

"We spoke of the reports from America, of plans for war."

Goering pulled back, horrified. "America will never attack us unless provoked." Goering shook his jowls. "Never. That is essential to our plans. We must not have the American industry, American resources enter the war against us."

Lindstrom nodded. Goering knew the limitations of his Luftwaffe. After the Battle of Britain, it was all over for the tubby air general.

"Good point, Hermann. But—"

Now Lindstrom leaned closer.

I need just a little adjustment here, he thought.

"My dear Hermann, I would keep those thoughts to yourself. You are, of course, the fuehrer's favorite. But—a word to the wise—he is determined to eliminate America before it grows too strong. If an opportunity arises . . ."

Goering's eyes narrowed, sinking into the flesh of his bowling-ball face. Like a truffle hunter who just uncovered an unsavory fungus, he backed up.

"Set on fighting America?"

Lindstrom smiled. I'm enjoying this, he thought. Actually having a damn good time pulling these strings.

"Most definitely. At the first good opportunity." Now Lindstrom clapped him on the back. "I would watch the next few days for such an opportunity, my dear Hermann. And you should be there first, suggesting such a daring course of action. It cannot fail but meet with the fuehrer's approval."

"Yes," Goering said, dreaming of the approbation he'd receive from Hitler.

"And now—" Lindstrom grinned. "I'm late."

And he left Goering, dreaming of glory and the day that he'd be fuehrer.

Lindstrom walked out the door, thinking.

Too bad you beat the hangman's rope.

Too damn bad . . .

She walked down the stairs, past officers, past secretaries, past everyone bustling about with crisp military efficiency.

Ali looked straight ahead, keeping one hand pressing firmly against her wound.

Have to get out of here, she thought.

But her steps were wobbly, uncontrollable.

She was nearly at the bottom step. And she heard noise. Excited voices. The sounds of people hurrying.

Could be nothing, she thought.

Could be.

Or maybe they discovered Stark.

An MP hurried up the staircase, taking the steps two at a time.

Ali reached the bottom, thinking:

They'll seal off the building. I'll be trapped here. A sharp pain kept jabbing at her midsection. Each step tearing at her, pulling the wound open wide, wider—

At the bottom, she turned and hurried to the hall. The voices and the steps of people bustling about echoed weirdly, dreamlike.

There didn't seem to be any alarm. I'm just paranoid, she thought, that's all. There's nothing here but the excitement of the War Department on alert. Nobody found Stark. Not yet . . .

She looked up.

The door out to the street was ahead. Two more MPs flanked the door. People were leaving, it was quitting time. The Saturday workers were leaving. Probably nobody would be here tomorrow, just a few people working code machines, looking at the Japanese messages.

Tomorrow morning it would be real quiet here.

She tried to force herself to walk normally.

Her feet didn't want to move. They grew heavier with each step. It felt as if it would be easier if she just dragged them.

The door, the guards, were closer.

Still no sign of alarm.

How long before the admiral's aide gets back?

A woman looked up at her, a secretary. She smiled. And then—no.

Ali thought her eyes trailed down, to Manly's hand, grasping at his stomach, to the spreading wet stain.

She kept moving.

Past the woman. Feeling her looking at her back, her mouth open. Debating whether to say anything.

Joining the people filing past the guards, a steady stream of Saturday workers ready, at last, to enjoy their truncated weekend.

These were dangerous times.

She moved into the stream. Then on, abreast of the guards.

Ali looked ahead.

She could smell the air. Hear the sound of the cars. The noises of the street. She took a breath.

She passed the guards.

Then she heard the whistle, the big-pitched shriek of a whistle. And voices yelling, telling the people to move away.

Ali tried to push past the people in front of her. Almost there, she thought, just about there.

She felt herself trip.

A voice behind her. "Halt!"

She didn't know that they were talking to her.

Again, the voice screamed. "Halt or I'll shoot!"

The workers screamed, and then they moved away from her. And she was alone, on the steps, looking down at the street. She saw the Capitol in the distance. It was so dark out . . . even though it was just near five. Dark, cold, and a light mist bathed her face.

"Halt!"

More voices.

And she knew that if she took another step they'd shoot her.

Bang. I'd be dead.

She pulled her hand away from her wound. It was sopping, coated with a dark slimy goo that could have been any color.

And then she collapsed to the ground.

A man in a dark, blue suit with ludicrous large lapels and tiny white pin stripes bowed to Ichiro and unlocked the door.

Ichiro bowed back.

Such a civilized gesture, he thought. A small nod of recognition, of respect.

Ichiro walked into the room. The door was shut behind him. He turned and locked the door.

And he looked at the machine.

The Japanese Encryption Device.

Something that the allies had broken well before Pearl, with their Decrypter, dubbed "Magic."

He looked at the code machine. There was a keyboard attached to a wood box. He saw metal disks and a wire leading to something that resembled a teletype machine.

He knew that no one at the consulate ever saw Takeo Yoshikawa's messages. And even Yoshikawa didn't understand the use his information was being put to . . .

Later, the Japanese spy would claim that he was just doing normal surveillance for the Japanese government. Yoshikawa was as surprised by the attack on Pearl Harbor as anybody.

Ichiro walked over to the simple wood chair before the desk, pulled it back and sat down.

The machine was on, ready.

Lindstrom had instructed him in the format to follow, so the message looked like any other from Yoshikawa.

Ichiro typed in the date.

As he worked, the teletype printed out the encrypted message using the code of the day.

Then the message.

He remembered the wording, the listing of battleships, cruisers, submarines, destroyers. No typist, it took him a long time.

The room grew stuffy and hot. Tiny beads of sweat gathered on his forehead, on his upper lip.

Then—he got to the last part.

Ichiro took a breath.

"There is no sign—"

He heard someone outside. Steps walking slowly past the door.

"Of the U.S. naval vessels . . . the *Lexington* and the *Enterprise*." Another breath. "The U.S. carriers are at sea . . ."

He stopped.

Then closed the message with his initials.

The teletype went silent.

He stood up and pulled the paper out of the machine. The rows of Japanese characters would make absolutely no sense.

Until they got to Yamamoto's Code Room and were translated.

And the admiral would learn the very bad news.

The news that wasn't true.

Not yet.

Ichiro turned and walked to the door.

He unlocked the door and stepped outside, feeling a bit of air hit his sweaty face.

Ichiro walked back to the consulate's radio room,

past grim-faced men who surely could taste the coming of war—so close that it stung their tongues.

Just how close they didn't realize.

Ichiro hurried into the radio room, the bogus message held tightly in his hand.

Murphy wasted no time hopping out of the plane.

"You—" he said, looking up at Jim—"are some piece of work. Not only do you nearly kill us, but how the hell am I supposed to go to lunch smelling like your upchuck? God . . ."

Jim fumbled with his straps, undoing the seat and shoulder harness. The cockpit was ripe, even with a breeze blowing strongly off the water.

He squirmed out of his seat, and up. "Hey, I'm sorry, Murphy. I really lost it up there—"

Murphy squinted up at him. "Lost what, Gorman? What the hell are you talking about?"

Oh . . . Jim thought. Inappropriate idiom.

"I felt like I was going to black out."

Murphy shook his head, and walked away.

Jim still could see the telltale residue of something sticking to the back of Murphy's shirt, flecks of goo glued to his head.

He saw someone running up to the plane.

A guy wearing a blue cap and sunglasses. He held a letter in his hand.

"Lieutenant," the man said. He held the envelope up.

Jim squirmed out of the plane. He pulled himself up, out of the cockpit. Awkwardly turning around, he lowered himself to a foothold on the side of the plane. And then he jumped down.

When he turned around, he saw the man wince. He's downwind, Jim thought.

"Er, a message sir. From U.S.S. *Arizona* . . ."

The *Arizona*.

I've seen pictures of the *Arizona*.

Before . . .

A ship crawling with men, one of the jewels of
Battleship Row.

And then—after, when it exploded. When all the
powder and bombs on deck exploded after the Japanese hit.

Over a thousand men killed. Some incinerated immediately. Others slow-roasted, dying agonizing
deaths below deck or in the burning swirl of oil on
the water. Many were sealed in nightmarish chambers of horror below the water line.

The explosion was so big, so damn powerful, it
sucked the air from a nearby ship, putting out the
fire on the repair ship, the *Vestal*.

More than any other ship, the *Arizona* represented
the horror of the attack on Pearl Harbor.

Jim took the envelope.

He opened it.

The messenger, some airstrip sailor, backed away.

Jim opened the letter.

And read the message . . . from his father.

22

She waited.

Toland was gone.

"Dr. Beck . . ."

Yoshira turned to Dr. Jacob, responding immediately to the name, this person who she was supposed to be.

"Dr. Beck . . . it's time I started," he said. "Dr. McManus made it very clear that—"

She heard a sound. A howl. A feral noise. A raccoon trapped under the tire of a car. A kitten moaning in the death-grip of some hungry, oversized rat.

"I guess you can begin, Julian." She looked around. Every light was on in the small lab. But still she felt surrounded by gloom, and darkness. Days were going by in the past. But—here—every hour crawled by.

Night was a bad time.

She heard the howl again.

And Dr. Jacob dared ask, "What was that?"

She shook her head. "I don't know . . . Toland is out there . . ."

More howls. Closer.

From the front, from where the iron door was.

"I have to bolt it," she said. "He said that he'd be right back. He said he'd come right—"

She forced herself to take a step towards the door. The sounds seemed closer.

Yoshira wished that Jacob would follow her, walk her to the alcove where the door was.

But he stayed by his machine.

It took forever to walk to the dark corner, to the metal door. Her hand reached for the bolt.

The door moved.

The handle rattled.

''Toland,'' she whispered.

The door flung open.

And she saw that she was wrong.

The blonde actress, whose principal talent seemed to be one of rather unusual dexterity, was modeling what Lindstrom would call ''dainties.''

He sipped the champagne.

Now this, he thought, wasn't so bad. A good day spent organizing things back here, and a little light entertainment, some good food, fine champagne while waiting for my ride home.

The woman—Elise Rackebrandt, star of a recent Norse cinematic saga, *Die Volsung*—extended a leg and slowly began rolling back her nylon. Pure silk, for which she had profusely thanked him. Apparently a package of such goodies had arrived today. All through the good offices of Dr. Josef Goebbels.

It was all so decadent. Down right evil. Still, there wasn't much he could do about it, now was there? Just sit back and enjoy the show.

Her performance went very smoothly up to the penultimate moment when the nylon got caught on her toe. A nasty old cuticle snagged the delicate garment.

She giggled, yanked it off, and then grabbed at her own glass of bubbly.

Elise sashayed over to him, one stocking on, one

off, and not much more than a Victorian-looking corset covering the rest of her.

"Would you like to take the rest off?" she cooed.

Her voice had a shrill, a strident beer-hall quality. Poor girl was born too late for her proper era, the days of the Silent Picture.

Lindstrom was about to decline the offer.

But his second—or was it his third?—glass of bubbly was prompting him to—what the hell—go with the flow.

He put down his glass.

"Why not?" he smiled.

Elise Rackebrandt extended her other leg to him, popping the straps of her garter with a satisfying snap.

And Professor Lindstrom reached out, thinking:

I hope I don't get pulled back *too* soon . . .

Men in white coats. People digging at her stomach, pulling away the jacket. The sounds of cutting, tearing.

Men in uniforms.

Someone looked down and sneered.

Bastard.

He says.

You'll hang.

Other words. Barely heard. Nazi. Spy Traitor.

And:

Hope you die . . .

And Ali remembered a prayer, from her Catholic school days, back when she believed, back when she was a little girl.

And hope to sleep before I die.

I'm so tired, she thought.

Why won't they leave me alone?

More white coats. A man with a mustache leaned over her and stuck a light in her eyes. One eye, then the other, is blinded. She felt pressure in her mid-

230 Matthew J. Costello

section. They're putting something there, she thought. A bandage.

She heard a siren. Another siren. All this noise . . .

She turned her head to the side.

They've found Admiral Stark.

They're mad because Admiral Stark is dead.

Not a good change, she knew. Too big. Lindstrom won't be happy . . . McManus. It might have other bad effects.

But it was the only way. What else could be done?

He was one of them.

She didn't know what to call them.

Now that she knew that they weren't the Iron Men, that they weren't really KGB hardliners.

That he really came from the future.

She felt herself being lifted.

They'll have a chance now.

Jim. McManus. They have a chance now,

Because—

She was carried inside the ambulance.

Because somebody else will be in charge of the U.S. Navy, in charge of the U.S. Fleet.

She heard the engine start.

And then nothing else.

Jim pulled the jeep out of the small parking lot.

It had been an awkward moment, when he asked someone, how do you get a car, a jeep, something that can take me down to the harbor?

One sailor gave him a strange look and said that, er, the motor pool might be a good place to try.

Duh . . .

Jim filled out some papers and then the jeep was his for the afternoon.

He took it slow moving on the road that left the naval airfield. The clutch was clumsy, grinding its way from gear to gear—no synchromesh here. But he got the jeep into third gear and was able to coast down the highway, heading south.

He thought of the last time he was in a jeep.

Funny. It was really only a month or so ago.

In North Africa, sitting behind Field Marshall Erwin Rommel.

I was a German then.

Yeah . . . at least I'm with the good guys this time.

He felt the afternoon sun on his back. The wind sent his hair flying straight back. The island was peaceful, sleepy.

Not for long, he thought. Not for long.

This letter confused him. His father—Tad Gorman's father—was captain Jack Gorman. And he asked him to come see him on the *Arizona*. The letterhead on the paper said Office of Naval Security, Pearl Harbor.

An important man . . . my father . . .

That's why I'm here.

But what am I supposed to do?

I don't have a clue as to why they sent me here. Why Tad Gorman? How can a navy pilot be so important to the attack on Pearl Harbor? And what's supposed to happen? Should the attack be stopped?

Or am I supposed to help it along?

He passed some Hawaiian children playing by the side of the road. They heard the jeep and looked up and smiled.

Jim waved at them.

And he saw something ahead.

He couldn't quite make out what it was. Someone standing in the road. No. It was a bicycle . . . and someone standing beside it.

Jim started to pull his jeep to the side, nearly off the road.

What the hell is the guy doing?

The man started waving. Waving at Jim, signalling him, as if he was having problems of some kind.

Reluctantly, Jim slowed . . .

The gear box started screaming. Jim hit the clutch and shook the stick shift loose, jamming it into second gear, then—changing his mind—first gear. The jeep lurched when he let the clutch free and the gear caught.

Jim pressed down on the brake.

It was a Hawaiian standing in the highway, the golden sun hitting his face.

Jim stopped the jeep.

No.

Not Hawaiian.

Japanese.

Jim waited.

Something's wrong here, he thought. The air seemed so still. There was just the breeze snapping the tall grass around. The sound of the wind whistling over the jeep.

The man stopped waving and walked towards Jim, leaving his bike there, blocking the way.

Something's . . .

Wrong.

Jim eyed the gear box. Reverse. Reverse will be down and back. Or maybe forward. Or maybe off to the side, and back and—

His hand touched the gear shift.

The man walked to the side of the jeep.

Jim's fist locked on the narrow nob of the shift.

Jim licked his lips. He looked at the man, dressed in a colorful orange and red shirt.

"Yes," he said. Expecting anything. "Something wrong? What is it?"

The man smiled.

A big smile.

And he said, "Hello, Jim."

The metal door flung open with an explosive force that sent Marianne Beck's matronly body flying back into the lab.

Yoshira moaned, as her back smashed against the concrete floor and her elbow hit hard.

She heard Jacob.

"Oh, God, no . . ."

She knew what was happening.

Even before she looked up.

The Pack was inside the lab.

They were ghastly creatures. Their clothes dripped off them, tattered, stained with blotches of red, flecks of gray. The first ones stopped. Stunned by the lights of the lab, the brightness.

Then they looked down at her.

She tried to claw her way backwards, away from them.

Jacob kept muttering over and over, "No . . . no . . ."

Their hesitation lasted only a few seconds.

And then they leapt on her, their mouths open, brown teeth gnawing the air, living machines, hungry, hungry . . .

Hungry.

Nearly all of Elise's clothes were off.

Everything, except a black bra that pushed her great melon breasts upwards and together.

She smiled coyly at him, waiting.

Lindstrom smiled back. But Goebbels' bony body was groaning under the weight of so much pulchritude. She wriggled her bottom back and forth, just a bit, urging him on.

Ever the gentleman, Lindstrom reached behind Elise's back and—with a deftness that surprised him—he unhooked her bra.

He thought he heard a pop, and the too-tight bra sprung free.

He saw a clock on the wall.

A disturbing thought.

I shouldn't be here.

I should have been yanked minutes ago.

"Come, liebschen . . . what is wrong?" Elise took his head in her hands and redirected his attention to the great valley in front of his nose. "You don't like the present when it's finally unwrapped?"

Lindstrom smiled.

"Yes," he said. "Wonderful. It's just—"

Back to the clock. Maybe it's wrong. Maybe the clock is wrong. Happens sometimes. Off by a few minutes.

No. This is Deutschland. The Third Reich.

If there's one thing you can be sure of, the clocks work.

There's been a screw-up.

McManus. Jim. Alessandra. Something went wrong somewhere.

Elise leaned closer, wriggling around a bit more feverishly on Goebbel's bony lap.

Another possibility occurred to Lindstrom.

The Time Lab. The Cloisters. That's where the problem is.

He watched another minute tick by.

But then Elise pulled his face into her creamy hillocks, quickly muffling Lindstrom's feeble words of protest.

When she opened her eyes—

For just a second.

—the bright lights were all aimed down. Ali felt bathed in light, the warmth adding another sensation beside the throbbing pain at her midsection.

There were people in white—the doctors—moving around, talking with muffled voices through their masks. The clink of metal, the dinner table being set.

Mom coming home for dinner.

Driving back from Montauk, from visiting her friends.

The slap of china hitting the table. The sun glinting off the ocean. The yellow of the beach.

Hushed voices there.

Mom drove fast. Pushed her Jaguar so fast. Loved it more than any of the other luxuries.

Loved it.

Hushed voices.

And Ali never heard that sound again. Never heard the Jaguar kicking up a spray of sand and pebbles as it pulled into the driveway of the beach house.

Never.

The clinking stopped.

Surgery.

They're going to operate on me . . .

The lights began to fade. White, to yellow, then to the dull glow of a late summer's misty sunset.

Then she heard nothing, and everything was black.

Jim stood there. His hand was locked on the side of the jeep to steady himself.

He shook his head.

Down the road, he saw a truck coming towards them.

The man, this Japanese guy, smiled.

"How do you know my name, how—?"

The man interrupted him. "Jim—it's me. Dr. McManus. I'm *here,* Jim."

The truck kept coming up towards him, barreling up the road, a ghost truck. Some mechanical augur, bringing news . . .

Jim looked at the stranger.

"Dr. McManus . . . I—"

Jim caught himself. There are two sides to this game, he reminded himself. Two sides. Don't jump to conclusions . . .

Jim pushed his hair off his forehead. Best test this man.

"Where did I just come from?"

The man smiled engagingly.

"From up there." The man pointed to the blue sky. "But before that—assuming all went well—the sixth century, A.D."

"Dr. McManus . . ." Jim said with genuine wonder.

"Yes, Jim, and—"

He turned. The truck was nearly there. "Best to get my bike off the road, eh?" McManus ran to the bike and dragged it to the side. Then he hurried back to Jim's jeep and got in.

"Let's go," McManus said. "I have so much to tell you. And there's not much time."

The truck slowed, as if checking out the action between McManus and Jim. But then it roared past them, onto the airfield.

Jim got in the jeep.

He started the throaty engine up and popped the car into gear.

It bounced forward, sending McManus flying. The physicist threw his arms out to stop himself. Then Jim got the jeep moving in a somewhat less jerky fashion.

"You're not much better down here on terra firma than you are up there."

"You saw that?"

"Just the last few minutes, the precipitous dive to the ocean, the near-stall. You'll have to do better than that next time, Jim. Much better."

"Next time. What do you mean 'next time,' Dr. McManus?"

"I'll explain everything but—Jim—"

He felt McManus looking at him.

"Jim, let's start with a clean slate. Let's start with you using my real name."

Jim had his hand on the nob of the gear shift. He yanked it out of second and pushed it—reluctant and screaming—into third. Jim thought that maybe he had misheard him.

"Your real name?"

Why do I feel that things are about to get weirder, Jim thought? How can all this get even more strange?

"Jim, my real name, my real personality, if you will, is someone named Dr. Ichiro Shirato."

First he's Japanese . . . then he's McManus . . . and now he's Japanese again.

McManus . . . Shirato . . . took a breath. "And, Jim, I come from a distant future that you might only dream about . . ."

* * *

Yoshira felt the teeth scraping at her neck. She heard them snap closed with a nasty click. Then again, closer.

But she kicked at the floor, and screamed, and her attacker just couldn't get at her.

Two others grabbed her. Then she felt heat, moistness on one leg, her calf.

''No,'' she yelled. Then, again, screaming.

She felt the teeth bite down, tear into her. She kicked her leg. Flailing. But the teeth held on.

Someone yanked her hair, snapped her around like a doll, dragging her close to the three . . . or four of them that held her.

And—for an instant—Yoshira saw some of the Pack, the human animals prowling among the sleepers, the time travellers. Fingering their bodies curiously, wondering—perhaps—if they were alive or dead.

One stopped near the body of McManus.

''No!'' she screamed. ''No!''

She felt another bite on her leg. The pain made her eyes shut. It was agony, the sensation rippling through her body, a terrible wave.

And then again.

The sensation—

Of being eaten.

She heard Dr. Jacob cry out. She pictured him, a plump little meal. A feast for the Pack.

They were back at her neck. She shook her head wildly, but she was held, her hair wrapped around one of their fists.

It will get worse, she thought. Much worse.

Then—there was another sound.

A popping noise. A scream. More of a yelp. Then another sound. The smell of something cooking. An explosion.

Then—as her senses returned—she heard that the pop was something being fired.

A gun.

Her leg didn't get bit again.

Another blast, and she felt her head released.

Again, and again, a succession of explosions that filled the room with the terrible reverberations of gunfire. The smoke filled Yoshira's nostrils.

She looked up.

Toland was there. He had his rifle at hip level, and he swung it cooly left and right, blasting away, so close that Yoshira thought that he'd surely hit her, or Jacob, or one of the others.

But the only other sound was the Pack creatures, the starving humans dedicated to eating their own kind, flying off the floor, screaming as Toland's powerful shells ripped into them.

Then . . .

It was quiet.

Toland walked over. Stood before her.

Yoshira tried to move into a sitting position. She tried to pull her legs underneath her. But one just didn't move. She struggled to brace herself with her arms.

"Oh, you came back . . ." she cried.

He stood there, looking down at her.

She didn't think there was anything odd about that. Not yet.

"I didn't know what had happened to you. I thought that they had gotten you. That they had killed you. I didn't know what we would do."

The tachyon generator hummed behind her.

She looked down at her leg. She saw the blood, the great chunk of exposed flesh and muscle.

She was a doctor. She knew what it meant.

"I need—" she looked around. "I need my kit. Bandages. Peroxide." She looked at it again, wishing it belonged to someone else. Wishing it wasn't currently her leg.

The smoky smell of the shells lingered. But they were joined now by another smell. The smell of the

Pack, the gamey smell from their ratlike scavenging, the smell of their own bodies, blown-open, exposed.

Dr. Jacob spoke, "I'll get some bandages," he said, quietly. "And—"

Toland cleared his voice.

She looked up at him.

And then she saw it.

He shook his head. "No. Don't bother," he said. He smiled. "Don't worry. Dr. Shirato doesn't need any bandages."

"Dr. . . . Dr. Shirato?" Jacob repeated.

But Yoshira Shirato kept looking at Toland, seeing the smile on his face.

Toland had been out of the room, she thought. Away from the shielding.

A chance they had been waiting for.

"You're not Toland," she said.

He nodded.

"Yes. And now you will tell me where everyone is—and what they're supposed to be doing."

"Her leg," Jacob said, whimpering. "Can't you see—"

Toland held up a hand, a finger. A stern teacher calling for attention. "Yes, where everyone is . . . and what they are doing."

She shook her head.

Turned away. Looking at her wound.

At the puddle of blood, building into a stream.

The room was filled with death, and—right now—she tasted it inside her mouth.

Sure, Jim thought, listening to McManus . . . listening to Ichiro Shirato.

He's from the future. It's all from the future. Should have seen that one coming. Don't know why I missed it. The technology was way beyond anything appropriate to the end of the twentieth century.

"I couldn't tell you, Jim," Shirato said. "It would

have made everything we did before—in Africa, in Vietnam—well, nearly impossible. You needed to *think* that you were dealing with local events.''

Jim nodded.

He didn't say what he was thinking now.

Which was:

How can I trust you? How can I simply take what you say now and know that it's true? Maybe you're the one changing history?

''This time, though, it's been an all-out effort by the Genetics to shape—''

''The Genetics?''

Shirato sighed. ''Yes. The group that used bio-engineering to increase their own power base. Mind you, not only on the Homeworld. Most of the off-world colonies have given themselves up to the allure of that kind of power.''

There was something in Shirato's words. Something that he wasn't saying.

Then Jim saw it.

''You're in revolt,'' Jim said. ''You're a rebel— you're the one fighting the power structure.''

Shirato looked away. The road looping around, and then down, opposite Pearl City. Jim saw the Naval Yard ahead, the ships, another airstrip with the lines of planes, close together, sitting ducks.

''You could say that, Jim. Yes. There were cells fighting the Genetics—almost from the start. But only recently did we learn that they had broken the Time Code, that they had begun dabbling in this century with the time stream. They knew how hard it was to track them in this century. The background radiation is just too—''

''But they changed time?'' Jim asked. God, he thought, what can I believe?

''Oh, most definitely. Absolutely. They changed time, just a bit here and there. Their first major venture, as you know, was in North Africa. But by then they were too powerful for me and my accomplices to go against directly. That's when my wife and I hit upon the idea of a safe point . . ."

"Your wife?"

"Yoshira. Oh—you know her as Dr. Beck. I didn't want her to come. But she was the most qualified. We needed to have our twentieth-century volunteers carefully monitored, and Yoshira is the best . . ."

And Jim realized something . . .

"This is only the beginning," he said.

He looked over at Ichiro. And Ichiro, his tanned face grim, bronze in the setting sun, looked back. "Yes. Only the beginning, Jim. Perhaps—" he turned away, to the harbor—"it might be the last battle in this century. There's a limit to how much they can play with the time stream. That limit may have been already reached. But there are other centuries . . . they won't give up."

"But they're in power . . . they've won, according to you."

Shirato shook his head. "No. There are still laws. Watchdog committees that attempt to control the mutations, the use of Time Transference—the Time Code. The power of the geneticists is still governed by laws. They want—need—the freedom of a completely fascist state. Total government, total power. Playing with the past will give that to them."

Right, thought Jim, just as playing with time could give Ichiro Shirato and his group more power.

And how the hell can I know what's real time?

Another thought . . .

Was Pearl Harbor supposed to happen?

Did it really happen?

Or did Shirato make it happen? Am *I* helping to make it happen?

He's Japanese . . . centuries removed from Imperial Japan. But still—

Jim shook his head, I'm thinking like the paranoid

assholes in Washington who incarcerated the Nisei—
the Americans of Japanese descent.

Still—how the hell can I tell what's supposed to
happen?

The only thing I can do is trust this man.

Who—only now—has told me where he really
came from, who he really is.

Jim decided that he best hear him out.

The clock was running . . .

"Okay . . . what am I supposed to do?"

Ichiro smiled. "Good. I felt your doubts. I was
worried—"

"No. Go ahead."

"Okay. You're going to see your father—Tad Gorman's father, head of Naval Security at Pearl?"

"Yeah . . ."

"Here's what has to happen, Jim." Ichiro Shirato
dug a piece of paper out of his pocket. He looked
up and smiled.

"I'll tell you about the plane later."

Jim shook his head. He wasn't kidding.

I *am* going to have to fly again.

Lindstrom felt sober. And whatever randiness he had
been luxuriating in, had—mysteriously—vanished.

Instead, he smelled something acrid that burned
his nostrils.

He heard—a whimpering, a crying.

He opened one eye. Tentative.

He saw the Time Lab. But he also saw the hazy
cloud of gunsmoke that hung in the room. There's
been trouble, he thought, that's why there was the
delay. Something went wrong back here.

He didn't turn his head.

He heard voices, made out who was talking.

"I'll start with your husband, Ichiro Shirato.
Where is he?"

Her husband? Then she's not Dr. Beck and—

Another voice—high-pitched, excited, scared—interrupted his thoughts. It was Dr. Jacob.

"I don't understand this. Who is this Shirato? What about Elliot . . . what about Dr. McManus?"

Good question, thought Lindstrom.

Then Toland spoke.

"Shut up. Shut up, Dr. Jacob, or you can join the happy dead people on the floor."

A pause.

Lindstrom felt cold, he felt gooseflesh sprouting up and down his arms.

He tried to breathe shallowly. He thought about closing his eyes. Lying there until it was all over.

Toland's snapped.

Toland's gone crazy.

No, Lindstrom knew that wasn't right. Somehow the other side, the Iron Men, got into Toland. And—and—he wanted to know what was being done so he could stop it.

"Your blood is making a rather large puddle, Dr. Shirato. I suspect you will not be conscious for very much longer. There is a chance that we could let them live . . . your husband, the others . . ."

"No," she moaned. "You wouldn't let anyone live. When you know what you need to, then we're all dead."

The man laughed.

He took a step. Lindstrom heard it. A step.

Then nothing.

I've got to get out of this chair, Lindstrom thought. Somehow, I have got to get out . . . and—

A soft thud, and then a scream. A pitiful sound. Dr. Beck—this Yoshira—moaned, and cried.

Toland—*whoever* was inside Toland—had kicked her.

Lindstrom turned his head just a bit.

And he saw Dr. Jacob looking at him. Good work, old boy. You got me back. Just in the nick of time.

But he looked down at his arms, his wrists strapped to the chair. If only Jacob could get over to him to undo the straps.

Jacob saw his frantic looks. He nodded. He started moving slowly, sliding towards him.

Toland swung around.

"Just where the hell do you think that you're going?"

"I—I need to check on them."

Lindstrom closed his eyes.

In case Toland looked over.

"They're fine, Dr. Jacob. Besides—isn't that this woman's job?"

"Yes, but—"

"Then stay right where you are." Then, talking to the woman, to Yoshira . . . "I'll give you five minutes to tell me where everyone is . . . and what they're doing. After that, I will kill one of them. And then the clock starts again . . . and you'll have another five minutes."

Lindstrom opened his eyes again.

The damn wriststraps were so tight. He tried pulling against one. But his hand wouldn't slip through.

He turned his head just a bit.

"Four minutes . . ."

Toland's voice was flat.

Just doing his job.

Lindstrom looked at the other wrist strap. And either his left hand was a bit less meaty or the strap wasn't quiet as tight, but it appeared that he might just have a bit more room.

He started squirming against the strap.

It made a leathery squeak.

And he froze, his eyelids quickly falling down.

He forced his breathing to be shallow, regular.

"Three minutes."

Lindstrom went back to work.

He pulled his hand tight against the strap. It felt like a cork stuck in a bottle. Harder, he pulled more, and his fingers were mashed together, a wriggling bouquet. Forgetting himself for a second, he grunted.

"Eh?" Toland said.

Lindstrom made himself freeze.

He felt his chest rising and falling much too quickly.

Please, he thought. Don't let him notice.

Then . . .

"Two minutes."

Lindstrom opened his eyes again. His hand was halfway through. Or—looking at it differently—halfway stuck.

He pulled back against the strap.

His fingers went white, the pressure forcing the blood out of them.

Each millimeter was gained through a complicated to-and-fro action of wriggling, and writhing. Lindstrom thought:

If I can just get my pinky through I'll have so much room . . . I'll be able to get my hand out.

The gun rattled. A chamber being prepared with another powerful shell.

Perhaps he'll pick me, Lindstrom wondered. Just as I get my hand free.

Forgetting the noise, he pulled back harder than before, jerking his hand back with his whole arm.

And the hand slid free.

Got to undo the other strap. Do that and get up, and—

And Toland's countdown interrupted him one last time.

"One minute . . . Dr. Shirato . . ."

24

Jim trotted up the gangplank. He felt the breeze off the ocean trying to blow him right over the side, into the clear water of Pearl Harbor.

As he reached the top, an ensign saluted him and said, "Welcome aboard, sir."

And Jim stepped onto the *Arizona.*

How many hours left, Jim thought? How much time do the men on board have before they die one of the most violent, grizzily deaths of the war?

Jim stopped for a second, smelling the air laced with a heady mixture of salt and oil and paint. He looked back to the mainland, to the link fence that surrounded the U.S. Naval Station.

McManus is over there now, he thought, watching me get on board. And by the time I'm done here, he'll be gone. Takeo Yoshikawa will be back to being a Japanese spy, just the way he's supposed to be . . .

He turned to the ensign. "I'm looking for Captain Gorman, I have a—"

Jim felt a hand touch his shoulder.

"Hello, Tad."

Jim turned around. He saw a tall man, his face bronze, lined with deep cracks that could be the result of too many laughs, or too many scowls.

Now he was smiling.

"Thought I'd come and get you . . . before you went looking for me."

Jim nodded. How to make this work, he thought. How to act as if he is really my father . . .

What's our relationship? Do we get along or is there a chill between us? Did Tad Gorman join the Navy to share his father's life or to compete with him?

"Hi, Dad," Jim said.

His father nodded, a half-smile flickering across his face.

"Right. Well, let me take you below." His father turned, and started aft, heading to an opening just rear of a battery of guns pointing at the sky, looking ready, deadly.

His father went into a dark hatch, leading Jim down into the ship.

"I spoke to your sister," he said.

"Yeah?" Jim said. And he tried to conjure up an image of Tad Gorman's sister, something from inside, something to help him. And it occurred to Jim that this time there wasn't any help. No little bits of memory, no mental flotsam and jetsam floating by at crucial times.

This time, things are different.

He wondered:

How different?

His father led him down one level, then another, past sailors laughing, talking, some getting ready for a night of shore leave.

"She's doing well. Might come out and see us at Christmas." His father turned and looked over his shoulder at him. "Depending on how things turn out."

At the next deck, his father walked to his left, down one passageway, then another, until he stopped at a door. He opened it and led Jim inside.

Jim followed. It was a small cabin, with a simple

platform for a desk, a bed, a mirror, and not much else. There was a chair. His father gestured to it and Jim sat down while his father went to shut the door.

"A bit tight, eh? It will have to do until they find me an office on shore." He paused. "Tad, you're probably wondering why I asked to see you?"

Jim cleared his throat. "Yes, sir. I was—"

"I know you still blame me, Tad."

Come on, Jim begged the consciousness buried inside him. Help me, damn it. "Your mother didn't have an easy life. A Navy wife never does. And I didn't make it any easier." The half-smile again. "But you have to understand . . . I didn't know how bad it had gotten. Her drinking was . . . something she kept secret. I—"

His father looked away.

A bit of an image began to come into focus.

A woman. Pretty, but with sad, lonely eyes. Jim saw her.

Jim closed his eyes.

"I should have been there for her," his father said. Jim heard the man's voice shaking. But Jim was fighting his own battle now. The image melted away but the feelings washed over him, a pang, a sadness.

"She's getting help now. That's the important thing."

"Is—it's—" Jim tried to say something.

He opened his eyes.

His father was looking at him. "I don't want us to go on the same way anymore, Tad. I lost your mom. She's better off without me. But I don't want to lose you, too."

Jim nodded, not knowing what Tad Gorman would really do.

The captain, his father, took a step closer. He rested a hand on Jim's shoulder. "I need you, son."

Jim looked up. All these feelings now. And I have

other things to do. I have to tell this man . . . that's why I'm here—

His father squeezed. "That's why I sent for you. When I saw you up there today, in your plane, dropping out of the sky . . . what happened, son?"

Jim shook his head. "One of the—" he thought a second, not wanting to display too much ignorance—"the flaps jammed. Then we started stalling."

His father's head moved up and down gravely. "I want you to be careful."

Got to do it now, Jim thought. I have to bring it up now. And God . . . it has to be hopeless, absolutely hopeless . . .

"Dad, there's something I have to tell you. On patrol today, I had a thought. And you're with Naval Security here, I thought you should know."

Captain Gorman sat down on the bunk. The springs groaned, crying out. Gorman folded his hands in front of him and looked right at Jim.

"Go on."

Jim looked around the room. This was going to be tougher than holding the stick of that plane. He looked back at Gorman's father.

"Dad, when I was up there, flying over the south end of the island, over the harbor, I saw just how damn vulnerable we are."

His father laughed and shook his head. "Fortress Pearl? You'd have a hard time getting Kimmel to believe that."

Jim leaned forward. "The battleships, all in a row. Like sitting ducks. Planes clustered together to protect them against sabotage. But the carriers. If we were to lose the carriers, it would be all over."

The commander stood up. "That's for sure, Tad." He looked back. "And don't think that I haven't tried to tell Kimmel that. Our carriers should be on patrol. Especially with the alert."

Oh, great, thought Jim. Maybe he'll do something about it. Maybe there's still time . . .

But his father quickly cut off the thought.

"But even Kimmel's hands are tied. Washington wants the ships to stay in harbor during the emergency. Orders straight from the War Department."

And then—just like that—it was over.

"Tad, I have to go topside and see the captain. We're using the *Arizona* as a clearing house for information. I tell you—all these ships, and there's still no plan, no tactics—"

Jim stood up and grabbed his father's arm, hard. Hopeless, he thought. Absolutely—

"Dad, the carriers have to be at sea. You don't understand." And Jim thought of McManus, Ali, the others, depending on him. It isn't fair. How the hell am I supposed to do this?

"Dad. If they're still here, if the Japanese attack, they'll be blown right out of the harbor. We'll lose Pearl, the war—"

His father smiled oddly. "War? What war, Tad? We're not at war. Not yet. And I don't think we'll see a first strike here. Come on, son, walk me up to the bridge and—"

A knock on the door.

Jim's breath caught in his throat.

His father opened the cabin door.

A young, almost-baby-faced lieutenant stood at attention.

"A message, sir, from CinC-PAC."

He watched his father take it.

The lieutenant saluted and left. And Jim waited, feeling dizzy, trapped, while Captain Gorman opened up the envelope . . . and read the message.

Admiral Husband Kimmel put down the phone.

Dinner, to be followed by dancing, had just been cancelled. *Had to be cancelled.*

He sat in his office, looking at his desk, pristine, clear of any work, and problems—save the message crumpled up on his desk.

It was only the first message. There would be others . . .

The sun was low in the sky. Just a pale orange light sneaking into the room.

He sat there, looking at the message, knowing that General Short had the same message, that all his commanders were reading his own message sent in response.

It could only mean one thing.

He mouthed the word, the terrible word.

His lips moved.

He smelled the teak wood, the oil used to polish his desk, the floor, to a high sheen.

He mouthed the word.

War.

He picked up the phone.

"What is it?" Jim said. "What does the message say?"

His father scratched at his face.

"It's—it's not marked 'secret,' " the captain said. "So—"

What could it be, Jim thought? What has knocked the wind out of this old seaman's sails? His father looked up.

He handed the message to Jim.

And Jim read it.

As he realized that he wasn't alone in this venture.

Admiral Harold Stark was assassinated in his office at 13:20 this afternoon. In the wake of this tragedy, the local Pacific commanders have been given direct responsibility for the security of their areas. This follows the general alert issued yesterday. All officers are hereby ordered to remain

*at their posts pending further instructions to fol-
low.*

Jim looked at the name typed at the bottom.

*Admiral H. E. Kimmel, Commander of the
Fleet, Pearl Harbor.*

Jim looked up. His father was studying him.

"Damn," his father said. "What's going on?"

Jim reached out and grabbed him.

"Dad. The carriers. There were orders for them
to go to Midway, to patrol the south—"

His father's eyes narrowed. "How do you know
that? That was classified. How the hell—"

Jim gulped. "The orders were rescinded. At the
last minute. Kimmel wanted the carriers out." Jim
waved the message. "Now . . . now he can. But he
might need a push, someone to tell him."

His father turned away, looking glassy-eyed, confused.

Then back to Jim. "How do you know this?
How do you know about the orders to send the
Lexington to Midway, to have the other carriers on
patrol?" The eyelids narrowed even further. "How
the hell—"

"Time," Jim whispered. "There isn't a lot of time
. . . dad. You can call him, talk to him. The ships
are already on alert." He squeezed his father's arm
tighter. "They could be gone—" Jim took a breath.
"By dawn."

His father stood there, frozen, as if he was looking
at a ghost.

No one said anything. Jim heard the sounds of
sailors going up and down the metal stairs. Voices.
The giddy talking of young men, nearly boys, excited at a night off.

Jim felt the man looking at him.

Ready to ask.

Who are you? Really . . .

Who the hell are you?

But then his father nodded. "You may . . . have something. If there's an alert, if there's a real danger . . ." Jim took a breath. "Alright, Jim. I'll call Kimmel—if he isn't dining out, or partying. If he's at his goddamned post. I'll call him—"

His father got up and opened the cabin door.

"And I'll try, by God, to get him to give the carriers the order to sail."

And Jim let a breath out.

Thinking . . .

We have a chance. If he convinces Kimmel, we have a *chance*.

Now all I have to do is think about the last thing I have to do.

And suddenly he knew he'd better find the head as fast as he could . . .

Lindstrom felt his hand give way. It popped free of the strap and, still marveling at his success, he hurried to free his other hand.

He'll see me, he told himself. Whoever it is inside Toland, he'll see me, or hear me and—

He fumbled with the strap holding his other hand tight.

But then it was free.

Seconds left. *Only seconds.*

Toland started turning towards the sleeping bodies.

And Lindstrom jumped up from the chair.

Suicidal, he thought. Absolutely suicidal. Crazy, desperate.

He was on his feet, moving towards Toland, towards the gun.

"Time's up," he heard the man say.

And Lindstrom saw that he was too late.

Toland—this madman from the future—saw him. He smiled.

So much for any threat I might pose, Lindstrom thought.

"No," the man said. And he swung the rifle butt up and clipped Lindstrom in the chin. He felt his lower jaw smash up, noisily. He felt his teeth crunch together. He tasted something gritty.

Lindstrom flew off his feet, backwards. He landed on his backside, the pain rattling up his spine. He tasted something gritty in his mouth, a chunk of tooth. The salty aftertaste of blood.

Toland had his gun lowered, facing him.

"You know, you were going to be the person I selected to die," the man said. "But now—perhaps you'll be the one to talk."

"Don't say anything, Professor Lindstrom!" Dr. Beck said.

Except Lindstrom—feeling as if he had walked into this movie well after the first reel—knew that it wasn't really Dr. Marianne Beck anymore.

And she probably came from the same god-awful year as this impersonator of Toland.

"No, I can't kill you," the man said. "Not when you might be able to help me."

The man moved his gun up, and to the right. Passing over Ali—

No, thought Lindstrom, tasting his blood, the porcelain grit of his broken tooth. "No . . ."

Past Ali, to Jim. Lindstrom saw Jim's chest rising and falling, evenly, peacefully. Lost in his time sleep.

To McManus. Dr. Elliot McManus.

I love the old bastard, Lindstrom thought. Whoever the hell he really is. So calm and steady. Keeping us sane while we play with madness.

Toland's gun stopped.

"Please," Yoshira Shirato said. "I—"

Lindstrom heard a clicking sound.

God. No, he thought. It can't happen. It can't—

He heard the trigger click. The blast filled the small lab with a terrible roar, a bluish cloud, dreamlike, followed by a too-real stench.

Lindstrom closed his eyes at the noise.

And when Lindstrom opened them, looking right at McManus's body, the scientist's body marked now with a great, bubbling hole at its center, he cried . . .

25

Lt. Commander Mitsuo Fuchida read the secret message.

The carriers were gone!

The report, the terrible report had been passed to him by Admiral Nagumo himself. The old admiral tried to smile, as if to say: this doesn't matter . . . this is no great matter.

But the carriers were the *prize*. Their destruction would eliminate the Americans from the Pacific. The war would be won.

In his dreams, Fuchida imagined the great carriers, with their decks littered with burning planes, caught completely unawares. He imagined the great ships listing to the side, sinking in the harbor, burning monuments to the great American disaster . . . the triumph of the Japanese.

Now—now, it was all different. There would be plenty of prizes.

But nothing as great as the carriers.

Fuchida guessed that many of his pilots were also probably awake, still wandering the flight deck, others writing letters to their loved-ones in Nippon.

We will all feel better when we are in the sky.

Flying to Pearl Harbor, to the great American fleet. It will still be *omoigakenai koto* . . .

Something unexpected.

With our planes, my spirit will soar.

Jim parked the jeep in a place where he hoped no one would notice it. He wasn't going to return it to the motor pool. Not until this was over.

And—if all goes well—I won't even be here.

Gorman will be a hero . . . or dead.

He saw the rows of planes, clustered together. And he saw the plane that he had flown with Murphy, near the edge. There were lights on in one hangar. An empty hangar.

Jim hurried across the strip.

As he got closer to the hangar, he heard voices, laughing, talking, the clattering of tools.

Jim walked in. A PBY was off to the side and some mechanics were working on the plane. Her engine compartment was open.

One of the mechanics looked up—a big smile still on his face. "Oh, evening, sir."

Jim smiled back. "Tough night to be working," Jim said.

Another mechanic gestured at the exposed engine. "Clogged fuel line, sir. Might take us a while to get it. With the alert and all, they want us to get her flight-ready."

"Sure." Jim looked around the empty hangar. Empty, because all the planes were sitting outside.

He looked back to the mechanics, dressed in navy blue coveralls streaked with black. "Lieutenant Murphy and I had a problem up there today."

"Yes, sir?"

Jim took a step to the plane. Jim smiled. "I think it was just something with controls. They were . . . sluggish. Still, I'd like to look at them." He broadened his grin. "Personally. Since I'm flying her Monday."

The two mechanics smiled, and nodded.

Sensing more work. Just when they were about to put their tools down.

"No need for you guys to do anything. But, I'd like to take a look myself. Could you, er, give me a hand taxiing her in here? I'd really appreciate it."

The men looked at each other, took a breath, and then one said, "Our orders are for all planes to be kept out on the strip, sir, under guard."

"Well, guys, I can't fly her the way she is. If you want to work on her tomorrow morning—that's fine. But give me some time with her and I'll get it ship-shape."

The two men—nearly ready to leave—looked at each other. "Okay, sir," one said. "We'll give you a hand. Just a sec . . ."

"Great," Jim said. "And no extra work for you—I promise. Not tonight. Just help me steer her in here."

And Jim took a breath, as the two men ran to the hangar doors and began to slide them open.

Captain Gorman stood in front of Kimmel's desk.

I don't like this, Kimmel thought. I don't like it when things aren't under control. And this—this whole situation isn't under my control.

And I don't like Gorman.

He's been a perfect pain-in-the-rear since he showed up.

As if Pearl Harbor wasn't a nearly invincible fortress. As if there was a need for some further preparations to keep the island safe.

Kimmel looked down at his desk. There were lots of messages on it, and more seemed to arrive by the hour. Washington was very concerned. Something was coming . . . but when and where?

"Go on, Gorman," Kimmel said.

Gorman rubbed his cheek. "Admiral, I think that you should order the carriers out to sea."

Kimmel raised a hand. "No. Washington wanted them in the harbor after the alert. I—"

Gorman interrupted. "That was Admiral Stark's decision. He overrode your orders, Admiral."

Kimmel looked away. Orders. Gorman had no sense of orders. A maverick, even if he was over fifty. The admiral rubbed his eyes.

"Well, I was ordered—"

"You can read the new orders yourself, Admiral. You've been given responsibility for the security of the Pearl Harbor. Whatever happens, it will be on your head."

"I don't know, Gorman—I—"

Gorman took a step closer, right up to Kimmel's desk. I feel small next to this man, Kimmel thought. A big burly seaman who somehow made it to the rank of commander . . .

Gorman raised a hand. "The carriers are sitting ducks here, Admiral. They can't protect themselves, or Pearl. If we were to be attacked—"

"That's absurd, ridiculous . . ."

"*If* we were to be attacked, the carriers would be the first targets. In five minutes, they'd be sinking in the harbor."

"It's too shallow. How would the Japanese get them? It's too damn shallow for torpedo bombs."

Gorman shook his head. "Did you see what the English did in Italy? They were able to fly low and cut the depth requirements in half . . . *in half Admiral.*"

He's not going away, thought Kimmel. God . . . why won't he go away? I've made my decision, and—

"Admiral—go back to your original orders. Send the *Yorktown* to Midway. Put the other two carriers on patrol—close enough to intercept any attack, but at sea—"

Gorman slapped Kimmel's glistening desk top. "It's a full alert, Admiral. Stark is dead. The Japanese are about to move. Damn it, don't just sit here."

Kimmel took a breath. He felt like stepping backwards. But if he did, he'd tumble into his chair, a comic character.

He looked up at the clock. All ships officers were on standby. That wouldn't be a problem. Though no one expected anything, they were there, waiting—for the Japanese to go to Singapore, or assault the Philippines. It all seemed so far away.

Gorman glowered down at him.

Kimmel heard his clock tick, a noisy sound in the stillness of the room.

He looked up. Gorman was looking down at him.

He is advocating going back to my original orders, Kimmel thought. That's all.

I would just be following the original plan, honoring the request from the commander at Midway. Setting up a patrol south of Oahu.

He looked up at Gorman.

"Very well. I'll give the order. They can set sail tomorrow morning."

Gorman didn't move.

He shook his head.

"Admiral . . ." he seemed to be acting very patient, as if he couldn't take much more of this. "Admiral . . . get them out now."

Kimmel nodded.

Saturday night.

Well, he thought. Why not? How long would it take them to set sail. Six hours? Eight hours?

Sometime around dawn.

Perhaps that was *best*.

He looked up at Gorman and shook his head. "Very well, Commander. I will give the order for the carriers to set sail—as soon as possible."

262 *Matthew J. Costello*

"Thank you," Gorman said. And he turned and saluted.

And Kimmel was glad to watch him leave.

Toland's gun stopped at Jim.

"Please," Lindstrom said. "Don't point your gun at the boy, he's—"

Toland clicked something on his rifle, readying a shell.

Lindstrom looked at Dr. Jacob, frozen by his machine, a machine that doesn't belong to this time, and then to Yoshira—a stranger now, someone he wouldn't recognize if he saw her real face.

"Five," Toland said.

Counting the minutes.

Jim's body slept peacefully, unaware that it was about to be blasted by Toland's gun. Lindstrom felt weak, as if he was going to collapse on the floor. Steady, old boy, he told himself. Keep a grip on it. Can't give up now.

Even though everything looked pretty damn hopeless, pretty—

"Four."

Yoshira was crying, lying on the floor, the tears rolling off her face.

Staring at the body of McManus, oozing away its life in front of her.

Her leg, her calf was chewed. She had a hand pressed against it, trying to stop her own loss of blood.

Toland looked back at them. And he smiled. "Three," he said. "There's still time. You know . . . you'll all go, one by one. Until I know what I have to know. To undo the damage, your meddling."

Lindstrom saw Dr. Jacob move. Just a few inches. But enough for Lindstrom to see. He slid a bit to the right, towards the controls.

Lindstrom looked over, his eyes squinting, wondering, what? What the hell are you doing?

Jacob slid a bit more.

"D—don't tell him," Yoshira wailed. "Tell him nothing. Their—their world is evil, a world of twisted, soulless mutations. There will be no more real humans, if they have their way. Everyone will be designed, shaped, created for pleasure, or pain, to work for the few, the ruling class."

Lindstrom nodded. Kind of like Reagonomics.

Yoshira looked up at him and smiled. "Please, say nothing."

Lindstrom looked at Toland. He shook his head and said, "Two."

Lindstrom licked his lips.

Because time was running out.

Ichiro Shirato had his fingers locked on the mesh fence. He watched Jim disappear into the *Arizona*. And—when Jim came out—Shirato made sure that he wasn't seen.

That wouldn't be good at all. They're going to pull me back, any second. And if Jim came up and spoke to this Takeo Yoshikawa, this Japanese spy, well, it could get quite awkward.

So, he moved around to the back of the Naval Base, back behind the oil tank farm, the billions of barrels of precious oil that must survive the sneak attack.

If we don't screw up, he thought.

And he wondered whether Jim was up to all this. Ichiro shook his head. It was just luck that he ended up helping, and now—we treat him as if he was a seasoned warrior.

And the sad thing is that he doesn't know the half of it.

Can't tell Jim everything.

He might see for himself.

He might have to travel the other way, to the future.

If he lived, if he survived this.

He might get to see what we're really battling.

Ichiro let go of the fence. The sky was bluish-black . . . peaceful, the calm before the storm.

He stopped away from the fence.

He looked at the watch on Yoshikawa's wrist.

And Ichiro thought:

I'm late . . .

I shouldn't be here. I should have been pulled.

Something's wrong.

Something's wrong in the lab.

"Hey!"

Someone yelled at him from the darkness of the oil farm.

Then he saw a dark shape, a MP guard walking up to the fence. Ichiro backed up.

"Hey! What are you doing there, pal?"

Ichiro kept backing up.

"Nothing. I just—"

"Get a move on buddy. This is a restricted area. Military personnel only, pal. Get moving . . ."

Ichiro kept backing up. "Yes, I'm going. I—"

Stepping backward.

Thinking:

Why am I still here?

What's happening back at the lab?

What's wrong?

"One," Toland said. "I'm afraid that your time is nearly up."

Lindstrom watched the man wave his gun around, a little dance worthy of a wild-west saloon.

"And after this one's gone, then we'll move onto this young lady—"

Lindstrom looked on in horror as Toland reached out and caressed Alessandra's sleeping body, starting at her leg, then sliding across the bare midsection, and up, across her breasts—

Lindstrom was outraged. I've got to stop him, he thought. He's a monster . . .

Toland's hand touched her cheek, his fingers traced the outline of her lips, pressing against them.

"It would be—" Toland said—"such a waste, such a terrible—"

Ali heard the word.

"Bull . . . terri . . . bull"

And then, "Waste."

It was a voice she recognized. It was, yes, Toland's voice. But—somehow—it didn't sound like Toland. It sounded . . . dangerous.

She opened her eyes.

And he was standing there, his hand pressed against her cheek. She saw him, but his back was to her, and he was looking at the others.

Lindstrom saw her. His eyes popped open, wide with terror.

And Ali immediately grasped the situation.

Toland . . . isn't Toland.

She let her eyes drift to the left. And she saw McManus on the ground, a hole in his chest. She almost moaned, nearly whimpered at the blood, the opening. A human road-kill.

So clearly and totally dead.

She saw Toland move to her feet, pointing his gun at Jim.

"I'm so sorry you don't see it my way," he said. "It will only be harder for you in the end. And—" He looked over at Dr. Jacob. "I can only be sure that sooner or later one of you will tell me everything.. . ."

The gun was pointed high, aimed right at Jim's skull.

The gun stock—just inches away from her feet.

At least, she thought, I think that it's inches away.

There was quiet, a stillness. And she knew that the blast was about to come.

Ali brought her right leg up, fast, sharp, her toe pointed at the gun stock.

She felt the straps tighten around her ankles.

There's enough room, enough room, she told herself.

I'll kick the gun, send it flying.

But then she saw that there wasn't enough room.

Her foot fell short.

Toland heard the noise.

"Wha?" he said.

He turned pointing the gun at her.

And Ali yelled.

"Ay-aaah!" she screamed, using a shriek to startle Toland.

It made him freeze. Then she brought her leg up again, her toe pointed at the gun stock. Up, and this time her foot connected.

All my strength, she thought, all my strength . . .

Her foot hit the stock, and she pushed up like an NFL place-kicker.

And the gun flung free, out of Toland's grasp.

Whoever it was, she reminded herself. It's not Toland. Toland is somewhere else.

And—while the others watched, amazed, hopeful—Ali screamed:

"Get it! Get the damn gun!"

26 ═══════

Fuchida was up. Surely this night sleep was an impossibility.

So he dressed, pulling on the brilliant red shirt, then his flying gear. He talked to himself. He imagined leading his bombers over the mountains of Oahu, screaming with joy as they swooped down on a sleepy, unsuspecting Pearl Harbor. He imagined the morning sun glinting off the sea, the gray metal.

The men, young American men, like his pilots, looking up, smiling, not understanding. Maybe even waving at him.

Not understanding . . .

Fuchida reached down and picked up the bandana given him by his father. The words, the characters exclaimed the victory to come . . .

He pulled it tight around his head.

He picked up his flying hat, his lucky hat, threadbare and worn. Certainly in need of being replaced.

Not until it falls apart.

He picked up his gloves.

And he left his cabin.

Jim felt chilled, the night air had turned cold. The airstrip was quiet except for the few guards who walked around the perimeter of airplanes.

There was no light on inside the hangar.

Jim hurried over there.

Hoping the guards wouldn't see him.

Best not to have any interruptions now, he thought.

He looked at his watch.

It was still hours away . . .

But Jim knew where he had to stay.

(I can't do this, he thought. I can't do this. If it really depends on me, then it's lost, gone.)

He reached the door at the side of the hangar building.

A voice called out to him. "Hey!" Then again, "Hey. You? Where are you going. Stop!"

Then he heard the steps of the guard running over to him.

Jim's hand froze on the door handle.

He turned slowly. A bit of light from a distant lamp near the base entrance fell on his face.

Hopefully showing my uniform, Jim thought. My rank.

"Oh, evening sir," the guard said coming to a stop.

Jim smiled.

Jim waited, hoping the guard would just nod and move on.

Which he didn't.

"Sir, is there anything wrong? The airbase is supposed to be closed."

Jim smiled, and then gestured over his shoulder.

"My plane's in there. I had it wheeled in. Bad fuel line. Can't sleep and I thought I'd work on it a bit."

The young guard looked confused. He rubbed his chin. "Er, Lieutenant, the area's supposed to be shut down at night. Nobody—"

Jim made his smile broader, even as he felt himself sinking. "Hey," he said. "Take a look." Jim gestured at the window, dark and smeary. The guard walked up and leaned close to the window, peering in.

The dark half of Jim's plane—Tad Gorman's plane—was just barely visible.

"See. It's in there. And I'd really like it checked out by morning. Before I have to take it up."

The guard nodded, and then backed away.

"Okay, sir," he said, smiling. "I guess you better carry on."

Jim smiled. "And you better keep moving. It's chilly tonight."

The guard grinned, saluted and then walked away.

Jim looked at his watch.

Four A.M.

God, he thought . . . am I the only person on the island that knows?

Am I the only one that knows?

Ichiro Shirato sat down by the side of the road, hidden by the tall grass. He heard something skitter away when he pushed the grass aside. A little field mouse, perhaps. Maybe something larger, a rat or—

He worried.

Maybe a snake.

A snake . . .

Interesting, he thought. That this is the Japanese Year of the Snake, 1941. And like a snake, the Japanese fleet slithers closer and closer to a sleeping Pearl Harbor.

He heard a truck go rumbling past, at first its roar muffled by the wind whistling through the grass. But then it was there, full, raucous.

So primitive, Ichiro thought. It's hard to believe that the internal combustion was used for as long as it was.

Hard to believe.

And then this other thought.

Maybe I'm trapped here, with this engine. I should have been pulled, and I wasn't.

And this:

I'll get to see it all.

If I stand up, I can see the harbor, I can see Ford Island, the line of battleships, and beyond, the destroyers, and the submarines, so many ships sitting there, so tight together, waiting.

He licked his lips.

I don't want to see it.

What is wrong? Why haven't I been pulled back? I could have seen Jim, talked to him again.

But that was not in the plan. Everything—all the parameters—had been worked out for all contingencies up to the point where I leave Jim to see his father.

If I saw him again—if I spoke to him—

Well, there's no way to tell what the result might be.

How it might change things . . .

He heard a squeak.

Something crying in the grass.

Some animal made a small, terrified noise. Scared by the night, scared by something larger, scurrying through the grass. Scared . . .

Chilled, Ichiro pulled his arms tightly around himself.

He stood up. The carriers were still there. All lit up, people moving around. He imagined he heard noises coming from them.

They're still there.

Two hours until dawn.

And he thought:

I'm scared . . .

"Nice duty," Lockard said, "Real nice."

Elliot put his thermos of coffee down on the small table. He listened to Lockard throwing the switches of the radar station. The station, open to the air, had been thrown together so quickly. There were no walls and the wind just ripped through it.

"So damn bracing," Lockard said, throwing another switch.

"Want some coffee?" Private Elliot said.

"Sure. Why the hell not? Not likely I'll be able to sleep up here . . ."

That thought hadn't even occurred to Elliot. The station was supposed to operate from 4 A.M. until 7 A.M.

A three-hour test. The idea of napping up here, surrounded by rock, the wind, didn't appeal to him at all.

Elliot watched the circular screen, green, unfriendly, flicker to life.

"So what do you see?" Lockard said.

Elliot shook his head then—aware that his gesture couldn't be seen in the pale green glow—he said, "Nothing."

"There's a shitload of B-17s due back sometime this morning. From the west, northwest. We'll probably pick them up later."

Elliot rubbed his hands together.

"Right."

"Yeah . . . and I think I'll take that coffee now. Damn, it's sure cold up here."

Elliot looked forward to dawn . . .

Captain Bryant looked through his binoculars to just behind the target ship, *Antares*. He didn't want to jump to any conclusions . . .

It's happened too many times before, he knew. Reports of enemy ships, any planes—

Enemy subs.

But he was sure that he had something, just there. Following the target ship, moving towards the entrance of the harbor. Could be a damn fish he thought. A dolphin, a bloody shark, something—

Or it could be a sub. A small sub.

He had watched it move now for ten, fifteen minutes. Enough watching, he thought.

And he radioed the destroyer on patrol duty, the U.S.S. *Ward*. His message was straightforward, simple.

Maybe even a bit absurd.

"Suspected submarine of unknown origin on a bearing due north, towards the entrance to the harbor."

Bryant sent the message.

He took a breath. It was out of his hands now.

The gun, Toland's gun, flew into the air. For a few seconds it was party time, everyone looking at the gun, gaily spinning around, nobody moving.

Until Ali screamed.

"Get me out of this chair!"

Toland shot a look at her.

But then right back to his gun, clattering to the ground.

And Ali took a breath.

What if the damn thing went off? What if it went off and blew a hole in the generator and we leave everyone stranded, just where they are?

Forever.

She looked around.

Dr. Jacob was watching her.

Just as Toland turned around and started for his gun.

But then Dr. Beck leaped on Toland's back, wrapping her legs around his body, screaming, crying, and—

For the first time, Ali knew that the woman had a special connection to McManus.

Lindstrom moved toward the gun and Ali yelled at Jacob, "Undo the straps. Hurry!"

Jacob ran over and fiddled with the arm straps.

While Ali watched Toland stumble, carrying Dr. Beck to the gun.

But Lindstrom got there first. And she thought: what Lindstrom doesn't know about guns could probably fill a good-sized library.

But Lindstrom had the gun. He pointed it at Toland.

Good so far . . .

One of her straps popped free, and Ali fiddled with the other one herself.

"Dr. McManus," Jacob said. "He's still back there, and now I don't—"

"Stop," Ali heard Lindstrom say. "Don't take another step."

And she heard Dr. Beck, screaming, crying, beating her fists on Toland. "You bastard, I'll kill you, I'll—"

Until she slid off Toland.

Onto the floor, heaving horribly, her pain, her anger filling the room.

"Give me the gun," Toland said.

Ali saw Lindstrom shake his head.

Come on, she thought, looking at Jacob fingering one strap. Come on, come on, come—

"You don't know how to fire that weapon, Dr. Lindstrom. So, why don't you just stop this right now, okay? Just hand me the gun. And maybe no one else will get hurt."

Lindstrom took a step backwards.

Bad move, Ali thought. Not the thing to do.

Sending out the wrong signal.

Her hand popped free of the strap.

Ali leaped to her feet.

Lindstrom looked at her with relief. The gun

looked as if it might slide from his hands to the floor, useless, unwanted . . .

"Don't you fucking move," she said to the man who occupied Toland's body. "Not another step."

Her order was ignored.

The man took a step, he actually leaped towards Lindstrom.

But Ali moved fast. Even though her muscles felt asleep, and her body was as wobbly as if she had downed a magnum of champagne, she moved smoothly, two steps, and then she brought her elbow up.

Lindstrom backed up just out of reach of the man's fingers.

And Ali brought her elbow down, grunting, aiming it at just the right place, below the neck, where the spine reached the brain stem.

Too hard, and he'd be dead.

Which she didn't want.

But just enough, and he'd fall to his knees like a toddler sliding on a banana peel.

She yelled, and then—with an accuracy that surprised her—she jabbed down. She heard a little crack, as the bone of her elbow met the bone of Toland's lower skull.

Toland melted to the floor, sputtering to the ground.

Ali thought of an ad for a Medic-Alert system.

An old lad tumbles and then wheedles to the radio-alarm system,

"I've fallen down . . . *and I can't get up.*"

Ichiro Shirato sat there, expecting every minute that the cool breeze, the grass, the eerie night sounds would disappear. Like that. And he'd be back in the lab.

But each hopeful thought brought just another gust of wind, another lick of cool air waiting the warmth of the sun.

Until, nearly dozing off, almost ready to lie down in the scratchy, rough-edged grass, he heard a sound.

Loud engines, turbines, stirring to life. And voices, fading in and out as the wind whipped around, changing direction.

Voices. Engines.

He stood up.

The first thing he saw was there, to the east. The sky didn't look as dark, not as black. It was purple. Just a bit lighter.

Morning was coming.

And then, he looked down below, saving the moment, not yielding to the hope that it might happen, that it might all work.

He looked down.

And he saw that one of the carriers was moving.

So slowly, sleepily, trudging its way past the battleships, the sleeping destroyers.

As if it could take forever to leave. As if it had all the time in the world.

Ichiro stood there and watched.

He saw action on the other ship.

Tiny ant-men running around. The other carrier would soon follow.

But so slowly . . .

How far would they get, how far away will they be when the attack comes?

They'll move to the south. He was pretty sure about that. But would they be far enough away that the Japanese patrol planes won't spot them, that a third wave wouldn't be launched, an attack on the oil, on the dry-docks, and, out at sea, on the carriers?

He stood there.

The dark purple of the sky faded a bit, to a lighter shade. A great, color clock in the sky.

He watched the carriers steam away . . .

=======

27

Toland was flat on the ground and Ali jumped on his body, pinning him.

She watched his eyes roll around, and then shut.

Lindstrom took a step closer to her.

"Is he—?"

Ali pressed down on Toland's arms and looked up.

"I don't know. He didn't fall that hard, not hard enough to get knocked out."

Lindstrom held the gun awkwardly. "I think that maybe you should take this."

He started to pass the gun to Ali.

"No, wait a second," she said. "Wait until we can tie him up, or—"

She looked back at Toland. His eyes opened.

Ali yelped, startled by the guard's wide-eyed stare.

The gun was poised halfway between the floor and Lindstrom, stretching towards her.

Ali pressed harder against the ground.

"Hey," Toland said. "It's me. I'm back. I'm okay."

Ali took a breath. She smiled. She started to ease up on the pressure.

The man laughed. "I'm back. And boy, the things that I've seen . . ."

Ali began to release him.

But as she did, she saw his eyes dart to the left,

just a bit. Looking to the left, looking at the gun, eyeing it, figuring out his chances.

And she went back to pressing against him.

Too late . . .

He moved, squirming to the left, tossing Ali off to the side. She rolled off him, thinking: he's going to get the gun. He'll get the gun, and start blowing us away one-by-one.

And—

Why was I tricked so easily? I wanted Toland back so badly I was ready to believe.

She hit the ground, spinning on the cold stone floor, banging her elbows and knees.

She heard Lindstrom grunt.

And by the time she looked up, it was too late.

There was a thin orange line at the horizon. The carrier *Akagi* steamed towards it, into the wind.

Take off will be fast, Fuchida knew. The planes will be snatched off the deck, the wind will grab them, help them climb.

He heard the raucous roar of the engines, the lines of medium bombers, ready for takeoff. Underneath their bellies lay 1600 pound armor-piercing bombs. His men were scooting into their cockpits, waving at him, so proud, so excited.

Fuchida smiled and waved back.

He looked up to the bridge. He saw dark shapes there, looking down. Nagumo was there, watching. And he had binoculars so he could look out to sea and see the other five carriers, watch the 360 planes fill the sky, the zeros, the dive bombers, the torpedo bombers . . .

Filling the sky, and then heading south.

Fuchida looked at his watch. Nearly 6 A.M.

He climbed into his plane. The compartment of the bomber was tight, but it felt so comfortable to him, so reassuring. It's part of me, he thought. This plane is like part of my body.

He looked ahead.

The first planes waited for the go-ahead from the signalman.

The orange line at the horizon grew, bloomed, opening up like a flower.

Fuchida took a breath and muttered an ancient prayer to his ancestors, to other warriors who fought for their land, for their family.

He looked up. The signalman waved.

The first plane took off, then—quickly, hurrying now, the next, dipping as it left the flight deck, looking as if it was going to tumble into the sea.

But then beginning its climb, higher, higher, disappearing in the still-inky blackness above the carrier.

The next plane, the next, and then, Fuchida, the flight commander, was ready to take wing, ready to finish the first five-plane formation.

The signalman waved.

He pulled back on the throttle. The Mitsubishi engine roared sleepily, sounding smooth and powerful.

The engine reved higher, and when the revs were strong enough, Fuchida gave a signal. The wheel-stops were pulled, and he released his brake. The plane flew down the now so-short flight deck.

And then the edge of the carrier was there, the dark sea below it. The tiny crescent of the morning sun shot yellow spears into the sky.

The plane hurtled off the edge. The zero dipped, as if ready to plummet into the sea.

But Fuchida pulled back, slowly, steadily, and the zero began its climb.

To climb . . .

Climb Mt. Niitaka!

The code for the decision to commit to the attack. Fuchida followed the line of planes up, while hundreds of others waited, ready to strike against America.

The radio crackled. And someone on the *Akagi* said, perhaps joking, "Massugu oide nasai!"

Go straight ahead!

Fuchida laughed. He started banking his plane to the left.

And he said, "Hai."

Straight ahead, on to the sleeping American fleet.

Private Elliot looked at the green radar screen. The white line traced its slow arc over the top, and then the bottom and—

Elliot saw something.

To the north.

"Hey," he said. Lockard was sitting against a nearby post, a mug of hot coffee in his hand. "Hey, Lockard . . . I've got something here."

Lockard's chair, which had been tilted back, crashed down to the wood floor. "What?"

Elliot looked at him and then quickly back to the screen.

"We've go a blip. Damn, look. Here it comes.'

Lockard, smelling of coffee and too many Camels, stood next to him.

The white line crossed another sector of the screen.

And there it was.

A big blip.

The image registered, and then—just as quickly— faded.

"What the hell is that?"

Elliot looked up at Lockard. "Damned if I know. Maybe those B-17s. They might be coming in from the north."

They both watched the blip flash two more times, each time imperceptibly closer.

"Heading our way, that's for sure," Lockard said.

Elliot turned to him. "Shouldn't you call Tyler?"

Tyler was the duty officer at the Fort Shafter Information Center. Right, thought Elliot, he'd probably know what it was.

Lockard was already moving, digging out another cigarette. He picked up the receiver. "That's just what I'm doing, Georgie. Let them know we're up here, freezing our tails off, but doing our job."

Elliot waited, watching Lockard looking at the screen.

The blip seemed closer. And larger.

And Elliot thought, It's too large. There's something wrong with the machine. He looked at his watch.

We're due to shut down soon, he thought.

And they'll probably have to send someone up here to fix this thing.

Jim woke up, curled up under the plane. He smelled oil, and the thick powerful stench of machine grease and grit.

He saw light.

God, no, he thought. What time is it? What the hell time is it?

He looked at his watch. 6:55. 6:56 . . .

He sat up. His bones ached. He was chilled. The plane, this one plane pulled off the field sat over him. Jim looked at her wheels, her great wings, the narrow barrel of her gun.

I'm crazy, he thought.

Absolutely crazy . . .

Lieutenant William Outerbridge, skipper of the destroyer, *Condor,* made doubly sure that the message reached Admiral Kimmel. Right away, no delays.

He had sounded General Quarters as soon as he confirmed the report about the midget submarine.

Now, he saw the sub—dead ahead. And he had a number of possibilities. He could try to blow it out of the water. But a miss would only give the sub a chance to escape, to escape the mouth of the harbor.

The same thing went for a depth charge.

It was a small target. And there was no telling . . . it might ride out anything that wasn't a direct hit.

I'm going to ram her, Outerbridge decided.

He gave orders to the engine room for full speed. His first mate confirmed that they were on a perfect heading.

And then Lieutenant Outerbridge watched his ship bear down on the unsuspecting submarine.

"Five hundred meters, and closing," his ensign said.

Outerbridge nodded.

The submarine seemed slow, sluggish in the water. And—with the sun just breaking the horizon, too obvious with its small wake.

The damn thing looks lost, he thought.

"Three hundred meters," the ensign said. Outerbridge heard the excitement in the ensign's voice. The other people on the bridge held their breath, excited.

As well they should be. This is the first battle of—the war.

"One hundred meters." The ensign's voice nearly cracked.

The first battle in what?

Is this an attack? A spy mission? What the hell is this?

It's not my job to figure that out, Outerbridge thought.

Now he saw the shape of the sub, just below the water, quite clear, its wake catching the dull morning light.

Won't be pretty for the poor bastards inside.

"Here we go," he said to everyone in the room.

To himself.

Here we go . . .

Knowing that the big question is—

Just where the hell are we going?

Where will this road end?

The destroyer plowed into the sub. There was a dull thud. A banging, a rattling.

For a second, Outerbridge imagined the men inside, the water filling the burst shell of the small sub, then the crashing and battering of the sub as it bounced under the hull of the *Condor.*

"All engines stop," Outerbridge said.

For the small destroyer, the *Condor,* the war had begun.

Kimmel took a sip of his black coffee, and then looked at the message.

An enemy submarine, inside the harbor?

What in the world would an enemy sub be doing here?

His aide stood nearby.

"Any orders, sir?"

Kimmel shook his head.

"No. Just see that the alert is maintained." He smiled at the lieutenant. "I tell you, Tom, I don't know what the hell to make of this."

"Yes, sir," the lieutenant said, then turning sharply and leaving the office.

A spy submarine, probably.

Maybe up to some sabotage.

And Kimmel took a breath.

The carriers . . . they're gone. They're out by now, he thought.

He got up and went to the picture window that overlooked the harbor. Kimmel saw the spot where the carriers had been moored only last night.

And it was empty. There was a big hole where they used to be. As soon as Kimmel saw that, he

wondered: was that a good decision? Or should they
have stayed here? Give the island more air cover?

On the other hand—

He turned away from the window. Yes, on the
other hand, the carriers were probably more effective
at sea. Certainly, they'd be less prone to any sabotage, any midget submarines.

Midget submarines. Kimmel shook his head. Can't
trust those Japanese. No telling what they might do to
protect their Greater East-Asian Co-Prosperity Sphere.

I wouldn't put anything past them . . .

The sun cut into the windshield at Fuchida's left,
making it hard to see.

But when he brought his hand up, he saw the island straight ahead so beautiful, sleeping on a Sunday morning. So quiet, with no expectations.

Fuchida leaned forward and looked up, above his
formation of bombers. A line of Aichi dive dombers
were directly over him. Turning right, he saw the
Nakajima torpedo bombers. The pilot's skills were
honed to the point of an art, drilled, and redrilled,
on the technique of torpedo bombing in the shallow
water of the harbor.

And then, above them, the zeros, the fighters,
who—when not protecting the bombers, would amuse
themselves by strafing the airstrips, the naval station.

"Let it be a surprise," Fuchida whispered to himself.

Pearl Harbor had many planes, and the ships had
great anti-aircraft guns. He could easily imagine his
planes being blown out of the sky. The three hundred planes melting to a mere hundred.

Let it be a surprise.

The mountains were ahead, the famed windward
side of the island of Oahu. Fuchida's hand tightened
against the stick of his bomber. Kahuku Point was
directly ahead.

Everyone must see it now.

And the excitement, the joy, was something that they must all feel.

There was a gentle wind from the east. A few clouds hung over the mountains ahead. Otherwise, clear skies.

And in minutes, I'll know if we have surprised the Americans . . . or not.

"Shut her down," Lockard said.

Elliot kept watching the screen. Tyler had told them not to worry. It's probably just the B-17s making their way from California.

But Elliot was fascinated with the blip. It was *so* big. Something has to be wrong with the machine, no question about it. At only 90 miles away, it nearly filled the top of the screen.

God, how many B-17s were coming in?

"Shut her down," Lockard said.

"Okay . . . okay," Elliot said. "But no one's going to pick us up for a while. They're always late. Let me just watch this . . . see if it is the B-17s."

"Go ahead," Lockard said. "The damn thing's probably broken."

Broken or not, the blips moved closer to the radar station, to the island . . .

His plane coasted across Kahuku Point, feeling only the smallest of down drafts. One small cloud gobbled his plane, but then he passed it and there was nothing but blue sky ahead.

And no enemy planes in the air.

No planes. Except—

Fuchida looked down below. And there was a small commercial plane—he didn't know what type.

Making lazy circles in the sky, back and forth, over the valley.

It obviously hadn't seen the line of Japanese planes yet.

Fuchida smiled. Imagine the reaction when the pilot, the Sunday morning pilot, looked up and saw the planes.

Thinking that, yes, they are American planes on maneuvers. Until he sees the red sun. The red sun . . .

Rising over Hawaii.

Fuchida brought his plane down, trimming the flaps just a bit.

The other medium bombers followed his lead, getting down to their ideal strike altitude.

He spoke into the radio.

His first message. In morse code.

"To . . . To . . . To . . ."

7:49. The naval base was minutes away.

"Attack . . . attack . . . attack!"

28

Ichiro Shirato looked up. He heard nothing. The wind blew gently from the east, and—he knew—the planes were still too far away.

But then he saw them.

Little dark blotches streaming from the north.

Ten, then twenty, then others higher, and more to the side. A great aerial armada.

He stood up in the grass.

I didn't want to see this, he thought.

No desire, no desire at all.

And—since I'm stranded here—what else will I see?

The zeros, the fighters moved to the sides of the bombers, alert for any response.

Ichiro laughed.

No one sees them.

Or if they do, they think they're friendly.

So much for the preparedness of Fortress Pearl Harbor!

The first wave would be the worst. No one would expect, no one would see, until the horror was overwhelming.

Total.

Surprise.

Fuchida had his cockpit open. He sent out the message, the code word indicating total surprise.

"Tora . . . tora . . . tora . . ."

He raised his hand with the flare gun, pointing it straight up. One flare, to indicate surprise.

But as he pulled the trigger, his hand got buffeted, blown to the side, and the flare didn't shoot straight up.

No, Fuchida thought. What if it's not seen? The men are looking for the signal? What will they think?

He looked at the flare, trailing awkwardly down to the ground.

He shook his head. I have to fire another flare, so they all see the message, so they know we have total surprise. The harbor, the ships, are ours.

Fuchida reloaded the flare gun. He raised it up, holding it straight up this time, and fired.

The flare shot neatly overhead.

Fuchida looked straight ahead. No fighters were rising to meet them. Incredible! And then Fuchida saw the naval air station, the planes, the ships . . .

A game. Too easily won.

Jim pressed his nose against the glass. He heard the engines, the roar of airplane engines so close that he thought they must be ready to crash into the airstrips on Ford Island. In the background he heard dull explosions, and he saw giant clouds of gray-black smoke stretching to the now foggy sky.

The Japanese planes glided only yards off the ground, spraying bullets at the row upon row of American planes, protected against sabotage, but completely exposed to the aerial attack.

He saw a red fire-station on wheels. A cannister of foam, a nozzle. Jim laughed at it.

Might put out a small engine fire.

Maybe—

But this—

He felt the heat on the glass from the firecracker-like explosions. A few pilots scurried into planes not yet hit, trying to get their engines started, and up into the air.

A few actually got moving . . . only to career into a burning plane, explode, with the pilot trapped, hopelessly, in the cockpit.

And soon, too soon—Jim couldn't see any untouched planes.

There was just a black junkyard outside, dotted with a dozen bonfires. And men lying on the ground, some burned, some shot, some wounded, crawling on the ground.

Jim looked back at the plane, the one plane protected in the hangar.

There was still time.

Time to see, he thought. The glass burned his fingers, the glare made his eyes squint.

I have to see.

He reached down and grabbed the door handle. It was hot. He jiggled the latch, and went outside.

Toland lowered the gun at Ali.

"I think," he said slowly, "that I'll have to use you to make the others talk."

Ali stopped moving.

The barrel was level with her midsection.

She felt faint. All the air was out of the room.

There has to be something I can do.

She brought her hand up. A gesture. An attempt to say something, to buy some time.

But Toland smiled.

And pulled the trigger.

Ichiro watched four planes swoop in from the east, right overhead, heading towards battleship row.

So very low, Ichiro thought. The secret to the success of the shallow torpedo bombing. He watched them hug the water, heading right to the front of the line of ships. At first, he thought they were heading towards the *California*.

But now he saw that the planes were clearly aiming for the second big ship.

The *Oklahoma*.

He watched, until they seemed to be ready to overfly their target. The two lead planes let loose their torpedos. Then they soared up, climbing away from the line of ships.

The next two planes quickly followed.

And then there was just the silent, foamy trail of the torpedos streaming towards the battleship.

It took just seconds really . . .

There were two explosions. The first when the torpedos hit, and then a great black cloud escaped noisily from somewhere inside the ship. Fiery tongues started lapping at the deck. Then—in a flash—the other torpedoes hit, and the ship seemed to jump into the air.

Ichiro Shirato—no stranger to death, no stranger to destruction—watched as these small things scurried off the ship, the capsizing ship.

Men, jumping into the water. Some on fire, wildly flailing at oily burning patches, tumbling into the oil-covered water, fire water.

Another explosion.

And the *Oklahoma* completely capsized.

Another squadron of torpedo planes came from the north. He watched them bank and head towards—

Yes. They headed towards the *Arizona*.

I know what happens, he thought. No need to watch. I know what happens . . .

But he couldn't pull himself away.

The squadron of torpedo planes seemed to be hurrying. Maybe the pilots were younger. They released their torpedos early, too early.

They trailed towards the *Arizona* but—somehow—missed it. The planes pulled away, their day's work done.

Ichiro Shirato looked up.

He saw more planes, the medium bombers, hovering over the charnel house of the harbor.

The smoke, the burning oil stung his eyes.

He watched the bombers come closer.

Jim got the hangar doors open. The hangar quickly filled with the smoke from the airfield, filled with the screams of men panicking, not knowing what to do.

Jim looked out at the field.

And he saw something incredible.

He saw men shooting up at the zeros. Shooting with handguns, shooting with rifles, cursing the enemy planes, crying, laughing.

He saw one man standing there, waving his rifle at the air. The soldier took a shot. Jim saw the airstrip spit at him as the zero's bullets hit.

The zero roared away, no more than ten, fifteen feet overhead.

Jim walked out of the hangar.

Just as another zero roared over the hangar. The soldier turned quickly, his face locked into an angry answer. He raised his rifle.

As the zero's bullets cut into him.

The soldier fell to the ground. The sneer still there, a thin river of blood streaming out of his mouth, down his cheek. Dropping onto the ground.

Jim looked at the airstrip. It was useless. There's no way I can get the plane out, he thought.

No way . . .

He took a step. Little heat clouds buffeted him. Smoldering planes exploded as pockets of fuel caught fire and exploded.

The little red fire stations were pathetic, so ridiculous surrounded by so much incendiary violence.

Jim walked out of the hangar.

Over to the dead soldier.

He stood over him.

Jim looked at the gun, still locked to the soldier's hand.

Jim knelt down. He pried open the dead soldier's fingers, pulling the dead man's grip loose, and pulled the gun away.

Then he looked to the sky.

Kimmel stood at his window, shaking. I'm shaking, he thought. He clenched his fists, trying to force the terrors to stop.

I don't want to embarrass myself, he thought.

He watched four planes drop their torpedos, smoothly, gracefully. An aerial ballet. He watched them hit the *Oklahoma,* watched the ship heave, and turn, rolling over like a dead puppy.

"Sir," his aide said. "We're getting no report from Hickham, but Wheeler says that they're completely non-operational."

Kimmel said nothing.

Non-operational. No fighters. I should have kept the carriers here. At least we'd have them, at least—

But no . . . in that instant he could imagine the carriers being hit by the torpedos, the terrible sight of one of those great ships exploding . . . splitting apart.

"Sir?" his aide said.

Kimmel turned. "Keep trying to raise Hickham, Lieutenant. And if you—"

There was a high-pitched whine.

Glass shattered.

And Kimmel felt something hit his chest. Something hit him, and then fell to the floor. He heard something tumble to the wood floor.

The admiral reached up and felt his chest, expecting a hole, a wound.

There was nothing. He looked down, and saw the shell. Kimmel picked it up.

A spent shell. Enough force to break the glass, he thought. To hit me—and nothing else.

"My god, sir," his aide said.

And Kimmel, studying the Japanese shell, looking at the bent and twisted casing, said, "It would have been merciful if it had killed me."

And he put the failed bullet in his pocket.

Ali took a breath.

What she assumed would be her last breath.

She closed her eyes. A reflex she couldn't fight.

And she heard the click of the trigger being pulled. And nothing else.

"Ahem." Lindstrom cleared his throat. "I'm afraid I took the liberty of removing the bullets in the few moments I held the gun. I felt that it would be safer that—"

Ali smiled. It was so nice to get her life back again. And while she didn't want to permanently mar Toland's body—which she hoped he'd soon reoccupy—there was something she had to do.

She jumped forward and brought the flat of her hand sharply up to the bridge of Toland's nose.

The man screamed.

There was blood everywhere.

Actually, Ali knew, it was more messy than painful.

Her next blow, though, was calculated to end any thought of resistance. She made a fist, pulled back, and then corkscrewed her small fist into Toland's unsuspecting midsection, and up, forcing every bit of air out of the man.

He fell to his knees.

At which point, a side chop to the head removed him from any troubling consciousness.

Ali—breathing hard, but filled with this incredible exhilaration—I'm alive damn it . . . alive!—turned to Lindstrom.

"Thank you. I owe you my life."

Lindstrom shook his head and raised his hand. "No, my dear. We owe *you* our lives. Your timely arrival got the gun out of this imposter's hand."

Dr. Beck, kneeling on the ground, slowly stood up.

For a few moments, Ali had been unaware of her. Sitting quietly with the dead body.

She stood up and walked to Ali. The woman's hands were smeared with blood, from cradling McManus's head. She reached out for Ali's hands.

Ali fought her revulsion. She extended her hands.

"Thank you," Dr. Beck whispered. "I have to—"

Ali nodded. There was something in this woman's eyes, something new, something she hadn't seen before.

As if—now, with McManus gone—she would have to take over.

Then there was a noise.

The tachyon generator.

Ali turned. Jacob was running from one end of the machine to the other.

"Dr. . . Dr. Jacob, what is it?"

The small man stopped, turned and extended his hands in a hopeless gesture. "I don't know. The machine just started." Jacob turned and looked at the dials of the Time Transference Device, the readouts giving the current speed of the subatomic particles, their density—

Dr. Beck let go of Ali's hand.

She too turned to the machine.

"Something is controlling it, something from the outside or—" Jacob leaned closer to the machine.

"As if it was programmed . . ."

"Well, do something about it!" Lindstrom sputtered.

Jacob hit buttons, threw some switches. "No," he moaned. "Something is overriding everything. I can't do a thing—"

Ali watched Dr. Beck walk up to the machine.

She stopped before it and raised her hands. She touched the sleek metal, the dials.

She's lost it, thought Ali. She's coming unglued.

Dr. Beck touched the machine, and then she turned.

A smile on her face.

"Ichiro," she said. Then again, whispering . . .

"Ichiro . . ."

Ichiro watched the bombers fly down the line of battleships, heading towards the ships near the end of the row.

One bomber was in perfect condition.

He watched the bomber trim its rudder a bit, putting itself perfectly in line with the last two ships.

The U.S.S. *Arizona* . . . and the *Nevada*.

He watched the bomb tumble from the plane, wobbly, falling fast, so small compared to the ship.

He watched it hit the *Arizona*.

(He knew that there was gunpowder on deck; nearly a ton of blackpowder, waiting to be stored.)

The explosion was immense, tremendous. The flash blinded him, and then the roar was deafening. An explosion to dwarf any that came before it.

Ichiro imagined the men, the thousand men, trapped, burning, the lucky ones incinerated immediately.

He saw bodies blown off the nearby repair ship, the *Vestal*. Black, smudgy doll-men flying through the air. The repair ship had been on fire. Now, in an instant, those fires had gone out.

Ichiro shook his head.

No oxygen.

The blast on the *Arizona* sucked all the oxygen, all the air away . . . an explosive vacuum.

Something stung his eyes.

He rubbed at them. They kept on stinging, again, and again. He rubbed.

And when he opened them, everything was blurry.

And then more blurry.

Now, he thought. It's happening now.

And, as everything faded, he had only one regret.

I would like to see Jim, in the plane, for the finish. To see if he makes it.

But, as he now saw, that was not to be . . .

A zero backed to the left, firing scattered shots at the few planes not burning, not exploding.

And Jim fired the gun at the sky, pumping bullets into the sky, uselessly.

His face felt wet. And he wondered:

Why is my face wet? What is making it wet?

He let go of the gun stock and brought his hand up. He felt the wet trail.

Jesus, he thought. I'm crying. Standing here. Firing at the planes, like a fool, crying and—

He lowered the gun.

And someone grabbed him, and yanked him backwards.

Dragging him back to the hangar. Jim shook his head.

No, I want to stay out there. I want to shoot at them. I—

He watched another zero strafe the airstrip, and then pull away.

And Jim turned to see who was pulling him away.

* * *

Dr. Beck closed her eyes.

She's going to collapse, thought Ali. She's going to fall, right down and—

The woman reached it and touched the generator, getting her balance.

And then she opened her eyes.

Dr. Jacob was too busy with his machine, running independently, doing something, to help her. Ali ran over and gave her a shoulder to lean on.

And Dr. Beck looked at her.

Her mouth opened.

Shock, Ali thought. She's tuning in and out, her system overloaded.

"It's okay," Ali whispered. "Come, sit down and—"

But Dr. Beck pulled away.

She shook her head. Back and forth, slowly at first, then more violently. Trouble city, thought Ali. She's going to break down. And she's the medical doctor, she's the one who's supposed to take care of us.

"Please, come and rest," Ali said.

Lindstrom came beside her. He extended a hand. "Yes, Yoshira—"

Ali shot him a look. Yoshira? Who's Yoshira? God, is Lindstrom losing it, too?

And all this only made Beck go more wild-eyed.

Jacob spun around grinning, oblivious to what was happening.

"I have it! I figured it out! It's incredible, but I *know* what's going on. You see—" he turned and tapped his machine. "This Time Transference Device here, well—"

Ali shot him a look, trying to signal him that there might be a better time to discuss this.

"I should have seen this," Jacob prattled on. "If we have our device here, then there's no reason why—"

"Dr. *Jacob!*" Ali said sternly.

She turned back to Dr. Beck. The woman was cringing, backing up to a corner of the lab.

She opened her mouth, her lips trembling, bits of spittle gathering at the edges.

Dr. Beck spoke . . . the speech slurred. "Wh—who are you?"

She was looking right at Ali.

With no recognition whatsoever.

Ali froze.

Shock. Real bad.

The woman looked around, seeing the others. She screamed. *"Who are you people?"*

Ali froze. What's protocol, she wondered? What do you do with someone flipping out? Go to them? Or back away?

What the hell do you do?

The woman's eyes trailed down.

Ali followed where her eyes were looking. Right at the body, at McManus lying on the floor. And Beck screamed.

As if she hadn't seen it before.

"Elliot!" she wailed. "Elliot!"

And—now completely confused—Ali watched Beck run over to the body.

29 ====

"It's all over, buddy. The planes are leaving."

Jim heard the words, but he still looked outside, to the field littered with dead men, dead planes . . .

"It's over . . ."

He turned and saw Johnny Murphy.

"They're gone."

Jim nodded, thinking: I can't do this. It's a fucking *Bridge Too Far*. I can't do this. I've snapped, and I'm as crazy as anyone on this island.

Murphy's voice was calm, soothing. "You okay, pal? Do you need a doctor . . . something?"

Jim smiled. Then he erased it from his face, thinking how dopey it must look. How can you smile, here, today?

He looked at his watch.

8:45. The second wave, the second attack would hit in minutes, finishing off what remained of the big ships, going for the destroyers, scattered around the harbor.

Only now there would be some resistance. A few planes from Hickham would get up in the air. There would be some anti-aircraft fire. Slowly, a lumbering giant, Pearl Harbor—the United States—would start to fight back.

Jim heard the planes.

"They're coming again," he whispered.

"Right, Tad. But we'll just stay here, just ride this thing through. It's the start of the war, buddy. But not the end."

Jim nodded. Right. Maybe . . . if . . .

He looked over at Murphy's shoulder, to the plane. Murphy saw him look and followed his glassy-eyed gaze.

"Hey. Our plane! What the hell is it doing here? I thought all the planes were out there?"

How many planes would the Japanese lose, Jim wondered. Twenty-five, thirty? Certainly not any more than that. While here, on the island, there were over 300 planes destroyed, nine battleships, a dozen destroyers.

Nearly twelve hundred men on the *Arizona* alone.

Including Tad Gorman's father.

(And—for a second—it felt real. My father, he thought. My father . . .)

But not the carriers.

And—and—

"We have to fly," Jim said.

His voice cracked. It was an animal sound, barely intelligible. He tried clearing his throat, seared by smoke.

"We have to fly."

In the darkness of the hangar, Murphy smiled at him. "Sure, buddy. We have to fly. We'll get our licks in. Just as soon as this is over. Don't worry—"

Jim shook his head.

"No. Soon. We have to get up. Before the last planes leave, before—"

He nearly said the name, nearly said something that would sound so strange.

After all, how could I know that Commander Fuchida would be up there, circling the harbor, recording the damage . . . the last plane. How could I know that?

Murphy shook his head. "The airstrip's a mess,

Tad. You may have saved our plane. But it isn't going anywhere.''

Jim felt the wetness in his eyes. His hand reached out to Murphy, shaking. "No. We have to get up there. We have to try and get that last plane.''

Murphy shook his head.

"Tad, there's no way. None at all. We just gotta sit tight.''

It's going to happen, Jim thought. I'm not going to be able to stop it. And history will change. The last move of the game. And we lose everything.

Everything.

No.

No . . .

He grabbed Murphy's shirt.

"Listen to me. Just . . . listen. There's going to be a third wave. If we don't stop it. They'll get the fuel . . . billions of gallons.'' Jim heard his voice, crying, pitiful. "And they'll take out the drydocks. And Pearl Harbor will be useless. Just an island. We'll be forced back—''

Jim coughed. He spit to the side.

"Back to California. Do you understand what I'm saying? There will be no Pacific base, no Pacific fleet?''

Murphy stood there. Jim heard explosions in the distance. The sound—at last—of anti-aircraft fire.

Then—Murphy looked at him, all reassurance gone.

"What the hell are you talking about, Tad? How can you know—''

Jim held onto his shirt.

"I *know*. There will be one plane, a last plane to report back to the fleet, to Nagumo, and—''

"Nagumo?''

"We have to stop it. Make it so that third attack never happens. It's what—''

His emotions slipped a notch or two, he felt himself losing it.

"—what's supposed to happen. And it won't happen unless we make it happen."

And Murphy said nothing.

For a long time.

Jim let his hands slip from Murphy's shirt. It was hopeless, he thought. Completely . . . hopeless . . .

He stood there.

And Murphy took a breath.

And took a step closer to Jim, right up to his face.

"How the hell do you know this . . . how the hell—?"

Jim shook his head. Can't tell him that. He'll think that I'm crazy. Can't tell him—

Murphy looked up, past Jim, to the field outside. Some of the airplane fires were going out of their own accord. Ground crews struggled with others.

Jim felt Murphy stare at him.

Murphy licked his lips. He looked up at the sky.

And then he nodded.

"Alright, flyboy. I don't know how you know this—but I'm with you. C'mon," Murphy said. "We have to get them to clear some of those wrecks . . . give us some damn room to take off."

And Jim followed Murphy out to the chaos of the airfield.

30 ═══════

Jim slid into the co-pilot's seat. And then Murphy got in beside him.

"Here we go, Tad. Let's strike a blow for God and Country."

Jim nodded.

And the patrol plane's engine roared to life, echoing too loudly inside the hangar.

Looking outside, Jim saw an army truck pushing at some smoldering wreckage, clearing a space for the plane.

"Okay. Let's ease her out. Check flaps. Brakes off . . . and—"

Jim looked at the controls in front of him. He shook his head. I was going to fly this myself? What the hell could I've been thinking? What—

"Brakes off?" Murphy repeated.

Jim scanned the controls and found a lever labeled brakes. He pulled back, pressing a button, and suddenly the plane began rolling.

Out of the hangar, onto the nightmare of the airstrip. The plane rolled over something, and it tilted to the left.

"Great," Murphy said. "Getting this baby to takeoff is going to be a miracle, a damn—"

"I'll do it myself," Jim said. "If you don't want

to go—"

Murphy looked over at him. "Don't worry, pal. Just like to—"

More revs, and the plane bounced down the alleyway cleared by the trucks.

"Bitch . . ."

Murphy flashed a toothy grin.

Once past the wreckage of the planes, they could see the airstrip. It was clear, but it had been bombed.

Murphy stood up in his seat and looked out at the tattered strip.

"Damn. This thing is littered with craters. Giant potholes. I'm going to have to maneuver around them. Goddamn . . ."

He sat back down.

"See anything up there, Tad?"

Jim looked up. But the sky was empty, clear of enemy planes. The second attack was over. And maybe we'll be too late. Gotta get up.

Got to be there when Fuchida makes his survey.

Bring him down.

Murphy taxied the plane to the corner of the strip, and turned.

"Brakes on," he said.

Jim pulled back on the brakes.

The engine whined.

"Oh, Tad. You take the gun. Once we're up there."

Louder, the propeller sending a storm whipping over the open canopy.

"All—set!" Murphy said. Then, "Let her go . . ."

Jim released the brake. And the plane lurched forward, immediately hitting a hole. Jim felt the plane tilt left.

But then it righted itself. It hit some debris, and then bounced a few inches into the air. "Come on, baby. Just a few more yards. Come—"

Another hole.

And this time Jim thought it was going to swallow the tire, and hold on, sending the plane cartwheeling down the strip, one more crashed hulk.

Murphy hit the flaps, and somehow the plane lifted out of the hole. Then he quickly lowered the flaps.

"That's it," Murphy spoke to the plane. "Just a bit more, just a bit—"

Jim licked his lips.

Except this time he wasn't scared. He wasn't going to get sick.

He just prayed that there would be one plane, one Japanese plane in the air when they got up.

"Okay . . . okay . . ."

Murphy nearly whispered to him.

"Give her full flaps, Tad. Let's get the hell off this garbage."

Jim moved quickly.

And—miraculously—the patrol plane lifted into the air, above the airfield, above Pearl.

And he could see *everything*.

The planes. Not recognizable anymore. Twisted, smashed together by the domino-like effect of the concussive explosions.

The ships. Some split in two, others capsized. Men still in the water, perhaps just dead, oil-soaked bodies. A graveyard of battleships.

And then—

Murphy banked the plane to circle the harbor.

The buildings, the squat Quonset huts with enormous craters, or riddled with bullet holes. Fire everywhere, smoke, burning oil. A nation brought to its knees.

Almost.

The carriers were still out there.

The *Enterprise*.

The *Lexington*.

Still out there.

"Tad, hey, I don't see anything up here. Going a bit higher. Play hide and seek in the clouds. But it looks like the party is all over."

There was the distant sound of gunfire. A dull thud as a shell hit the patrol plane.

"Damn. They're shooting at us. Our own people. We can't stay up here, Tad. Stupid fools will blow us out of the sky."

"Not yet," Jim said quietly. "Just another loop."

But Jim thought, We're too late. We missed the plane.

And the third wave is going to come.

He rubbed his eyes.

And then—just below their plane—he saw something.

A bit of movement.

A plane, a small bomber.

A Japanese plane.

Circling the harbor.

"There he is," Jim said quietly.

"There he is."

Fuchida looked down. He expected to enjoy this spectacle, a success beyond anyone's imaginings.

The destruction was nearly total.

But now, alone—in the aftermath of the attack—Fuchida looked down and saw the dead.

He saw the survivors being fished out of the water.

He imagined the men trapped in the capsized ships, struggling for a way out, trapped by water rushing to fill the ship.

It's not good for me to be here, he thought.

I'm feeling too much for the enemy, his *seishin*.

He saw enough to give his report to Nagumo, to tell him to send the last wave, to finish the job.

And then—as if sensing something—Fuchida looked up . . .

* * *

"Here we go, Tad. Just hold our fire. Wait until we're . . . as close . . . as we can be."

Jim nodded. He held the co-pilot's stick, felt the button that fired the gun.

The plane began its dive on what looked like an unsuspecting Fuchida.

"We got him, pal. Doesn't even see us. Doesn't—"

But then the Japanese plane quickly cut left, peeling away from their diving attack.

And Jim was left staring at a whispy cloud and blue sea.

"Damn," Murphy said.

And Jim—with no responsibility to pilot the plane—looked around. And he saw Fuchida to their left, drifting behind them, and—

Out of sight.

He's behind us, Jim thought.

"He's behind us," Jim said. "You've got to—"

"I know. I know where the hell he is. But this isn't a fighter. I can only do so much. So . . . much."

Jim heard a gun firing. A bullet hit something in the back of the plane, giving off a clear ping.

"Great," Murphy bellowed. "This is great. Who the hell is that pilot?"

Murphy looked at Jim, and Jim knew that he expected an answer, wanted an answer.

"Lieutenant Commander Mitsuo Fuchida. He led the attack."

Another ping at the back.

Murphy looked at Jim.

His mouth opened. He started to say . . . something.

But instead, he pulled back on the stick, gave the engine more power, and started to climb.

Jim felt his back plastered against the seat. The plane screamed out as it climbed. There was the rattling, burping sound of Fuchida's guns. But—this time—no hits.

Finally, Murphy leveled off.

And Fuchida's plane sailed below them.

"Got him, buddy. Got the bastard. You'll get one chance. Just keep those bullets pumping."

Jim nodded.

And Murphy now brought the nose of the patrol plane down and started for Fuchida's tail. Already he was turning, but it was taking time, and Murphy was now watching for every small maneuver.

"Okay. Hold on a sec. Just a little closer . . ."

Jim's finger tensed against the button for the plane's gun.

"Just a . . . bit—"

Then Fuchida's plane dropped down, suddenly, leaving a hole in front of them.

"Damn!" Murphy said. But he quickly got the patrol plane to follow, catching Fuchida as he banked right this time.

And then Fuchida's plane was right in front of them.

"Fire!" screamed Murphy.

Jim pulled the trigger.

And shiny yellow spray erupted from the front of the plane, right at Fuchida's bomber.

Fuchida felt the shells hit. And then the plane seemed to wobble.

No, he thought. I'm going down. But then the plane righted itself. Fuchida tried to steady the rudder. It appeared loose, as if it had been chewed up.

And he thought:

Another burst, and my plane will go down.

And then, what will Admiral Nagumo do, old conservative Nagumo?

But Fuchida knew the answer to that.

There would be no third wave.

I have to stop the Americans . . . and then get back to the *Akagi.*

And though he was piloting a sluggish bomber, though his rudder had a problem, Fuchida tried a trick that he learned many years ago over the clear water of Osaka Harbor.

"What the—"

The bomber looked like it was going down, straight down.

"We got her," Jim said. "We got his plane . . ."

But then Jim watched—amazed—as the plane looped around. It was a circus trick, something you'd do in a biplane, barnstorming the heartland of America.

And even from this distance they heard Fuchida's plane protest the maneuver.

They passed over Fuchida.

They couldn't see him.

"He's behind us."

Jim looked at Murphy, expecting him to do something, to get them out of this.

Instead, he seemed frozen, bested.

Finally—still not moving—Murphy said something. "Okay. What we do is—"

Shells ripped through the navy patrol plane.

Blood spattered the windshield.

Jim thought that Murphy had been hit. He's wounded. God, and I'll have to fly this plane, land it . . .

But then Jim looked down, at his leg.

There was a great open gash, the tattered material of his pants melted to blood, and skin, and torn muscle. No pain, he thought, I feel no pain.

Murphy looked over, then down to the leg. He had the plane in a dive. Jim felt his body lurching forward.

"Got to get us out of here, Tad. Got to land. We're shot up bad. Going in the sink if we—"

Murphy banked the plane left . . . or was it right? Jim couldn't tell. It all felt so shaky, so wobbly. "Got to land."

Jim nodded.

And that means . . . that means . . .

He looked up, seeing the blue sky, the few wispy clouds.

Fuchida's plane.

"He's not coming after us," Murphy said, sounding happy.

Yes, Jim thought.

But he's getting away.

We lost.

Jim closed his eyes.

We lost, he thought.

The last play of the game. And we lost.

And when he opened his eyes Jim couldn't hear the plane anymore. The clouds had thickened, filling the windshield, then the cabin, until his eyes were filled with a filmy white gauze.

He couldn't feel his leg, the wound. He felt nothing.

I'm going back, he thought—with no joy, no pleasure at all.

Going back.

To see what will happen.

Now that we lost.

31

Admiral Nagumo watched Fuchida's plane approach the *Akagi*. The admiral had given orders for the carrier to steam due south, to greet Fuchida's plane.

He saw it wobble in the air, watched how Fuchida carefully trimmed his plane, trying to make the approach as smooth as possible.

But Nagumo saw the chewed-up rudder.

The fire squads were ready.

Fuchida made it back.

But not completely unscathed, *hai?*

Nagumo kept his binoculars on the plane. Dropping a few feet, then rearing back, the plane responding wildly.

Nagumo thought about all that had been accomplished that day.

And he thought of the many battles that would be ahead.

Fuchida's plane dropped a few more feet, unsteadily approaching the carrier.

And Nagumo raised his hand.

To give the order to be sent to the fleet.

For the attacking fleet to set a course due east.

It has been a good day, Nagumo thought. A tremendous surprise, a crippling blow to the enemy. Yamamoto had delegated the final decision entirely to me.

Fuchida's plane dropped, hit the runway, tilting this way and that, nearly out of control.

And Nagumo thought . . .

It's best we not test our luck for a third time.

Nagumo put down his binoculars.

And he hurried to congratulate Fuchida . . . and tell him of his decision.

Epilogue══════

1

Jim shook his head.

There was this tremendous ringing, giant bells, rattling inside his skull.

He opened his eyes.

He saw Ali, Jacob, and Lindstrom standing near the Time Transference Device.

Dr. Beck was on the floor, kneeling by McManus . . . or was it Ichiro Shirato?

By his dead body. She was wailing.

"Hey," Jim said. But his voice was faint, barely audible. My body's still half-asleep. Then, louder. "Hey!"

Ali turned.

And a smile came to her face.

"Jim!"

She walked to him—and was it his imagination, his slowed-down state-of-mind?—but it seemed to take forever.

"Jim," she said.

She threw herself on him, and hugged him close.

He tried to hug her back.

"The straps?" he said. "Could you undo the straps?"

Ali looked up. She was crying, laughing. "Yes,"

she laughed. "I missed you, Jim. I felt so alone, back there, wondering where you were."

He tried to smile back.

"I blew it," he said. "I didn't do what I had to."

He looked down to the floor. And he thought: Is Ichiro dead because of me?

But Lindstrom hurried over.

"Jim . . . there's something wrong with the Time Transference Device. It started operating by itself, as if it was programmed. It yanked you back, took away—" Lindstrom gestured to Dr. Beck. "And now—"

Dr. Beck . . . Jim thought. So she was from the future, too?

Then Dr. Jacob turned around.

"The machine's circuits are failing, one after the other, as if it was some kind of self-destruct program."

Jacob's round face was scrunched up in a hapless attitude of genuine confusion.

Ali finished undoing his straps.

Jim got out of the chair and pulled her close.

"I blew it," he said again. "I didn't stop—"

But then two things happened. First, Dr. Beck— or whoever she was—stood up and started yelling.

"You people . . . you killed Dr. McManus," she screamed. "Who are you?"

Ali leaned close to Jim. "She doesn't know us."

Jim turned to Lindstrom.

Lindstrom whispered to him, barely audible. "The Dr. Beck we knew was really McManus's wife, actually Ichiro Shirato's wife—"

Jim interrupted. "He was with me—at Pearl. Is that—" he pointed at the body. "Is that him?"

Lindstrom shrugged. "No. At least, I don't think so. That's the real Dr. McManus. I—"

But the woman came up to him and started beating

Jim on the chest. "You—you people killed him. Who are you?" she wailed.

Why me, Jim thought? Why do I get blamed?

Lindstrom moved to his desk.

"Hey, wait a minute," he said, oblivious to the beating Jim was getting.

Ali, at least, tried to pull the woman off.

"We didn't do it," Ali said.

Lindstrom grunted. "I think—yes, by god. Look at this. Come here, Jim . . . Ali . . . I think we're out of the woods . . ."

Jim started for the desk, to Lindstrom's small computer.

Could it be?

Did Fuchida go down?

Did something happen to stop Nagumo, stop the third wave?

Jim looked around and saw Toland in a chair, asleep.

"What happened to him?"

"Oh. He was taken over. When he left the Time Lab. I guess he might be back to his old self by now. As soon as the sedative wears off. But Jim, my boy, I think you did it. I think—"

Jim heard other voices. From outside. At first, Jim thought they were the Pack, feral creatures hungering for dinner.

But then a side door opened. A door that shouldn't be there.

And a man opened it. A man dressed in a gray suit, with a natty Prince Albert beard, and glasses that were balanced on the tip of his nose.

"What is this? What in the world?" the man said.

Jim stood there, like the others, frozen at this apparition from *Gentlemen's Quarterly* strolling into the Time Lab, through a door nobody knew about.

"What on earth? This is a museum. The string

quartet is about to begin and I heard—who are you people? And—''

The man—unprepared for the shock—looked down and saw the body.

''My God! There's been a murder in my museum!'' He backed up.

Screaming, as he went. ''Guards! Security!'' His voice cracked. ''Help!''

Lindstrom grabbed Jim's arm, and then Ali's. ''We've got to get out of here. Now. The back way. Then scatter. Try to find out what your lives are supposed to be . . . pick up the pieces . . .''

''But what about—'' Jim started to say.

Jim looked at Dr. Beck, back on the floor, next to McManus.

''She . . . knows nothing of us. We have to go . . .'' Lindstrom insisted.

Dr. Jacob was already scurrying towards the back.

''But the machine?'' Jim said.

Lindstrom kept guiding them towards the back. They heard steps outside, hurrying towards them.

Jacob looked over his shoulder as he made his way to the exit.

''It's useless,'' Jacob said. ''All the micro-circuits, the silicon chips, all burned out. It's just another high-speed particle generator now. It's as if it was supposed to happen . . .'' Jacob said with some interest.

The steps were closer. Jim heard the man, the curator scream. ''In there . . .''

''Please. Go!'' Lindstrom ordered.

And they all ran as fast they could.

2

It was cool outside.

But Jim saw cars on the George Washington Bridge, blessed traffic. And there were no cannibal people waiting to pounce on them.

"We have to scattter," Lindstrom said. "Maybe later, after some, er, time, we can meet. But for now—"

Jim looked at Lindstrom, then Ali.

"We actually did it? We stopped them?"

Lindstrom rubbed his beard. "It would appear so. There's just—"

"What?" Ali said.

"Nothing. I—well—I just wondered whether Ichiro died? Is that him on the floor back there?" Lindstrom gestured at the Cloisters lit up for an evening concert, a cultural vespers. "And his wife, Yoshira . . . did she go back to their time, or someplace else? And there's something else . . ."

Jim waited patiently. He pulled Ali close.

Even Dr. Jacob huddled close.

Lindstrom shook his head. "Now, how the hell will we know what's real time—and what's been changed?"

Nobody said anything, pondering the enigma.

Then Dr. Jacob's tiny bowling-ball face lit up. "Why, I know—"

But the sounds of sirens cut through the trees, screaming from the Henry Hudson Parkway.

"Look, we must split up! See what this world is like. If we're lucky, you can all go back to where we were . . . before the *Intrepid* disappeared."

"But my idea—" Jacob said.

"Later," Lindstrom insisted, putting a hand on Jacob's shoulder.

"For now, get as far away as you can."

Jacob nodded, looked around in an almost cartoon fashion, and then disappeared down the slope, to the street lamps of Riverside Drive.

"Well, goodbye," Lindstrom said, giving them both a great bear hug. "It's been . . . an adventure."

Ali leaned close and kissed Lindstrom's beard.

The history professor smiled in the darkness and then he pulled away. One last wave, and then he went in the opposite direction to Jacob, heading into Fort Tryon Park.

Good luck, Jim thought.

"Maybe we should stick together," Jim said, to Ali. "It will be—"

Ali shook her head.

She leaned forward and gave him a kiss.

Full, on the lips.

"It will be safer if we split up," she said. Jim looked at her eyes, glistening from the faint glow of distant lamps in the park. "Don't worry," she smiled. "I'll find you . . . when it's safe."

And then she ran away, both, down towards Henry Hudson Parkway, to the decrepit overlook that loomed over the Hudson River as it streamed past the bridge, out to the blackness of the Atlantic.

The sirens were closer.

Jim looked around, wondering if there was another direction to run, another way to go.

He saw a path leading down to the Cloisters Cafe, and—past it—to streets that wandered through the north Bronx.

In minutes I can be lost in bodegas and lotto shops, he thought.

And then—he too ran away.

3

It was, of course, as if nothing had happened.

Jim's apartment was exactly as he had left it. The bills were still unpaid. The letter from the Columbia registrar requesting overdue tuition for his Master's Thesis was still held in by the miracle of magnetism to the ancient refrigerator.

Some Burger King onion rings—oily, probably indigestible—sat in a stained white sack. They were next to some skim milk and grapes which—if all was unchanged—unfortunately had seeds.

He was flush from running.

The adrenaline gave him a strange buzz, like too much caffeine.

Not a nice feeling.

He grabbed the bowl of grapes and sat down in front of the tv.

The news was on.

The lead story.

The strange death at the Cloisters. The hidden lab. The amnesia that afflicted the two survivors. The description of the fugitives, poor sketches, hopefully useless to the police.

The woman, Dr. Marianne Beck, was hysterical.

Maybe crazy.

And scientists were already asking to study the particle generator. Some from NYU, someone from Columbia University.

Jim was sure that they would find it completely nonfunctional.

A reporter on the scene mentioned the possibility that the device was a super weapon, something to hold the city hostage.

Jim spit out a seed.

So, everything's the same . . .

Except.

It's not. Someone's dead. Here. And who knows what other changes might be in place, subtly changing time.

Jim took a breath, his exhaustion setting in.

I'll wait a week before seeing Ali, to find Lindstrom . . .

But he had to wonder.

What was going on . . . ?

In the future.

Where the real war was taking place.

Was Ichiro there, his wife? What are they facing?

And—despite everything—Jim had this one last thought, sitting in the third-hand easy chair, before his eyes slammed shut.

I should be there. To help them.

He grinned. Sleepily.

Life is strange.

After all.

I'm a Time Warrior . . .

THE END

About the Author

Matthew J. Costello is a Contributing Editor at *Games* Magazine, and writes for *Sports Illustrated* and *Writer's Digest*. His interviews have regularly appeared in *The Los Angeles Times* and *Amazing Stories Magazine*. *Time Warrior #1: Time of the Fox* was published by ROC in 1990. He is also the author of *Darkborn* and *Home*. Costello lives in Ossining, New York with his wife and three children.